Wolf *Kissed*

SUPERNATURALLY *Yours*

BOOK TWO

S LUCAS

Wolf Kissed

(Supernaturally Yours Book Two)

S Lucas

Cover design: Blue Crescent Covers

Editor: TS Arthur

Proofreader: Proofreading by Mich

slucasauthor@gmail.com

To my grandad, the man who even though he didn't know I wrote smutty books supported me nonetheless.

Miss you every day you are gone, Poppy.

Content Notice

While Vampire Kissed was potentially on the more brutal side, this story still has some scenes that may make readers uncomfortable.

This is a paranormal why choose romance and has dark themes throughout, some of which may be triggering to readers including:

- Abuse (past mentions)
- Blood and gore
- Cannibalism (bad guy)
- Death
- Graphic descriptions of violence
- Murder
- Non consent (FMC and minor characters)
- Sexual assault including rape (past memories, and one scene for FMC and on page minor characters)

There are scenes of M/M action between the men in the harem, with existing relationships before the FMC arrives.

Please be aware that this book includes the POV of the bad guy. His chapters can and do contain a majority, if not all of the bullet points above. To give you some prewarning his chapters are: 12, 21 and 30.

Prologue

Lila

The world has changed so much since my parents were children. At one time humans ruled the world. Not anymore. The supernaturals took over, and the vampires, wolves, and demons claimed the United States. They split into territories for each faction. West for the vampires, central for the wolves, and east for the demons.

I was born into the wolf sector of the United States. Each year, the wolves held balls, which were mandatory for every woman of age that wasn't already married or mated, whether they were human or she-wolves. Only the males succumbed to a curse, making them even more driven to find their mates.

Every year without fail as soon as a female turns eighteen, an invitation inlaid with gold would land on our doorstep. The idea is for the male wolves to find their true mates and whisk them off to live happily ever after.

My mom went to a few before she met my father, but there were no wolves in attendance that she ever matched with. She'd seen her friends being chosen and taken away to be mated to their new packs. I never fully believed in true mates, though. For all I knew, the women were dragged away against their wills by brutish wolves whether they wanted to or not.

My mom was different, though. She believed everyone had another half to their soul, whether human or wolf. It just so happened that her soul mate was not a wolf. That didn't stop my mom from taking great pride in dressing me up each year from the age of eighteen to see if I would be privileged enough to be picked and find my one true love.

Bleugh.

The balls were the greatest event of the year in my sector. They spared no expense. Full of drinking, dancing, and male wolves sniffing around the women in attendance. The men approached each woman who caught their eye, hoping they would find their mate.

I hated them—men of all ages wanting to touch me, plying me with alcohol, and some even propositioning me even though they knew we didn't have a connection. I'd do my best to spend as little time as possible in the main halls before disappearing to hide until they were over.

The previous year was different, though. Both my parents had died in a freak accident. A car jumped the sidewalk as they were heading back to their vehicle. While my father died on impact, my mother clung to life. I spent weeks at her bedside, waiting for her to wake up after brain surgery. She never did. When I got back to the house we'd lived in my entire life, that golden invitation had been sitting on the mat.

Tearing the invitation to shreds, I threw the ripped-up paper in the trash. I thought nothing of it as I arranged my parents' funerals. I'd had enough. I didn't want to be forced to go to another ball, to have to mate with someone I didn't care about, even if they say the mating is voluntary.

When a job offer in Portland, the vampire sector, came up, I sold my parents' house and headed West. I wanted to leave the wolf sector and have a fresh start. Things didn't go to plan though.

After landing in Portland and finalizing everything with my new job, I went out to celebrate. I never made it to my first day, though. Going out had led to drinking, which led to dancing, which led to me being kidnapped after leaving the club.

I ended up in a cage, naked, and surrounded by several women in the same situation as me. Wolf shifters had snatched us. They'd been driven from their own sector after some sort of curse had taken them and they'd left their packs.

Instead, they chose to become rogue while they searched for their mates. But they didn't care about finding their true mates. They collected women to use and abuse for their own pleasure, occasionally blood bonding with women against their will.

One wolf, in particular, took an interest in me, and he made my life a living hell. He took me whenever he wanted, whether or not I was conscious. As far as he was concerned, I was his and he planned to blood bond with me on the blood moon.

Chapter One

Lila

Jolting awake, my heart races in my chest. I feel it pounding so hard I'm surprised it hasn't come straight through my rib cage. All I ever see when I close my eyes are fangs and fur, blood splattering over my skin as the murderous, depraved pack of wolves kills another woman. Rubbing my eyes, I brush the sleep away and look around until I'm satisfied that I'm safe. It's still light out.

Stretching out as much as I can in the cramped car, I let out a yawn. My body is barely even functioning anymore from the lack of sleep. I only let myself rest during the day now, and even then my sleep is fitful. It's the best bet I have of chasing the nightmare away, but they still come. Savage men abusing my body, and those of the other women locked in cages in a darkened cave like animals.

That was until she came. Demi. I was almost out of hope before her, too exhausted and broken to take anymore. Alaric was going to claim me as his own, to blood bond with me, and until then I felt like there was nothing I could do about it.

I'd prayed for it to end, for Alaric to get too rough and kill me as he took from me. My body was battered and broken, and my mind was splintering. When Demi arrived, she knew her men would come for her no matter what it took and that they'd save the rest of us.

And they came. They whisked us away from that nightmare and took us to a women's sanctuary run by the magic born, where our wounds were healed, and our minds slowly started to be glued back together again. But it wasn't enough for me.

I had to get away; I needed to protect everyone from what I thought was following me. The magic born kept telling me there was no way any of the wolves had survived the vampires' attack, and even if they did, we were safe within the shields surrounding the sanctuary. I wasn't so sure. For the last few weeks, it's felt like something was coming for me, or more to the point, someone. Even in another state, I don't feel like I'm far enough away.

The nightmares of Alaric assaulting me plagued me every time I closed my eyes, and I was exhausted. So I ran, and one of the magic born helped me. She believed me when I told her I didn't think he was dead and that he'd come for me. She gave me a car, albeit a little run down, enough supplies and money to get me at least a few states away.

Checking myself in the rearview mirror, there are dark circles below my eyes from the lack of sleep, and the red veins all but take over the white. The blue is dull and lifeless, and my pale skin looks sickly and wrong. It's been like this since they rescued us. The other women went to the therapy sessions; they were sleeping and eating well and looked better and better each day. But that didn't happen to me. Instead, I look exactly as I did when I was rescued.

I stifle another yawn that threatens to be unleashed, but it's no use. Leaning over to the passenger seat, I rummage around for another energy drink and come up empty. There are countless empty cans flung into the footwell, as well as various food wrappers.

I've spent my days driving throughout the night, not daring to stop even as my eyes grew heavy. Brief stops during the day give me enough sleep to be able to get back on the road. I'm running on fumes, though.

I need to stop for more supplies.

Starting the engine, the car sputters to life and I guide it back onto the asphalt. Glancing at the fuel gauge, I wince. Even if I could go without food and drink, I'm definitely going to have to stop in the next town whether I want to or not.

Peering out of the windscreen, I notice the tree line edging further away from the roadside, opening up into large, empty fields. In summer, I imagine the fields will be filled with all sorts of produce, but right now they are covered in a few inches of snow. The sun glares off the whiteness, blinding me momentarily. Hopefully, I'll be pulling into a town soon. Then I can get gas, snacks, and give my legs a small stretch.

Since leaving the sanctuary, the panic surrounding me has lessened, as though the further away I get from my nightmares, the less grip it has on my soul. I'll take it while it lasts. I turn my gaze back to the road in front of me; it looks like it could go for miles in a straight line, but as more and more buildings appear, I know I have to be close to the town.

Tapping my fingers on the steering wheel, I hum along to a tune only I can hear, keeping my eyes peeled for somewhere I can pull over to refill the tank. The small town I'm pulling into is quaint.

Most of the buildings are made of wood, and I drop my speed as I cross the city limits, taking in everything around me. There are people wrapped up in thick coats to stave off the cold, and I shiver at the thought of only having a sweater thrown in the back seat.

I spot the gas station just ahead and sigh in relief as I pull onto the forecourt. Turning off the engine, I reach into the back of the car and grab my sweater. As I come back around, I spot someone out of the corner of my eye and let out a shriek as he lifts a hand to knock on the driver's side window.

He's an older man, with a head full of gray hair, wearing coveralls with the name of the gas station embroidered in red on his chest. The name Burt is just below it. I place my hand over my chest to calm my racing heart. Pulling up the lock on the door, I grab the key and slowly open it. Burt holds the door open for me as I exit.

"Afternoon, miss," comes Burt's cheery voice and he smiles widely at me. "What can I get you?" He must notice the look of confusion on my face as I just stare at him. "How much gas?"

"Oh, right. Sorry." I shake my head, remembering how in Portland the attendant had to pump the gas for you. "Fill the tank, please."

"Right away, miss. If you just head inside to pay, Ol' Sammy will help you out." He gives me his back as he reaches for the pump.

Quickly, I throw my sweater on, shut the car door, and head inside, shivering as the cold brushes against my face and freezes my hands. A little bell tinkles above the door, announcing my arrival, and heat blasts from the vents just above it.

Heading straight for the aisles, I browse the snacks and grab some before I move to the refrigerators. My back prickles and I glance around, but there is no one there apart from Ol' Sammy behind the counter. When my arms are loaded with potato chips, candy, and a few energy drinks, I go to the counter to pay for my haul and the gas. Ol' Sammy has his back to me as he moves a few boxes around.

"There's a cold snap heading this way." My head snaps up and the old man is staring at me from the other side of the counter. I nod and smile weakly.

I gather my things and head back outside, dumping the items on the passenger seat. Burt gives me a smile from across the forecourt.

"Now, you be careful, miss. The roads are getting icy."

"Thanks." I give him a small wave and climb back into the car. Starting the engine, I blast the heater, holding my hands in front of the vents until I get some feeling back into them.

When my fingers no longer feel like blocks of ice, I put on my seatbelt and head for the exit, slipping back onto the main road. It doesn't take me long until I've left the town and I'm back surrounded by trees again. I stifle a yawn, covering my mouth with the back of my hand. Even my nap at the side of the road wasn't enough.

I need to stop for a rest, but not just yet. I still want to get more distance between me and Portland. It's only been a couple of days since I left. I have no idea when the next town is, but I'll stop there. Hopefully, I can find a motel close to the main road. The sky seems to darken as the surrounding trees get larger and closer together, the sun almost blotted out by their looming presence.

It feels almost like I'm driving through the night, even though I know there's still at least another hour of daylight left. Turning on the car's lights, I blink a few times. My eyes are so heavy, the darkness isn't helping how tired I am. Movement within the trees at the side of the road grabs my attention and I whip my head to the side. Whatever is there is moving fast, keeping pace with my car.

It seems to move closer to the edge of the tree line, but I still can't make out what it is. Goosebumps erupt across my skin, and a shudder races down my spine. My breath quickens as my mind imagines the monsters of my nightmares chasing my car. When the shadow dashes out of the trees and in front of the car, I let out a shriek, yanking the steering wheel to avoid it.

There's nothing I can do as I hit a patch of ice on the road, the lurching movement of the car sending me to the other side of the road. I slam my foot onto the brake, but nothing happens as the car slides across the ice. I know before it happens that I'm going to crash into the forest edging the road and I brace for the impact.

The sound of crunching metal hits my ears, just as my head is jerked forward and my face smacks into the steering wheel. Blackness takes me as pain ricochets through my body.

Chapter Two

Grayson

Sprinting through the woods, the branches whip across my sides, but I ignore the sharp stings as I continue my run. I'm on a mission to catch my prey. It's my sole focus right now. I hear their thumping heart as they try to flee. But I have their scent now, and I'm not planning on losing them.

The full moon is high in the sky, and there's not a cloud in sight. I'm at my strongest when the moon is in this phase. My senses are beyond anything a mere human could ever grasp. As I close in on my prey, I smell their fear. Their flight response urged them to get away. But they won't.

The scenery whips by me as I bound over boulders and fallen trees. I threaded in and out of the colossal trunks as I followed closely on the heels of my meal. The thought of sinking my teeth into them and tasting their blood has me picking up speed.

As I break into the clearing, I see them only a few paces ahead of me. I have them now. Leaping onto their back, I sink my fangs into their neck. Their body crumples to the ground beneath me. Tearing into the flesh, their warm, coppery blood floods my mouth. I rip away a chunk of meat and swallow it whole.

Pulling my head up, I dig my teeth into their soft side, splitting skin and muscle as I go. My mouth and head are covered in their blood and it's a glorious feeling. I feast until my belly is full. Leaving the deer carcass on the ground for the scavengers, I head to the lake I know is nearby.

It doesn't take me long to get there; the air grows cooler as I get closer to my destination. When I get to the water's edge, I glance down, seeing my reflection. But it's not a man that is staring back at me, it's an enormous wolf.

My black fur is flecked with silver, and my mercurial eyes match that of my human self. There is blood all over my muzzle and claws. Leaning down low, I lap at the water, sending ripples across the otherwise still surface. The blood from my kill mixes with the crystal-clear liquid, staining it red.

A branch snaps to my left, and I lift my head up, scenting the air. There's a human here. There should never be humans here.

How dare they encroach on my land? The darkness whispers in the back of my mind.

I hunch down low, my hackles raised, and a low growl escapes from between my teeth. They're coming closer now. They really shouldn't have come here.

Kill them and protect your pack. The whispering voice comes again.

A figure stumbles out of the brush, a gun held at his side. He's wearing tatty jeans and a lumberjack coat. There are a few dead rabbits strung over his shoulder. A growl rumbles from my chest and draws his attention.

Raising his gun, he aims it in my direction. Bad idea. The darkness pulls me under. Moving quicker than he expected my wolf shoves off the ground. His eyes widen as we leap. He pulls the trigger; the bullet grazing my side. But it doesn't hinder me. I land hard on top of him and crush him against the hard ground. His gun is flung to the side.

End him, make him bleed. The voice penetrates my mind again.

My lips pull back as my bloody teeth come into full view. The man beneath me tries to scream, but it barely escapes his mouth before I slam my jaws over his neck. My teeth sink deep, and his blood explodes across my tongue. I bite down until I hear a crack, crushing his windpipe and breaking his neck.

Letting out a grunt, I release my hold on his neck and take a few steps back, away from the dead man. With a shake of my head, I come back to myself and look at the man below me. He really shouldn't have ventured into my territory. There are enough signs around the area and a fence to deter people. But some never learn, and they end up like this guy.

My bones crack, and my body contorts as it shifts. Crouched low on the ground, with my legs underneath me, my hands drop to my sides. My torso stings as I glance down at the wound from the bullet, but it won't for long. I already feel the skin knitting itself back together.

Searching the dead man's pockets, I look for some sort of identification, but he has nothing on him aside from a set of keys. A quick glance tells me the serial number has been filed off the gun laid beside him.

He's probably someone that no one is really going to care about; only criminals and the nefarious sorts go around with unmarked guns. This means I won't have to call Achilles to come to sort out the dead man, instead we have a special bonfire with his name on it. It's not like I'm rolling in cash to be able to pay the warlock off again, so I'll take care of this one myself.

Leaving the body behind, I head back toward my cabin. The journey back would be quicker in my wolf form, but I'm so full after my meal, I meander back at a more human pace. The leaves crunch under my feet as I tread across the forest floor.

Even in my human form, I can hear for miles around me: deer grazing a few miles away, rabbits burrowing in their dens, and birds flitting around the trees above my head. It's more muted than when I'm a wolf, but if I wanted to I could still track a specific sound to its location. A gentle breeze caresses my naked skin, but I don't feel cold. I never do. A bonus of being a wolf, I guess.

By the time I hit the clearing where my cabin lies, the wound on my side has completely healed. Strolling up the steps, I stride across the porch and shove through the front door, slamming it behind me. Hunter startles and glares in my direction. His eyes widen as he takes in my appearance.

"Again, Gray? Really? How many times have I told you about trailing mud and blood in here?"

A growl rumbles in my chest and I snap my jaws in his direction before lifting my middle finger at him. He chuffs out a laugh and turns back to his book, shaking his head. Stomping through the cabin, I make my way to the bathroom just off the hallway.

"Want me to wash your back?" Hunter's voice calls from the main room.

Grumbling, I slam the door shut and turn on the shower. I don't even wait for the water to warm before I plunge under the stream. Blood, mud, and all sorts of debris I've picked up from the forest swirl around the drain as the water rains down over me.

Grabbing the soap, I scrub at my body. When the water finally runs clear, I grab a towel from the rail and sling it around my hips. I don't bother retrieving clothes from my bedroom as I head back into the main room of the cabin. Hunter is perched at the table still reading his book.

"GRAYSON!" My name is bellowed from behind me. Cayden stomps down the stairs that lead to the loft and his bedroom.

"What?" I snap back.

"Why the fuck is there human blood in the cabin?" He cuts his gaze over to Hunter. "And you, how did you not smell it?"

Hunter shrugs at him, giving about as much of a shit as I do by the fact that it's human blood and not just animal blood that I trailed into our cabin. Moving to the fridge, I open it and pull out a beer. I pop the top and guzzle it down, the liquid quenching my thirst. Cayden appears beside me. He's a little bigger than me in stature, but that's the alpha in him. I could still kick his ass in a fight if I wanted to.

"Found a hunter on our land again." I look up at Cayden.

"When will humans learn to read the damn signs? What are they, stupid?" Hunter sighs before going back to his book.

"You can't kill every human who comes onto our land, Grayson."

"The asshole had a gun and shot me. I wasn't exactly going to stick around while he tried to kill me, was I?" It's not exactly the truth, I wanted to kill him before I even realized he had a gun, but I won't admit that to Cayden.

"But you were in control?" Of course, he was going to question me about that.

"Completely." Cayden eyes me warily, but I didn't exactly lie in my answer to him. Rolling his eyes, Cayden shakes his head.

"Go put some clothes on and I'll sort out the pit. You can retrieve the body." With that, Cayden spins on his heel and stalks out of the cabin.

Gazing over to Hunter, he smirks at me; he loves it when Cayden is pissed at me, taking way too much pleasure in my admonishment. Considering that's all I get from Cayden most of the time, it's definitely the main source of Hunter's enjoyment.

Chapter Three

Lila

My head throbs as I blink open my eyes and dizziness sweeps over me. Probing my head, I wince. I feel something wet and sticky on my skin. When I take my fingers away, they are covered in blood. I try to recall exactly what happened, but I can't remember a thing.

I'm still in the car, but I can't see beyond the snow covering the splintered windscreen. Turning the key, there's nothing. Not even a splutter from the old engine. Wrenching the key from the ignition, my shoulders droop as I admit defeat.

My breath comes out in shuddering white plumes as my teeth chatter. Shivering, I shove my hands into the sleeves of my sweatshirt. Not that it will stave off the cold that sinks into my bones. I need to get out of here before I freeze to death.

My fingers curl around the handle. I push it a few times, but it doesn't budge at all. I undo my seatbelt and clamber over to the other side of the car; I try the other door, but it's just as jammed as the first one.

Fuck my life.

I grab the window handle and roll it all the way down. A yelp escapes me as the snow covering it lands straight in my lap. Maybe I should have left it closed, at least then I wouldn't have ended up with wet jeans. I brush as much of the white powder off my legs as I can, but it's no use. It's already thawing and leaves dark patches on my jeans. Grabbing my backpack from the back seat, I toss it out of the window.

Teeth gritted, I kneel on the seat and lean out of the window. The front end of the car is crumpled around a tree, I can just about make out where the road lies between the pathway of trees on either side. Even then, it's hard to see with the snow lying on top of the tarmac.

I shove myself further out of the window and lose my balance. I can't stop my fall. I land hard on my shoulder, sending a stabbing pain through my collarbone. Already I feel the snow melting against my clothes. With a grumble, I roll onto my hands and knees. My fingers sink a few inches into the snow before I get the energy to push myself to my feet.

Swiveling slowly on the spot, I gaze up and down the road, but with the snow and lack of light, I have no idea which way I came from. Reaching back into the car, I gather my snacks and drinks together from the gas station and shove them into my backpack. There are a few clothes in there but nothing more than clean underwear, socks, and a few t-shirts.

Retrieving a pair of socks, I shove my hands inside them, trying to ward off some of the cold. It's not much, but it will have to do for now. A wolf howls in the distance, startling me, and the back of my head bangs off the roof of the car before I push myself back out of the window. My gaze flits around in every direction, but all I see are trees and shadows.

My body shudders as I think about my last encounter with wolves, the nightmares flood my mind and my heart races.

I can't let them take me again.

There is another howl, only this time it's closer. Without thinking, I shove my bag over my shoulder and move in the opposite direction of the howls. Bolting straight into the trees, without another care.

I have no idea what direction I'm going in, but it doesn't matter as long as I get away from the monsters chasing me. Branches whip against my bare face, catching my cheeks so hard they're sure to leave marks. I don't know how long I've been running when I bring myself to a halt. I'm panting and sweat covers every inch of my skin, but now that I've stopped, I feel the tendrils of cold gripping my body again.

A scan of my surroundings does nothing; I'm surrounded by trees. I can't even see the car anymore.

Fuck, I'm lost.

Opening my pack, I pull out a bottle of water and take a small sip. It's icy cold, but I need to stay hydrated. There has to be something out here, a place where I can find shelter until morning. Then I can try to find my way back to the town. The moon peeks through the foliage, and I see a glint of silver in the distance.

Putting the water away, I fasten up my pack and head in that direction. Snow crunches underfoot with each step, leaving small indents in the white powder. As I get closer to the silver, I notice it's a huge wire fence. It stretches as far as the eye can see to the left and right. If there's a fence, there have to be people out here. Picking a direction, I head left, following the fence as I go.

Every ten feet, there are signs warning trespassers to keep out and not to enter. If I can find an entrance, I can try to flag someone down within and see if they can help me without even entering the grounds. Carrying on in the direction I've been following, I inspect the fence a little more.

Considering how many signs there are telling trespassers to stay out, I find it odd that the spikes are facing the wrong way. Instead, they are pointing inside, as if they are there to stop someone from getting out. I shiver at the thought of what was inside. Running my fingers over the chain link of the fence, I keep walking.

My hand goes through the fence as I stumble, and I have to stop myself from face-planting it with the other. I push back from the metal and notice the gap between the posts, the fencing bent inwards as though someone has pushed their way inside. No one should be stupid to go inside somewhere with this many warning signs.

I twist away from the fence and shriek. I'm face-to-face with a wolf. It lowers itself down, showing me a set of wickedly sharp teeth as it growls. Without thinking, I spin back toward the fence. Shoving myself through the hole, I push against the metal, but with my pack on my back, there's no way I'm getting through. I pause my struggling for a moment to raise my gaze to the wolf.

It's closer now, sniffing the air before growling at me again. Dropping my bag on the floor, I dive for the gap in the fence. Burning hot pain explodes around my calf and I tumble to the ground. The wolf's teeth are deep in my skin, pushing down on the bone until there's a snap. I can't suppress the scream that rips from my lungs. I kick with my other foot to dislodge it but it's trying to pull me back through the fence.

I claw at the ground, attempting to get any sort of purchase so I can pull myself away from the wolf. A thundering howl explodes all around us. I don't even know what direction it's coming from, but then I'm free.

The wolf that was turning my leg into a chew toy releases its powerful jaws and cowers. Whatever else howled has the wolf scared. With a yip, it spins on the spot and gallops away.

Dragging myself fully inside the fence, I let out a shuddering breath. The wolf's appearance brought back too many memories. I knew I'd have to go through the wolf sector to reach my cousin's in the demon sector, but I was hoping if I stuck to the roads and didn't stray, then I wouldn't come across too many.

I sit and check my leg. My jeans are torn and blood trickles from the savaged skin. Reaching for my pack, I pull it closer and grab a t-shirt from inside. The fabric tears as I rip it into strips and use them as a makeshift bandage to stem the bleeding.

When I've done the best I can, I let my body flop back into the snow, not even caring for the cold anymore.

Chapter Four

Cayden

Grayson is going to be the death of us.

Stomping out onto the deck that surrounds the cabin I share with Grayson and Hunter, I clench my fists together. My nails bite into my palms, drawing blood and a spark of pain before the wounds heal themselves again.

If it isn't bad enough that we had to leave our pack for their safety, the fact that he keeps killing humans who trespass on our land is going to draw the wrong attention. We seclude ourselves from wolves and humans alike for their protection, but even with the signs on the fencing around the cabin, some are still stupid enough to enter.

I make a mental note to get Hunter to recheck the fencing and seal any breaches in the metal. There are only so many times we can afford to pay Achilles to clean up Grayson's messes. This really isn't how I expected to be spending my evening, not that I had any plans, but this definitely wasn't on the agenda.

It's a mile walk to the pit and another five miles to the perimeter of the fence on this side. As I move past the wildlife in the area, they all quieten down, recognizing the predator in their midst. Scrubbing a hand through my shaggy brown hair, I let out a sigh. I need to get a leash on Grayson soon before I have to put him down myself.

We've been friends for decades, he's the beta to my alpha and my brother in everything but blood. But last year, we had to leave the Blackwell Pack behind; the insanity poisoning our minds finally becoming a problem. I could no longer trust my decisions.

Grayson is suffering the most, spending more and more time in his wolf form. If we don't find our mates soon, then it'll be the end for us. The darkness will take over our minds and make us feral—the beasts will take over.

Reaching the charred pit, I pull my focus back to the present. There is a pile of logs beside it, covered in a tarp. It's barely recognizable now, with the snow covering the surface. Grabbing the edges of the plastic, I rip it away, balling it up before slinging it to the ground. Moving logs from the pile to the sunken earth, I arrange them ready for the bonfire we will need to burn the body.

As soon as I'm finished, I recover what logs we have left in the pile, taking note to replenish it. Pulling the lighter from my pocket, I light the edge of the tinder and place it within the logs. I add more as I walk around the edges until there is enough to set it all alight. Hunter once suggested adding gasoline, but he soon went off that idea when he nearly set the whole forest and himself on fire.

Shaking my head at the memory, I watch as the fire engulfs the wood. I feel the heat on my face as the flames grow. A crunch of foliage sounds behind me, but I already know Hunter is approaching. I could smell him as soon as he left the cabin.

"Once we're done, I need you to check the perimeter." I don't even turn to speak, keeping my focus on the flickering flames as they dance before my eyes.

"He's getting worse," Hunter comments.

"I know, brother," I reply. He's seen the madness taking over Grayson, the same as I have.

We attended the balls each year, even before the darkness sunk its claws in. While others in our pack were bonded, we never found our true mates. We'd once spoken about taking a blood mate between the three of us. It would freeze the blackness in its tracks for now, but Grayson would never return to how he used to be.

Could we really bring in a blood mate, one who could end up fearing for their lives when Grayson was lost in one of his spells? No, the chances of him killing them was far too high. We'd keep going until we couldn't go anymore, resigned to the fact that finding our mates was never meant to be. Grayson was losing more of himself every day, and we wouldn't leave our brother to face the darkness alone.

We'd rather go together, fulfill the promises we made to each other. When the madness gets too much, we'll end each other, and the last one will take their own life. The fences surrounding us will only hold us back for so long and we won't let our curse be the end of others.

The Blackwell pack would lose its alpha and betas, but before I left, we put things in place. If we don't check in every two weeks, then Beck, the interim alpha, is to contact the pack's lawyer and get the letter I left for him. He then has strict instructions to hold a vote for the next alpha of the pack to be chosen.

At least the pack will carry on, even without us. They'll be safe. For now...

A hand on my shoulder has me shifting to look at Hunter. I can see the stress lines on his handsome face. He shows nothing around Grayson, but when we are alone, I see the toll that the curse is taking on him. He won't say it out loud, covering his pain with jokes, but he's hurting. Hunter desires nothing more than to find his mate, like his parents did when they found each other, but even now he's losing hope that it will ever happen.

Placing my hand over his, I squeeze his fingers as he steps up behind me, resting his chin on my other shoulder. I feel the heat of his body as he presses up against me. With the flames in front of me, and Hunter behind me I'm wrapped in warmth. If only we had been destined for each other instead, we could have been mated and the darkness would never have gotten this far.

While I enjoy his company, Hunter isn't my true mate. Neither is Grayson. We use each other for release, and while we are connected as pack mates, that is the only connection we will ever have together. The only thing that could truly bond us would be if we shared a mate.

While rare, it isn't unheard of, much like the bonds we already have with each other. It would make it so much easier if our true mate was the same person.

For now, we will help each other when we can, and sometimes it beats down the darkness for a little longer. Or at least that's what we tell ourselves as we wring pleasure from each other.

Chapter Five

Grayson

Trudging from the cabin, I'm frustrated by Cayden and what our lives have become. We are part of one of the strongest packs in this area—the Blackwell pack. But because we haven't found our mates yet, we are succumbing to the curse. It burns through all male shifters' bodies, though some don't start succumbing to the curse till much later in life.

Cayden knew the signs; he saw them in all of us. It was how his father died, he'd blood bonded with Cayden's mother, even knowing she wasn't his true mate. But blood bonding only temporarily holds off the darkness and once it returns, the descent into madness is swift and brutal. Cayden's father lasted longer than most. He was well into his sixties before the curse finally got him; it turned him into a savage beast.

No longer man and entirely wolf, his father had attacked members of the pack on the night of a blood moon. Killing men, women and children indiscriminately, we had overpowered him, and Cayden had been forced to rip his own father's throat out.

As soon as I showed the first signs, Cayden kept a close eye on me. Hunter assumes I haven't noticed the madness in his eyes, but I see it even if he tries to keep how it affects him to himself. The final straw came when Cayden nearly killed the other beta in our pack. Beck had only made a small comment, but my alpha had lost his shit. He'd tossed Beck against the wall before kicking him in the side and fracturing a few ribs.

When Cayden came out of it, he panicked. He all but forced us to leave the pack. He left Beck in charge as the interim alpha, and we'd announced to the rest of the pack that we were going to search for our mates. Really, we were going to die. We'd been to every ball we could attend and we'd still not found our true mates.

You don't need anyone. We're stronger alone. A voice whispers in my mind.

I know the voice is lying to me. It's the darkness sinking its claws into me and propelling me further into the darkness. No good will come from letting it have its way, only death and misery. I chuckle to myself because death is all that's coming for me, anyway. Without my mate, I'll give in eventually and it will force Cayden to end my life just like he did his father.

Thinking about the past leads me further towards the hunter's body than I expected. I'm already coming up on the lake. As I get closer, I smell his blood in the air again, but it has a rancid and toxic scent now. Coming up beside him, I kick his limp body with the toe of my boot before leaning down and hefting him over my shoulder. I grab his gun in my free hand and start heading back for the cabin.

As I cross through the line of trees bordering the lake, I hear a shrill scream. Dropping the body from my shoulder, the transformation explodes through me as my paws smack the ground with a thud. My wolf is moving before I even consider which direction to go in. I take a moment to realize I'm heading towards the fence.

Has another human come through?

If they have, we'll be burning two bodies in the fire pit tonight. I let out a howl and it echoes through the surrounding forest. Every creature around me stops at my warning. Even the predators pause in their stride. Galloping through the trees, I get closer to the fence. And then I smell it, the sweet scent of blood.

Pulling to a stop, I see a figure in the snow and I let out another growl, but they don't move. They don't even make a sound. I stalk closer toward the prone form and as I get closer I realize it's a woman. Her blonde hair spreads out across the snow. It's tinged red with blood by her forehead. But it's the blood coating the lower half of her jeans that gets my attention.

When I'm looming over her, another growl rips from within me. My teeth drip with saliva as I prepare to rip her throat out. The darkness is baying at me to end her life. I'm about to strike when a soft moan drifts from her lips and my movements still. Sniffing the air again, I drink in her scent of roses and jasmine and the darkness ceases its incessant call.

My body creaks and moans as I shift back to my human form. Kneeling beside her in the snow, I reach out a hand and brush her bloodied hair away from her face. My fingers graze against her cheek, and an electric shock races through my hand, up my arm, and straight to my heart. I nearly fall down on top of her, but quickly brace my arm on the other side of her body and scan her face.

Her eyes are shut, but I see movement under her lids. Her lips are parted, and I wonder what it would be like to taste her. I lean my body closer until my chest is pressed against hers. I can feel and hear the steady beat of her heart and it makes my lips curl up in the corners.

She's ours. My wolf cries. I feel him stir under my skin. He hungers to taste her as much as I do.

My lips trace over her cheekbones. Her skin is so soft beneath me. A small whimper escapes her as I drag in one more breath of her delicious scent before I push back on my heels, gather her in arms, and turn toward the cabin.

I run the entire way back, not caring for my nakedness or the sticks and stones that ravage the soles of my feet. Jumping up the steps, I slam my shoulder into the door, almost busting it off its hinges. There's no one inside. Cayden and Hunter must still be at the pit waiting for me to bring the hunter's body.

Opening the link that connects my mind to theirs, I call for them both as I lay the woman's body down on the couch. Cayden is the first to burst through the open doorway.

"What's going on?" Cayden pulls up beside me but pauses the moment he sees the woman on the couch.

"You were meant to bring the body to the pit, not to the..." Hunter's voice drifts off as he steps up next to Cayden. "She's not dead."

"No fucking shit, asshole," I bark at him. "I found her at the perimeter. We need to help her."

"Hunter, get your things," Cayden orders and I hear Hunter move to the hallway to get his medical kit from his room. "You didn't kill her?" Cayden's attention comes back to me.

I shake my head at him as I peer down at her unconscious form. Dropping to my knees, I slip the socks from her hands and take one of them in mine. I'm hoping to feel the same shock I did when I first touched her, but it's just a low thrumming tickle across my skin.

Hunter dashes back into the room and all but shoves me away from the woman. The minute I lose contact with her I let out a growl. I lunge to my feet and grab Hunter by the front of his shirt. His eyes widen as he takes me in, he can feel my wolf close to the surface.

"I'm here to help her, Grayson. But to do that I need you out of the way." Hunter attempts to placate me but all I do is snap my teeth at him.

"Grayson, let him go," Cayden demands, the air becoming thick with his alpha power. I feel it wash over me but the darkness is pushing back.

My fingers flex a little on Hunter's shirt, but I can't seem to get them to release him. Every time my fingers loosen, fear of him hurting the woman has me tightening my grip again.

"Grayson! I am your alpha. You will release him now!" Cayden pushes out with his power again and it crashes into me in a wave. My fingers finally open and I release Hunter. "Go and finish cleaning up your mess, Gray." Cayden's voice is softer now, but I shake my head at him.

"No, I need to stay. I need to keep her safe." I stomp around the back of the couch, leaning over it so I can watch her. Still I didn't care about my nakedness.

Cayden looks between me and the unconscious woman on the couch, shaking his head and letting out a huff. Hunter has his medical kit already half open and is already wearing surgical gloves.

Unwrapping the strips of t-shirt from around her ripped jeans, he grabs a pair of scissors and he reaches for the woman's pant leg, cutting it to the knee. I let out another growl as I see the bite mark on her calf. Hunter raises his eyes to mine before getting back to work.

"Fine. Hunter, clean her up and situate her upstairs." He turns his gaze on me. I feel his eyes burning into me. "And I guess I'll be clearing up your mess... again. At least put some clothes on. You don't want to scare her with the monster between your legs if she wakes up."

With that, he twists, grabbing a discarded pair of sweatpants off the rack by the door and flinging them at me. I grab them without even looking up at him and yank them up my legs.

Chapter Six

Lila

Every inch of my body hurts, from my head all the way to my toes. But the worst pain is in my calf. Images of a wolf sinking its razor-sharp teeth into my flesh springs in my mind and I scramble to sit up.

Agony ricochets through my lower leg. I slam my eyes shut and clench my teeth together. When the throbbing becomes an ache once more, I let out a sigh and release my death grip on the comforter underneath me.

Slowly opening my eyes, I look around. I'm sitting on an unfamiliar king-sized bed. The walls around me are made entirely of wooden logs. There is a small dresser against the wall on the right, a set of drawers on either side of the bed, and that's it. At the end of the bed is a wood railing with stairs leading to a lower level.

Pausing, I listen and wait to see if I can hear anything coming from the floor below, but there is nothing but silence. I swing around on my ass, moving my legs over the edge of the bed and look at my wrapped-up calf. There is a bandage from my knee to my ankle.

I tense and remember the sound of cracking as the wolf locked its jaw around my leg and the intense pain that followed before I passed out.

Did the wolf break something? How much damage did it do? Why am I not in a hospital?

I assess the rest of me. My jeans are gone. But apart from those and my missing hoodie, I still seem to be dressed in the clothes I had on in the car. There are a few bumps and bruises on my arms and legs and a dull ache in my head. I lift my fingers to where it hurts the most and feel the paper stitches that hold a cut together.

Pushing up from the bed, I place my weight onto my good leg before trying to shift to the other one. As soon as I put even a morsel of weight onto the injured limb, I cry out in pain and fall to the floor in a crumpled heap. Burning agony sweeps up my leg and tears flood my eyes.

Frustration swells within me. I need to get out of here. Wherever here is. *He'll* be coming for me, and I need to keep moving. If I don't, *he'll* capture me and finally complete the blood moon ritual. Fear and determination fill me as I push up onto my knees.

I check out my surroundings again and shuffle across the floor for the drawers. I don't know who lives here, but the last time I was outside snow had been falling. There is no way I can go outside in the clothes whoever owns this place has left me in.

When I reach them, I push up fully onto my knees, opening each drawer and rooting around for what I need. Pulling out a couple of pairs of socks and some gray sweatpants, I put them on. They aren't perfect, but they should help fend off some of the cold in the lower half of my body.

My leg twinges again and I wince. I grind my teeth together. Everything is taking too long and my frustration grows further. I check another drawer and find a pile of sweaters. Plucking the first one from the top of the pile, I hold it up in front of me. It's going to drown me, but it'll work until I get back to civilization and find some help. I drag it over my head. The sleeves are too long, and I have to roll them up slightly.

That's when the smell hits me. Cinnamon and vanilla. I can't stop myself from lifting the material to my nose and inhaling. Slumping down, I get lost in the smell that comforts me and calms my nerves.

Pulling myself out of the fog that seems to take over my mind, I shift back onto all fours and crawl across the floor, heading for the opening in the railing. When I reach the stairs, I sit at the top of them. Below me is an open-plan living room. I can't hear anyone downstairs, but that's not to say there isn't someone hiding in a dark corner. There must be someone else here. It's not like I bandaged my own leg.

I want to push myself to my feet and sprint down the stairs, but with the damage to my leg, I'm not sure that's going to be possible. Instead, I take one step at a time on my backside. It's hard going with only one leg, but it's better than the alternative. I'm halfway down the stairs when I have to pause and take a breather.

This is going to be more challenging than I thought. I have no idea how I'm going to get back to my car, where it is, or even how to find the road when I can't even get down some stairs. Maybe I can persuade whoever brought me to take me back, but I don't know if I can trust them. Who lives in a cabin in the middle of the woods, surrounded by a fence that looks like it's trying to keep something in?

Is it even safe to go outside? What if the wolf who bit me is still out there?

My mind races. Shoving those thoughts away, I continue my journey down the stairs. When I get to the bottom step, I'm exhausted and frustrated. Lifting the leg of the sweatpants on my damaged leg, I spot the blood slowly spreading through the bandage.

Fingers gripping the railing, I use it to pull myself upright. I'm not steady on my feet, but maybe I can find something to lean on once I make it outside. Looking up, the door I could see from the top of the stairs seems so much further away than it was before.

I take a tentative step, putting weight down on my injured leg. The minute I do, I crumple into a heap, landing funny on the bottom step. Pain shoots up my spine and my leg. It's at that moment that the tears start, the droplets streaking down my cheeks. I let out a whimper and stretch my bandaged leg out in front of me.

There is no way I'm going to get anywhere. The damage to my leg is too great and unless I plan on crawling back to the road, which I don't then I'm stuck here. I hear a creak outside and lift my head, staring at the door as tears blur my vision.

Someone is coming. I don't know if they are friend or foe.

Fear floods my system and I let out another whimper, closing my eyes tight. It could be *him*. Has *he* finally found me?

Chapter Seven

Cayden

The snow crunches beneath my booted feet as I stomp out of the forest. The smell of the fire in the pit clings to my clothes and skin. The first thing I need to do when I get back to the cabin is grab a long, scalding shower to scrub the smell of ash from every part of me. Grayson shakes the snow off his fur as he bounds up the steps and onto the porch. As he gets closer to the door, he lets out a whine. It's then I smell it.

I rush through the cabin door, leaving Grayson behind, and the scent of fear hits me full force as I shove my way inside. Her whimpers ring in my ears as I take her in. The blonde beauty that Grayson found just inside the perimeter is sat at the bottom of the stairs. Tears streak her face and the smell of blood tinges the air.

At that moment, I realize she's stolen some of my clothes—not that I mind. It's better than her coming down here in what Hunter left her in after checking her injuries. From the fresh scent of blood, I assume she has reopened her wound. Something Hunter won't be impressed with, not after all the work he put into stitching up the gnarly laceration on her leg. He had even removed a broken wolf tooth from it.

Grayson's response to the events had been the most surprising thing. The fact he had wanted revenge, or that he'd brought the woman home confuses me. Not just that, his protective instincts are rarely triggered by these sorts of things. His scars prove his worth as pack enforcer, but he hasn't cared about anyone or anything since the darkness dug its claws into him.

Something is changing. I can feel it.

Her head whips up and her eyes widen as she takes me in. I must look like a mess to her, my skin speckled with dirt and ash. I wouldn't be shocked if there is the odd blood stain on my clothing too, but the all-black materials hopefully hide it well enough.

The smell of fear gets stronger as the woman attempts to push herself up from the bottom step and back up the stairs, but all she does is fall down. Her cries of pain shake me to the core and kick me into action. I'm in front of her in a split second.

I drop to my knees in front of her and try to make myself as small as possible. A difficult task when the alpha in me desires nothing more than to make sure she knows I'm the predator and she is the prey. He feeds on her fear and his hackles are raised, but I won't let him overwhelm me.

The poor woman is absolutely terrified, and my wolf bristling at the surface is going to make her more afraid of me than she already is. With my hands out in front of me, I try to soothe her. I hum softly, but her body still quivers.

"I will not hurt you." I finally find the words to calm her. Her head tilts up and she stares at me with those glistening blue eyes. I see the tears in the corners and all I want to do is reach forward and wipe them away.

My hand reaches toward her, but as I do, she leans away from my touch, and I quickly withdraw.

"Please, let me help you to the couch. I need to check your wound." I point at the spreading red on her leg and her eyes track to the spot.

A small nod is all I get in response. I scoop her into my arms and her hands claw at my shirt as I carry her to the couch. Sitting her on the edge, I lift her foot onto the coffee table. The minute my fingers grace her skin, a shot of electricity races up my nerves and my heart skips a beat.

Mine. The alpha in me claims.

My fingers trail down her pale skin from her knee until they reach the edge of the bandage. Unhooking the safety pins holding it in place, I carefully unwrap it. I deposit the soiled cloth behind me and grab the medical bag that Hunter left on the floor, dragging it towards me.

I assess the bite mark on her leg. The wound is still clean, but the trip down the stairs has ripped a few of the stitches. The worst parts of the wound are now open and blood is dripping down from the torn skin. I grab the saline solution and gauze from the bag, and I methodically clean the fresh blood away. I put pressure on where the wound is bleeding from.

As I press down, a small whimper escapes her throat. She's been silent since I sat her on the couch, but now my eyes jerk to her and my wolf whines. He wants to comfort her and snatch away the pain I've caused her.

"I'm sorry," I murmur. "If I could take away the pain I would." I continue to hold the pressure on her leg. "Do you remember what happened?"

"I was running. I found the fence, there was a gap. I wouldn't have come in otherwise." Her voice is like music to my ears. "But a wolf attacked me and I panicked. Why is it always wolves? Why are they always coming for me?" Her words gain pitch as she reaches the end of her sentence.

"I promise you, the wolves won't come for you here." The real wolves in this forest know not to come on our land; we've marked every inch of it, especially Grayson. Even with the fence broken, they daren't cross the perimeter. They know who the true owners of this land are, and they fear us.

"I need to keep moving." She suddenly moves, brushing my hand away and trying to rise on her uninjured leg. The minute she stands on the wounded one, she falls.

I'm on my feet in the blink of an eye and I wrap my arms around her slender form. I can't stop myself from bending down and brushing my nose against her neck, inhaling deeply. It's like freshly cut roses, jasmine, and a hint of my scent from the clothes she has stolen.

Mine, mine, mine. My wolf whines.

My hand brushes through her hair and I pull her head back slightly until my eyes lock with hers. Her pupils are dilated and I feel the pull between us. I want to lean down and kiss her and I edge closer to her. My lips graze across hers and I give her a soft kiss even though my wolf demands I claim her.

Her lips tremble against mine for only a moment before she responds to my kiss. Her hands grab onto my hair, holding me against her. I brush my tongue against the seam of her mouth and she parts for me, letting my tongue slip inside.

We devour each other, the push and pull setting my blood on fire as I hold her body against mine. In the next moment, she is ripping herself away from me, her hand pushing against my chest, my heart rapidly beating under her fingers. Our breaths are labored and all I can smell is her.

"We can't," she mumbles, keeping her weight against my chest as if she is using me to keep herself upright.

Of course we can't. She doesn't know me. I know this, or at least I should. But all my wolf is doing is pushing against my skin, craving to lay her down, to savor every touch and the feel of her skin as we claim her. To feel her tighten around my cock as she takes my knot.

I pull myself together; I take a small step back from her, and then another. She stands on one leg, swaying slightly before lowering herself down onto the seat and staring up at me with wet eyes.

Did I cause those tears? My wolf whines at me again. He wants to wrap around her and soothe her. Instead, I take another step back.

"I'm sorry." Grabbing another bandage and gauze from the medical case, I hand them to her.

The minute she takes them from my grasp, I spin on my heel and stalk out of the cabin. The last thing I want to do is leave her behind, but if I don't, I'm unsure what my wolf will do. He's too close to the surface to trust myself.

The door slams behind me and I pass Hunter on the steps. I had sent him to secure the opening in the fence that the woman came through after Grayson returned and to check the rest of the perimeter for any more gaps.

"Cay, where are you going?" He shouts after me, but I ignore him. As soon as I'm far enough from the cabin, I strip out of my clothes and drop to the snow-covered floor. The transformation sweeps over me, and I take off into the forest.

Chapter Eight

Lila

The man storms away, leaving me with the bandage and gauze in my hands. I blink rapidly. My body feels hot, and my skin is clammy after that kiss. A kiss that completely devastated me. As soon as he held me in his arms, I could smell the same delicious scent I picked up on the sweater when I put it on and I couldn't stop myself.

It wasn't until memories of *him* forcing himself upon me flash before my eyes that I pull away. Holding the man with gorgeous, shoulder-length russet hair at a distance, my breath comes out of me in pants. My heart is on the verge of bursting out of my chest. But then he moved away from me, taking cautious steps back until he was no longer within reaching distance.

Sitting on the couch, I want so much to tell him that the tears streaming down my cheeks were not caused by him, but I couldn't seem to find the right words. All I managed was a feeble refusal. His expression went blank before he apologized and he raced out like the hounds of Hell were on his heels, the door slamming behind him.

I grip the bandage and gauze tighter in my hands. The nightmares of what happened to me in that cave are never truly going to leave me. I have no idea if I'll be able to get that close to a man again. While the kiss left me with an ache for more, the terror of my past isn't far behind it.

A gentle knock at the door startles me and I sink back into the couch. Could it be the man? Did he come back? The door creaks open and I don't even realize I'm holding my breath. But it isn't the same man. This is someone new.

He looks to be a little shorter than the first man, and his blond hair is swept back away from his face. Eyes that I can only describe as being close to amethyst look over at me before they glide down my body to my legs.

"Oh no, you opened the wound." His voice is soft and angelic as he shuts the door quickly behind him. The complete polar opposite of the other man. "Let me see about getting that closed back up for you."

I should be scared that there is yet another man in this cabin, but something in his voice calms me. He approaches where I'm sitting on the couch before dropping to the floor in front of me.

"At least he cleaned it before he ran out of here." He's talking to himself, but I don't care as long as he continues speaking. With a shake of his head, he pulls the bag the other man left on the floor closer to himself and rifles through the contents. He pulls out a bottle of clear liquid and a syringe.

"I should probably introduce myself before I stab you with sharp objects." He raises his eyes to mine and grins, showing a little of his teeth as he does. "I'm Hunter, resident doctor of this rat pack group." He places the syringe and vial down on the table and reaches a hand out toward me.

With a shaky hand, I reach toward him. As we touch, I swear I feel a small static shock race through my fingers. It's like when the other man touched my leg. The man, who hasn't taken his gaze off me since he entered the cabin, eyes go wide. His hand wraps around mine and he shakes it firmly before he gives my fingers a small squeeze.

"And what about you, gorgeous? Is there a name to go with such a stunning woman?" He keeps my hand in his as he raises an eyebrow.

"Lila," I mumble.

"Ah, a beautiful name for a beautiful woman. It's lovely to meet you, Lila. Welcome to our humble abode." Finally, he releases my hand, reaches for the syringe and vial before he turns back to me. "May I? It's nothing sinister, I promise. Just some anesthetic, so I can redo the stitches that got pulled out." He tilts the bottle toward me so I can see the label.

I read it and give him a nod. He jabs the needle into the vial and withdraws a small amount of liquid into the syringe.

"I'm sorry. It's going to sting, but only for a moment." He gives the syringe a flick before he moves it closer to my leg.

The needle slips through my skin with a pinch, but I barely feel it. Hunter's other hand lies next to where he's injecting me and his touch makes me forget what he's doing. With a nod and a smile, he pulls back and recaps the syringe before he places it on the table. Hunter leaves his hand on my leg, and his fingers caress my skin. Slowly, the area goes numb until I can barely feel his touch anymore.

"See, I told you. Just a sting. Now let me just find what I need." Hunter twists his body away from me as he reaches back into his bag. "So, pretty Lila, tell me about you?" I don't say a word. I just stare at him. "Not a talker, huh? I see. It's all good. I can talk enough for the both of us."

With his focus back on me and a suture kit in his hand, he begins to close up the ruptured stitches. All I feel is a slight tugging sensation as the thread pulls through my skin.

"As I said, I'm Hunter." Another stitch. "And the buffoon that went running out of here is Cayden." The needle pushes back through my skin. "There's one other, he's the one who found you—Grayson. He spends a lot of time in the woods, so don't expect to see much of him."

My entire focus is on Hunter's face. I watch his lips move as he speaks. His eyebrows pinch together with each stitch he adds and ties off.

"We live out here together. It's much quieter in the forest than it is in the town." He places the suture kit back down and inspects his work before he smiles up at me. "All done. Now, where was I?" He reaches forward and grabs the bandage and gauze that lie now forgotten in my lap. "Oh, yeah, so we live out here. Grayson found you in the forest and brought you back." He places the gauze over my wound. "The cabin is closer than the town. It made more sense, for sure." His fingers brush over my skin again, and I feel a tingle beneath his touch. "You were cold, too. We didn't want you to get hypothermia."

Hunter continues to wrap the bandage around my calf. "Sorry, this was the best I could manage at such short notice. You might want a little more support to help you walk."

"Broken?" The single word slips through my lips.

"No, not broken but if the wolf's tooth had hit any further to the right it'd have been a different story."

My eyes widen and my body stiffens. This is about the only time I wish I was supernatural so I could heal quicker and get out of here.

When he's finished, he pulls the leg of the sweatpants back down and busies himself, depositing everything back into his bag. I haven't noticed, but while Hunter has been talking to me, I've sunk further into the couch, my fear now at a manageable level. Hunter rises to his feet and places his bag on the table before he turns back to me.

"I was thinking of making a sandwich and some tea. Would you like some?" He doesn't wait for me to answer and heads for the open plan kitchen I hadn't even noticed when I first came down. I track his every movement. "Don't fret, I'll make you something anyway. If you don't eat it, I'm sure Cayden or Gray will later."

There's the banging of metal and the running of water as he fills a kettle and places it on top of the gas burner.

Hunter hums to himself as he works. He moves around the kitchen with the grace of a cat, his footsteps barely even making a sound. The kettle whistles and he turns off the burner before grabbing a box of tea bags out of one of the many cupboards lining the walls. Dropping one in each cup, he fills them before he carries them over to the dining table between the couch and the counter.

Hunter adds a few more things to the table before walking over with two plates. He places them down on a huge dining table on the other side of a dark hallway before he heads back over to where I'm still sitting on the couch.

"Now, I don't want you to split your stitches again. So, if it's okay with you, I'd prefer it if I could carry you to the table."

"Okay," comes another mumble from my mouth. With a smile, he leans down and sweeps me up.

My arm loops around the back of his neck and I lean my head against his chest. The sound of his heartbeat against my ear continues to calm me. Inhaling deeply, the smell of him—old books and coffee—soothes me. My hand around his neck tightens and I let out a sigh. I swear I hear him sniff the top of my head as he carries me.

Reaching the table, he slowly lowers me to my feet. I lean on one leg and grasp onto his arm as he pulls a chair out. Taking my hands in his, they tingle as our skin connects. It's only mild, but it makes my heart rate increase.

"Take it slow." Hunter helps me down onto the chair before he moves to the space at the head of the table.

I shift my focus to the hardwood in front of me. There's a plate with a ham sandwich on white bread and a handful of potato chips. My stomach grumbles. I haven't eaten properly in what feels like forever. Mostly I've snacked on junk food I've picked up from the few gas stations I've stopped at along the way.

"How do you take your tea? We have some creamer, sugar, honey, and lemon. You name it, we have it." Hunter's voice startles me enough that I jump.

"Creamer, one sugar." He nods and finishes my tea exactly how I requested. Once he's done it, he pushes the cup closer to me.

I wrap my hands around the cup; the heat seeps into my skin and I sigh once more. Lifting the cup to my mouth, I take a small sip and then another. Before long, I'd drunk over half the cup. Few people know how to make a decent cup of tea, but this is perfect. None of that using a microwave to heat the water and putting the milk in first nonsense.

I edge the cup back onto the table and bring the sandwich to my mouth to take a bite. Chewing slowly, I let out a small moan. It might not be much, but it's better than microwaved pizza and two-day-old hot dogs.

"Wow, if that's all it takes to make you moan, pretty Lila, I can't wait to see what you do when I make you more than a sandwich," Hunter comments. His sandwich is just in front of his mouth as if he is about to take a bite.

My cheeks heat as embarrassment floods me. I nearly choke on the bite still in my mouth and quickly swallow it before I grab the cup of tea again to take a swig to wash down the bread that now seems to be stuck in my throat.

"Don't be embarrassed. You should hear the sounds that come out of Cay and Gray's mouths during dinner. They're like animals."

A small laugh bursts from my lips. I can't stop myself. The chuckle that comes from Hunter makes butterflies take flight in my stomach. Trying to distract myself, I take another bite of my sandwich. This time I'm a lot more successful.

Hunter and I sit in companionable silence as we eat. Before long, we both finish our sandwiches and tea. I place the cup on top of the plate and go to stand. Hunter is on his feet before I can even get my legs in front of me. He places a hand on my shoulder to keep me in place.

"What sort of gentleman would I be if I didn't clean up too? Especially with you being injured." Hunter swipes the plates from the table and strides into the kitchen. He ditches the empty dishes into the sink with a clank.

I lean back slightly on the chair and take a deep breath. This is the first chance I've had to relax in months. Even at the sanctuary my nerves were always on edge, constantly checking over my shoulder. When I was outside, it felt like there were always eyes on me. Eyes I know in my heart were *him*. But here, I'm feeling the safest I have in forever.

Chapter Nine

Hunter

This is the closest to the surface my wolf has been for months. The scent of roses and jasmine permeate the surrounding area. *Lila.* Her pale blue eyes followed my every movement from the minute I entered the cabin. Even as I was making us both something to eat, I could feel her stare burning into my back.

Now, as she relaxes at the dining table, I can't stop my eyes from roaming over to her while I wash the dishes we used. She's wearing Cayden's clothes, but I wish she were wearing mine so I could smell myself on her. After I patched up her leg the first time, Cayden decided his room in the loft space would be the best place to situate her. The area is bright and airy, with little furniture. At least we could keep an eye on her without the need to open and close any doors.

I'm not sure if she realizes she's been out for almost an entire day. She didn't wake as I disinfected the torn skin of her leg, or when I had pulled the broken wolf tooth from her wound and sewed it back together. We had cleaned her up the best we could, but there was no hope for her jeans.

I towel-dry the dishes and place them back in the cupboard as quietly as possible. Lila closes her eyes at some point. When I reach for the towel and from the soft sounds of her breathing, she seems like she's on the verge of falling asleep again. She hasn't picked the most comfortable place.

I move over to her and carefully lift her from the chair. Her head settles straight back onto my chest like when I brought her to the table. She mumbles something that's not coherent, even to my enhanced hearing. I carry her over to the couch and lay her down. Pulling a blanket from the back of the cushion, I tuck it around her small form.

My ears perk up at the sound of paws on the ground outside the cabin. Grayson must have returned from hunting the wolf that attacked Lila. I had wanted to ask Cayden about it when I got back, but he'd hightailed it out of here so quickly I hadn't had a chance.

I leave Lila on the couch and head to the door to let him inside. He's still in his wolf form. As he steps over the threshold and brushes past me, he focuses on Lila and lets out a soft whine. His muzzle and paws are still covered in blood, and it's definitely animal blood that I smell.

"Keep it down, you'll wake her." I hush him and he glares up at me, flashing his fangs. I know he won't attack me, or at least I hope he won't. His wolf has been unpredictable for a few months now.

Grayson heads straight over to Lila and I follow close behind him. With how his wolf has been, I'm not sure I can trust him alone with her. He glances toward the bloodied bandage and gauze on the floor and those silver eyes of his train straight back onto me.

"She reopened her wound when she tried to get downstairs. None of us were inside when she woke up." Grayson huffs at me, or at least huffs the best he can in his animal form. "What, you can't blame me? You went off to kill the wolf you could smell on her. Cayden sent me to check for any more holes in the fence and he went to finish disposing of your hunter."

Grayson lowers himself onto his haunches and rests his chin on the edge of the couch by Lila's head. He doesn't even seem to care that he looks like a savage beast with all the blood around his jaw.

"Couldn't you have at least cleaned up before you started lying all over the furniture?" I glare at Grayson and he snarls at me before he turns his attention back to Lila as her chest rises and falls.

Lila lets out a sigh and her eyes flutter open. She lets out a blood-curdling scream and slams herself back into the couch. Her arms rise to protect her face and Grayson growls.

I rush and grab him by the scruff of his neck to drag him away from her. He struggles against my hold and thrashes around. He smacks straight into the table and pulls from my grasp as he attempts to scramble away from Lila.

"Lila," I shout. I try to reach her, but she doesn't stop her screams. "He won't hurt you." I can't get through to her.

My fingers latch onto Grayson's scruff again and drag him to the door, fumbling to get it open before I propel him outside. I slam the door behind him and engage the lock. The door rattles as he heaves himself against it. I feel his need to get back to her but I can't let him. Not while she's in this state.

My attention returns to Lila. She's curled up in a ball in the corner of the couch, and I drop down beside her. My arms wrap around her shaking body. "Lila, please listen to me. I promise he won't hurt you," I murmur against her ear, but the shivers that race through her body don't stop. Her fingers latch onto my arms, and her nails dig into my skin, sure to leave small crescent moon imprints.

"Keep it away from me. Don't let it near me." Her voice trembles as she speaks.

"I won't let him back inside. But please, I need you to breathe. Take a deep breath in and count to four." She inhales deeply. "Now let it out on the count of four." Her breath comes out in a rush, but as she continues, I feel her tremors subside.

"The wolves—they're evil. They take and they take. They take what isn't even theirs." She rushes her words out between her inhales and exhales. "They hurt people." I'm not sure at this point if she is talking about actual wolves any more or shifters.

Lila's not entirely wrong if she is talking about shifters. I've heard rumors of wolves taking women to force them to become their blood mates.

I run my hands up and down her back. Her body still trembles weakly and I feel her tears. They make my t-shirt damp where her face presses against my chest. Her grip on my arms gets weaker and finally, she wraps her arms around my waist. I move my hands to her hair and brush it out of her face.

If there is any time to tell her we are wolf shifters, this certainly isn't it.

"He's gone. It's okay now." Lila still doesn't let go of me.

I shift a little on the couch and pull her toward me, so she is perched on my lap. I drag the blanket from where she was and drape it over us both. Lila barely moves, only a subtle change to lie the side of her face over my chest. I trace my thumb over her exposed cheek and wipe away the tears.

"He would never hurt you." Even though I know what Gray is like, I believe my own words. The fact he brought her back here alive after he found her on our side of the fence speaks for itself.

Any other human would be dead; his wolf would enjoy the hunt and the blood he would spill. The darkness would drag him into the depths and claim its pound of flesh. But there's something about her that seems to calm his beast. He's been the most like his old self that I have seen in a long time. Even my darkness is being held at bay.

Lila relaxes in my hold and her breathing evens out. I can only assume that exhaustion has pulled her under. It's not every day you get attacked by one wolf and then come face-to-face with another soon after.

As Lila sleeps quietly in my arms, I can't stop myself from touching her. The connection between us is a live wire that burns through my veins and sets my very soul on fire. I trace my fingers down the side of her neck before I hit the fabric of the jumper she wears. My hand skims down her arm. The heat of her body radiates through the fabric. When I reach her hand, I lace my fingers with hers. Her hand is so tiny inside my own and I marvel at how delicate she is.

Her fingers tighten around mine and she lets out a whimper before she releases them again. I want to chase away her nightmares, erase whatever haunts her mind. She was absolutely terrified of Gray. I'm not entirely shocked after a wolf attacked her in the forest. Seeing another wolf, especially one as huge as Gray in the cabin, is enough to push anyone over the edge. But what does she know of wolf shifters? Where has she even come from? If she's from this sector, she must have been to the balls and come across our kind before.

I sense Gray's return. He's in his human skin now, completely naked without a care in the world. Well, apart from her. He stands in the cabin's doorway and looks over at Lila curled in my lap. A sneer crosses his features before it's gone again, but I don't miss it.

Blood is still smeared around his mouth. Lifting my finger to my lips, I gesture for him to be quiet and point toward the bathroom. He storms off down the hallway to his room. The door shuts hard behind him, but it's not enough to stir Lila from her sleep.

Lila shifts against me and I feel my cock twitch. Her scent overwhelms everything. I know even when I take her back to bed and leave her there, my clothes will smell of her. And as much as it will leave me rock-hard, I don't want to wash her scent from them.

Deciding it's best to take her back to the loft, I carefully lift her and stand. I take the steps two at a time and approach the bed, placing her down as gently as I can. The blanket pools over her hips and I quickly make sure she's fully covered. I let my fingertips brush against the side of her face, and she nuzzles against my hand.

A door opens and closes downstairs and I drift away, pausing at the top of the stairs to glance back at her. I'll come and check on her later, but for now, I need to speak to Grayson and Cayden—if I can find him. I head back down the steps to the lower floor and head straight for Gray's bedroom. When I open the door, he's sitting on the edge of the bed, still gloriously naked. His mouth and hands are now clear of blood.

I make my way over to him and plop down beside him. The fact he's semi-hard doesn't go unnoticed by me.

"She hates me." There is a slight tremble in his voice.

"I don't think it's you she hates, Gray. She seems to hate all wolves, animals and shifters alike. Something has happened to that woman, and I don't just mean the fact a wolf bit her at the perimeter. There's something else going on there, too."

"I don't want her to hate me," Gray grunts. He's not usually the type to give a shit what others think of him, so this is different.

"You came on a little strong. Can you imagine being attacked by a wolf in the forest and then coming face to face with, well, you? You still had blood on your face, for Christ's sake." I let out a soft chuckle. "I think even I would crap my pants a little."

Gray snorts and looks over at me. He shrugs his shoulders. "There's something about her, I want her. My wolf does too."

"You're not the only one, buddy." I run a hand over my crotch and adjust my hardening cock that's trapped in the confines of my jeans. "We need to talk to Cayden when he comes back. Maybe she's the one we've been looking for."

I rise and reach out a hand to Gray; he grasps it and I pull him to his feet. When he's upright, I yank him towards me until our bodies are flush. My arms wrap around his waist and hold him close.

"We can't overwhelm her though, Gray." I feel his cock against my own. Only thin fabric is between us. If I can't get close to Lila yet, maybe Gray can take the edge off like we always have in the past. I wrap my fist around his cock and give him a tug.

A growl bursts from Gray's mouth and then his lips are on mine. We both attack my clothes and as I kick off my boots, his lips trail down my neck to my pulse point. He bites down hard on my skin. Hard enough to leave a bruise in its wake. I relish in his touch, even as he divests me of the materials that smell like her.

Once I'm naked, Gray shoves me down on the bed. He crawls over the top of me and his lips connect with mine again. Our hardened cocks rub against each other. A moan escapes from my mouth and Gray takes his fill. He thrusts his tongue into my mouth in time with his cock rubbing against mine.

"Fuck me, Gray. Fuck me hard. I need you to fill me." At my words, Gray leans away from me.

Gray flips me over and he reaches for the lube in the bedside drawer. He cracks open the lid and I hear it as he squeezes the bottle before he chucks it back onto the bed beside me. A calloused finger probes at my entrance and I relax for him. He presses knuckle deep and thrusts in and out of my hole over and over until all that leaves my mouth are pants and moans before adding another finger.

It doesn't take long before he pulls his fingers from me and I whine. I turn my head so I can look at him. Gray grabs the bottle of lube from beside me and slicks it up and down his hard length, adding more to my hole before his thick head is there. Nudging through the ring of muscle, I let out a breath as I relax.

Gray thrusts inside me, not even giving me a moment to grow accustomed to the intrusion before he's slamming home. The air is pushed from my lungs and I let out a grunt as my fingers wrap around the comforter. It's never soft or sweet with Gray. He moves at a punishing pace, setting my whole body on fire. The perfect blend of pleasure and pain.

I feel the change in thickness at the base of his cock as his knot pushes against me. A knot that I know for a fact won't swell when he comes. That only happens with wolves and their true mates.

I can't wait until I can watch him with Lila, as he cums and his knot swells inside her, locking them both together. Would she let me take her ass as he claims her pussy? Let us both knot her?

I have no idea where these thoughts are coming from. She doesn't even know us but with Gray deep inside me I can't help but wonder. Gray wraps his hand around my leaking cock and jerks me off, not even slowing down his thrusts.

The pace is hard and fast, and it isn't long before I'm grunting my release onto the bed. Gray follows close behind me. Spilling his seed inside my ass as he collapses on top of me, he takes us both down fully onto the bed.

We lie in a sticky, sweaty mess, both of us exhausted. But even now my thoughts shift back to Lila and as Gray's softening cock slips from inside me and his cum spills out, my length hardens again.

Chapter Ten

Lila

After my encounter with the wolf in the living room, I wake to find myself back in bed in the loft room. Someone has wrapped a blanket around me and voices are coming from below. There are at least two of them, from what I can tell. Shuffling up on the bed, I recline with my back against the headboard. The voices go quiet and a head appears at the stairs. Hunter.

"Hey, I thought I heard you. I'm making some stew if you'd like to come down and eat with us?"

"The wolf?" I question.

"He's outside. It's just me, you, and Cayden." At the mention of Cayden's name, I squirm. I haven't seen him since we kissed and I pushed him away.

"Okay," I mutter.

Hunter gives me a huge smile and makes his way up the rest of the steps. He approaches the bed slowly, his hands relaxed at his sides. When he reaches the side of the bed, he offers me his hand and I grasp it. Shuffling to the edge, he helps me to my feet. My leg still throbs. I don't even know how long it's going to take before I can put my weight fully on it again.

"May I help you to the stairs? Though, I might have to carry you down. Don't want you falling." I give Hunter a nod and he slips his arm around my back. My arm reaches around his waist as I lean my weight against him.

With small steps, we make the trek from the bed to the opening in the railing. I only stumble once or twice on the way while using Hunter as a crutch. Each time I slip, he tightens his grip on me until I'm confident to move again.

As soon as we reach the top of the steps, Hunter swoops down and picks me up bridal style. A shriek breaks from my lips and I laugh as I'm cradled against him. The low rumble of his laughter makes his chest vibrate. He carries me down and over to the dining table where we ate sandwiches earlier.

Lowering himself, he deposits me onto a chair that is already pulled back. Before he stands, he gently kisses my cheek and makes a hasty departure back to the kitchen. Shifting my attention to the table, I notice Cayden is sitting opposite me. His amber eyes bore into mine for a moment before he smiles.

"I'm sorry about earlier, Lila. It was very unbecoming of me." Cayden sounds sincere, and I accept his apology with a nod.

"It's okay." I tap my fingers on the table to distract myself.

"It's not. You're injured and I took advantage. It won't happen again." I slump in the chair at his words, feeling disappointed that he doesn't plan to kiss me again. Another part of me isn't sure if I'm comfortable with a man that close to me.

The door slams open, and hard steps stomp through the cabin's main door. Whipping my head around, I spot another man. He's absolutely huge with short salt-and-pepper hair and eyes that look almost silver. Stubble covers the lower half of his face like he hasn't shaved in a while.

A black t-shirt stretches across his torso and tight, ripped, blue jeans hug his legs. His eyes jerk toward me and he grunts slightly. Hunter moves around the counter, throwing an arm around the other man's shoulders.

"Lila, this is Grayson. Ignore his mean appearance; he's a softy, really." The comment earns him an elbow to the side from Grayson. Hunter lets out a grunt. "Okay, I lie. He's a total asshole, but he's going to be nice, aren't you Gray?" Hunter grins at Grayson, who shrugs Hunter's arm away and stalks over to the table.

Grayson drags out the seat next to Cayden. The legs scrape across the wooden floor before he drops into it. There's more grating noise as he pulls the chair closer to the table. His eyes never leave me and I feel my nerves tingling. I can't decide if I want to flee from this man or move closer to him.

"Hi," I offer him, but Grayson just grunts at me, earning him a stern look from Cayden.

"Foods up, kids," Hunter announces from the kitchen, appearing at my side and placing a huge steaming bowl of stew in the middle of the table. It smells absolutely amazing. I can't wait to tuck in but I don't reach for the bowl straight away, waiting to see what the guys do first.

Hunter moves back to the kitchen before he's at my side again. The scent of freshly cooked bread reaches my nose and I moan slightly. A groan echoes from across the table. I blink quickly, looking over at the two men opposite. They're both watching me with a laser focus and my cheeks heat.

"See. Told you I was the master of making people moan." Hunter chuckles, and Grayson glares at him. I don't hide the smirk that graces my lips.

"Shut up," Grayson grunts before snatching a bread roll from the bowl. He shoves half of it into his mouth and takes a huge bite.

Once all the plates and bowls are on the table, Hunter sits beside me, moving his chair a few inches closer so I can feel the heat of his body. Cayden reaches for the ladle resting on the side of the stew bowl and Hunter quickly slaps his hands away.

"Ladies first. Where's your manners, Cay?" Even Cayden is man enough to look sheepish at Hunter's words.

Shaking his head, Hunter loads the ladle with the delicious smelling concoction and reaches for the bowl he placed in front of me. He fills it almost to the top before depositing it back on the table. Hunter drops the ladle back into the stew and brings his attention back to me. He reaches over my body, grabs a few of the bread rolls, and puts them onto the plate beside my bowl.

Hunter rips one of the rolls in half, adding a generous helping of butter to each side that instantly melts from the heat of the still-warm bread. Grabbing a napkin, he opens it up and lays it on my lap before passing me a spoon. When our fingers connect, I shiver. He takes a moment to caress the back of my hand before breaking the connection once more and leaning back into his chair.

Grayson and Cayden are both watching us from across the table. Grayson looks grumpy as hell but I'm reckoning that might be his default setting. Cayden looks intrigued, but also a little annoyed as if he'd rather be on this side of the table with me.

"Dig in before it gets cold, Lila," Hunter remarks.

Dipping the spoon into the stew, I fill it before raising it to my lips. I can feel everyone's eyes on me. Opening my mouth, I wrap my lips around the spoon before pulling it back out. The taste explodes across my tongue as I chew the vegetables and meat. I have to cover my mouth to stop the moan that wants to escape.

"It's good. Really good." I dive back into the stew and get another heaping spoonful.

"Glad to hear it." Hunter grabs a few more rolls and adds them to his plate before filling his own bowl.

Once he's done the other two men follow suit. We eat in relative silence for a few moments, the odd grunt coming from Grayson who I notice is picking only the meat out of the stew with his fingers and leaving the vegetables. Cayden shovels the food into his mouth, not even taking a moment to breathe. The broth from the stew drips down both of their chins.

Hunter wasn't kidding when he said they ate like animals. When all that's left is liquid and vegetables, Grayson uses his rolls to scoop up as much of the broth as he can. Cayden at least used his spoon to eat, but as soon as the bowl is empty, he lifts it to his mouth and drinks what is left. He follows it up with a few rolls before reclining and rubbing his stomach.

Glancing over at Hunter, I observe he is definitely the most civilized of the three. Eating slowly, he seems to savor every mouthful of the delicious food. His eyes sometimes glance over at me to see where I'm up to. In fact, all three of them have been stealing glances at me as if I don't notice.

"Would you like some more?" Hunter asks as I use one of my rolls to soak up the last of the juices.

I shake my head. Two proper meals in one day is more than I've had in a long time and now I feel ready to pop, and a little sleepy.

"I'll clear up," Cayden exclaims as he rises from his seat. He gathers up as many of the dishes as he can carry before taking them to the kitchen.

Hunter follows suit, picking up what's left of the stew and trails behind Cayden. Grayson remains where he is, his silvery gaze watching me as I fiddle with the napkin in my lap.

I'm not sure what to do with myself. It's not like I can get up and leave the table without help, preferably from Hunter. He's the only one who has really touched me, and his body against mine calms me. Cayden unsettles my mind, making me hot all over, and Grayson...I'm not sure I want to risk what could happen if he gets close.

The thought of Cayden touching me sends heat straight to my belly and then lower. I clench my thighs together. The scrape of a chair being shoved back pulls me back from my thoughts as Grayson practically flings himself out of his chair.

"I'm going to check the perimeter again." His voice is gruff and strained as he rounds the table and stomps out of the door, slamming it behind him.

What's his problem?

As if reading my mind, Hunter lays a hand on my shoulder and I look up at him. "Don't worry, Lila. He's not used to it being more than just us three."

"If you can take me into the town I passed, I can get out of your hair." I don't want to leave. I feel oddly safe here, but I don't wish to cause disruption to their lives either.

"No, it's Gray's problem, not yours." Hunter kneels next to me, taking my hands in his. "He'll get over it. If it's okay with you, I'd like you to stay a little longer so I can keep an eye on your leg. I don't want to risk you getting an infection. I'll see if I can get Cayden to pick up more medical supplies in town."

I should demand he take me to the town, preferably to a hospital where I can get my leg looked at properly. But a part of me knows that I'm safe here, that I'm no longer being watched. The trek back to the town without my car wouldn't be possible, and even though Hunter has said they go there, I have no idea where their vehicle is.

If something happens en route, I have no way to escape. I'll stay for a while until I'm back on my feet. Then, they can take me back to the town and I'll continue on my journey out of this hellhole to my cousins. For now, I feel like these three could actually protect me. I don't know why, but deep in my gut, I know they can.

"Want to get a shower?" Hunter asks. The rapid nodding of my head confirms my answer. I can't remember the last time I got a proper shower. Using the sinks in restrooms to do a quick wash before getting back on the road didn't exactly count. "Come on, then."

Hunter stands and pulls me straight up to my feet. I lean against him as we make our way down the hallway I spotted earlier. We enter the first door on the left and I'm startled by what I see. The cabin might not be huge, but the bathroom is well-equipped. There is no bath but instead a huge shower is on the back wall, with enough space for at least two people and multiple shower heads.

The toilet and sink are modest in comparison, with a small mirror above the taps. Catching sight of myself, my mouth drops open. I see the bruises on my face where I hit the steering wheel and the butterfly stitches that hold an inch-long cut together. My hair is in total disarray. It resembles a bird's nest and looks greasy as hell.

I'm suddenly embarrassed at my appearance. I can't believe Cayden kissed me when I looked like such a hot mess. Itching to get clean, I move closer to the shower.

"Slow down, speedy. I'm going to have to get something to cover your leg while you shower so it doesn't get wet." Hunter kisses my cheek again and leans me against the side of the shower before he leaves the room.

Chapter Eleven

Hunter

Rushing out of the bathroom, I move back down the hall. When I round the corner, Cayden is still in the kitchen, leaning against the counter. His arms are folded across his chest as he looks in my direction.

"I kissed her," he blurts out as I get closer.

"I want to do nothing but kiss her, you lucky bastard," I snark. "Grayson feels it too. Do you think..." I trailed off.

"She's the one?" Cayden finishes my sentence for me. "Whenever I touch her, my wolf hungers to claim her. I had to leave earlier, or I don't think I'd have been able to stop myself."

Opening the cupboard under the sink, I grab an empty plastic bag and a roll of masking tape. It's the only thing I have for the situation and the best thing to stop Lila from getting her leg wet.

"My wolf is calm around her. He hasn't been calm for a while, Cay." I stand back to my full height and look over at my alpha. "We need to be careful, though. There's something she isn't telling us. We can't tell her what we are."

Cayden nods in agreement. "Take care of her. I'm going to check on Gray." He spins on his heel and strides out of the cabin, leaving me and Lila alone.

I return to the bathroom with my supplies and pause outside the door. Knocking gently on the hardwood, I hear a small yelp and the sound of things hitting the floor. Without waiting, I nudge the door open to find Lila attempting to reach down to pick up the shampoo bottle, which is now pouring its contents out onto the floor.

"Let me." Brushing up against her, I grab a towel and throw it onto the liquid mess. I swipe up the fallen bottle with my empty hand and set it back on the shelf inside the shower.

"I'm sorry," she whimpers. Her arms wrap around her waist as she hugs herself.

"Think nothing of it. We'll get more from the store." I smile at her and hold a hand out.

Lila slips her hand into mine and I help her to the small bench seat just inside the shower cubicle. I'm not sure how comfortable she will be with me, but I need her to drop the sweatpants to add the bag and tape. It'll make both of our lives so much easier.

"Can I help you remove those?" I gesture toward the offending pants. Her eyes cut to mine and her lip trembles, her teeth nibbling on her lower lip as she thinks about my question.

"I guess..." Her voice trails off.

Resting the tape and bag on the side of the sink, I bring myself back to her. Looping my thumbs into the waistband, I lower them slowly over her hips and down her legs. When the pants are around her ankles, I lift her non-injured leg first and remove it from her foot.

Without me having to ask, she sits down on the bench and holds her other leg up to me so I can remove the sweatpants entirely. Lila shivers as my eyes start at her feet and slowly work their way up her bare skin. I can't stop myself from brushing my fingers against her pale flesh. Her body quivers under my caress, and I look up at her face.

Lila licks her lips. Her cheeks are flushed pink under the bright lights. Reaching over for the bag and tape, I work clinically as I cover her wound inside the bag and tape around the top of it. I've done my best to make sure no water can get onto the wound underneath it.

"I'm sorry. It's the best I can do until Cayden goes to town."

Tossing the tape into the sink, I rise to my full height and offer her both of my hands. Lila grabs them without question, and I pull her to her feet. She looks up at me but doesn't make a move to gain space from me. With her so close, I want to pull her into my arms and kiss her like Cay admitted to already doing.

I want to taste her lips, drink down her scent, and drown in it. Lila half-hops closer to me, her body pressing up against mine. I can't stop the blood rushing straight to my cock as the smell of freshly cut roses and jasmine envelops me. Lila's lips part and I'm drawn straight to her, lowering my head toward hers.

Our lips brush together, and I feel that connection again. The sensation of electricity zaps through my body. Her hands grab at my shirt, feeling their way to the bottom, slipping under the hem and onto my bare skin. My whole body is lighting up under her touch. She must feel it too, as she gasps against my mouth.

I take the opportunity and slip my tongue inside her mouth. Our tongues explore each other, lips molding together as we devour each other. Lila's hands explore the flesh under my shirt and I slip one hand around the back of her neck, holding her mouth to mine. My other hand skims down her back, curling around her ass, and pulling her against my hardening length.

The minute my stiff cock brushes against her core, it is like a bucket of cold water has been thrown over Lila's head and she flings herself away from me. The back of her knees smack the bench seat and she falls down onto it. Her head hits the glass wall of the shower. Her breath is coming out in pants as she pushes herself back even further from me.

Lila's scent turns acrid, and the smell of fear floods the bathroom. Her eyes are wide, and she stares off into space, no longer looking at me, but straight through me.

"Please don't...I'm sorry...please don't hurt me." Her body curls up on itself as she fumbles over her words.

Her words slam into me. Whatever haunts her is replaying in her head, and I'm not sure if I can pull her out of it. Lowering myself back to the floor, I make myself as small as I am able, making sure I am below where she is curled up on the bench.

"Lila, no one is going to hurt you." I reach a hand toward her, pausing before my fingers could skim over her bare legs. "We will protect you. Me, Gray, and Cayden. You're safe here."

Lila's body still quivers even as I try to soothe her with my words. My wolf wants nothing less than for me to wrap myself around her and hold her close. To fight away her demons and bring her back to us. Whoever mistreated her deserves to endure a slow and painful death for hurting such a beautiful creature.

If I ever find who damaged this sweet woman, I will make it my mission to give them a slow and painful end. I'll draw them to the brink of death, before piecing them back together and starting from the beginning.

"Please, Lila. I need you to come back to me, beautiful." Lila's trembling subsides, but she is still unfocused. Moving a little closer to her, I gently lay my hands on hers and carefully open her clenched fists. There are moon-shaped indents in her palms already.

"Hunter?" her voice questions.

"It's me. I've got you. I promise." I edge closer to her.

When I'm sitting as close as I can, her hands still in mine, I raise my eyes to hers. This time she's looking straight at me. Her cheeks are stained with tears. Without warning, she flings herself into me, her arms wrapping around my torso as she straddles my thighs. Her head lies on my chest and, cautiously, I bring my arms around her shoulders, holding her close as she cries against me.

Lila's body is shaking again, but this time from the tears streaming down her face instead of from the fear. Running a hand through her hair, I hum gently and let her get it all out.

After what feels like forever, but is probably only a few minutes, Lila's sobs finally quieten. Pushing back from me she rubs her hands down her cheeks, wiping the tears away. Her outburst has reddened her eyes, but she still looks beautiful.

"I'm sorry for whatever you've been through. But I'll keep my promise. I've got you and we'll protect you no matter what." I brush my fingers down her cheeks, wiping the last of her tears away.

I push up to my knees with Lila still in my arms, place her on the bench seat, and lean into the shower. Rotating the dial, I set the temperature to warm before I turn the water on. Moving back to where Lila is sitting, I kneel back in front of her and take her hands in mine once more.

"Let's get you in the shower. If you're anything like me, you'll feel a million times better."

Chapter Twelve

Alaric

My wolves surround the abandoned car. They sniff and paw at the ground as I approach. Her scent lingers in the air, but it's fading now that she's no longer here. I lean in through the open window and inhale deeply. The intoxicating scent of my soon-to-be mate fills my lungs and my eyes drift shut.

My cock hardens and I palm myself, letting the fabric rub against my tip. Lust fills me as I remember all our times together. My little bitch sprawled out on the floor, her limbs chained down, the metal links clinking together as she struggled. Oh, how she struggled.

Her blonde hair had fanned around her head like a halo. Her naked skin had pebbled with goosebumps after I dragged her to the showers and shoved her under the frigid water while I had my way with her. Her body pressed flush against the tiles as I sank my cock into her. Her skin might have been clean, but my cum still dripped down between her thighs.

I'd marveled at the sight as I dropped to my knees and used my fingers to jam my seed back inside her quivering body.

"Please don't," she'd whimpered, but I knew she craved me. Me and my little bitch have a connection.

While she had told me no, I knew she loved it rough. The sight of her blood turned me on further and without another thought, I'd ravaged her body over and over, taking every hole she had to offer.

Her cries and screams had only spurred me on to claim what was mine. It was no longer about us joining during the blood moon to impede the darkness. My body craved her. I wanted to drink in her screams and her cries of pain, watch her bleed for me and bathe in her blood. She was mine, and I was so close to bonding with her when they came and took her from me.

She had disappeared from the cave while I limped away to lick my wounds after they decimated my pack, but I knew I wouldn't lose her for long. The tracking chip we had embedded under her skin had taken me to the magic born's sanctuary. Not long after, the signal went dead.

It hadn't taken me long to realize I was no longer receiving a signal, but she hadn't gotten far. My mate had stopped at a store to buy supplies and I slipped another tracker into the car while she was inside. The rundown piece of crap wasn't the best for security.

The receiver beeps and I'm pulled out of my memories. My cock is throbbing, something I will need to take care of later. I shove my hand in my pocket and yank out the receiver. The small dot bleeps showing my little bitch is only a few miles away.

"Boss, the boys are exhausted. We need to rest so we are ready to get your mate back." Ryan, my new beta, ambles up beside me.

I've gathered the rogues along the way. We all want to find our mates and when I told them about how mine was stolen from me they followed me to help retrieve her. I might not be a true alpha, but they know I'm in charge and will follow my orders no matter what.

"Hunt, feast, and rest." I glance back at the tracker and the barely moving dot. "We have time to plan."

"Yes, boss." Ryan wanders away and gathers the wolves. He barks orders to them and they scatter into the forest.

I take one more whiff of my little bitch's scent and saunter away. Casually striding down the edge of the tarmac, I'm a few miles down the road when I smell humans—a man and a woman. A smile spreads across my lips. I drop my clothes to the floor and shift into my wolf.

Hunt. Feast, the voice in my head calls.

My paws move and I veer into the forest, tracking the scent of the humans. It's not long before I come across a vehicle near the side of a dirt track and not far from it is a brightly coloured tent. Tire tracks are clearly visible in the snow. I scent the area and confirm that neither of the humans are close. With one tire in front of me, I slash my claws over the rubber. A faint hiss escapes as the tire deflates.

I shift away from the now immobilized vehicle and sniff the ground. The scent of the male is the strongest and I track him first. When I find him, he's gathering wood in his arms. The only light comes from the torch on an elasticized band around his head. He hums to himself, not even realizing he's being hunted.

I slip through the darkness, my paws shifting silently over the ground as I stalk my prey. He stoops down to gather another piece of wood and I strike. My body lands on top of his and I take him to the ground. We are plunged into darkness as the light on his head smashes. My teeth snap over his shoulder. He goes to scream but I sink my teeth into his neck, severing his spine and arteries.

His blood spills from his neck and turns the snow red. I shudder with lust at the sight. I crawl off the man and flip him over.

Feast. Feast. Feast.

My teeth sink into his thigh and I rip him to shreds, feasting on his flesh piece by piece. His blood doesn't taste as good as my little bitch's, but the meat will sate me for now. When I've taken my fill, I leave his carcass for the scavengers and continue my hunt.

"Tommy," a soft voice calls. "Tommy, where are you?" It comes again and I move in that direction.

The small woman stumbles through the trees. Her headlamp lights a small area in front of her. Her blonde hair cascades down her back. I move closer. Her eyes are green, but that doesn't matter. For tonight I can imagine she's her. I'll sate my lust before I kill her.

Fuck her. Kill her, the voice screams.

My bones shift, and my fur recedes until I'm standing naked behind a tree. I crouch low. My claws slash across my side and I grunt. The pain only adds fuel to my blood. I need to make it believable. I tumble from behind the trees straight in front of the path of the woman and fall to the floor. A groan leaves my lips as I hit the snow.

"Please...help me," I add an extra thread of strain to my voice.

"Oh, my God!" the woman exclaims. "Tommy!" Her voice is like nails on a chalkboard. "Tommy, come quick."

That's it, come to me. Save me.

The woman falls to her knees beside me. Her hand lands on my shoulder and I shudder at her touch. She presses against my shoulder and I let her shift me onto my back. She scans my body until her eyes fall to the slashes across my side.

"Shit, what happened to you?" Her hand presses to my wounded side and my cock twitches.

"Wolf." I grimace. "I was bathing in the stream. It attacked me." A frown appears on the woman's face before it's gone again.

The woman reaches into her pocket and fumbles with her phone. She raises it into the air, wafting it around. "For fuck's sake. I've got no signal. Come on, I'll get you to our jeep and take you to town."

She moves an arm around my back and helps me sit. The wound on my side has begun to heal; I need to move this along. I let her struggle a little as she gets me to my feet and puts an arm around my waist, the other still over my side. We take stumbled steps and she mutters to herself about Tommy's disappearance and hopes he will be at the car.

I let her guide me. She imagines she is going to help me. She doesn't realize what's coming.

As we get closer to the jeep, she leans me against it. Her hand falls away from my bloody side and she tries the door handle. It's locked and she curses. Her eyes darted around the forest.

"Tommy, where the fuck are you, you asshole?" she screams into the trees around her, but she gets no response. She doesn't know that Tommy is no longer breathing. She makes her way back over to me. "I'm so sorry. My boyfriend's got the fucking keys. And fuck knows where he is."

I grin before her eyes move to mine and I quickly drop it. She moves a hand back around my waist and guides me towards the tent. "Let's see if we can stop the bleeding. As soon as Tommy gets back, we'll get you to town."

She drops to her knees and opens the zip at the front of the tent. She reaches out a hand to me and helps me down. I give the appropriate sounds of pain and discomfort and follow her into the tent. My knees hit the inflatable mattress and it sinks below my weight. In a crouched position, she grabs a few bottles of water and a towel.

She shrugs out of her thick jacket and lets it fall into a space next to the mattress. Her long-sleeved top covers her skin, but it won't for long.

"Lie down." I do as she asks and drop onto the mattress. She kneels over me, dampening the towel with water.

She presses it to my side and cleans the blood away. The towel comes back red, but with the blood gone and my wound already closed, there are only faint lines which won't be there for much longer.

"What the actual fuck?" She gapes down at me, and I strike.

With lightning speed, I spring up and grab her by the back of the neck. She screams, but no one will hear her.

I slam her body down into the mattress and hover above her.

My hand moves over her mouth to squash the shrill screams. My nails extend on my other hand and I make quick work of her clothes. The claws skim over her flesh, leaving shallow cuts all over her skin.

She struggles against me. Her nails scratch at the hand over her mouth, leaving welts in their wake, but it drives me on. My claws drag down her back, adding more shallow cuts until I reach her hips. I lift them so her ass is in the air. Gathering saliva in my mouth, I spit into my hand, slathering my cock with the fluid.

With one hard thrust, I'm seated fully inside her. Her pussy doesn't lie. Her walls squeeze around my length as I begin to pant. Her teeth dig into my hand making me groan. The pain adds to my pleasure. I release her mouth and she lets out another scream. It's like music to my ears and I draw my hips back before I pummel back inside her. Each thrust rips a scream from her mouth and I relish in the sound.

My skin slaps against her and from this angle, I can imagine she's my little bitch. My claws retract, and I suck on my finger to make it nice and wet before I jam it through the tight muscle in her ass. The mattress muffles her squeal as I take her in both holes.

"That's it, little bitch. Take it. You fucking love my cock. I can feel you squeezing me so hard." My eyes drift shut as I fuck her hard. Her screams continue, but so does the tightening of her walls.

I knew she was mine.

Thrust.

Fuck, she loves it rough.

Another thrust.

I'm going to claim my little bitch.

My hips flex again and I shove another finger into her ass. Her body lurches forward.

She loves to play hard to get.

My hand on her hip claws at her and I spear her on my cock over and over. My claws extend again as I fuck her. They pierce through her skin inside. The blood makes my fingers slick as they glide in and out of her ass.

My balls draw up, but I'm not done yet. I rip my cock and fingers from her holes and slather my cock in her blood before I force my way into her ass with my hard length. She hasn't ceased screaming and I grow tired of the constant noise. My fingers wrap around her throat and I pull her back against my chest.

They tighten and cut off any sound coming from her mouth. I'm so close. My thrusts grow harder as I fuck my little bitch's ass and lay my claim. My spine and balls tingle as I roar. The walls of her ass clamp around me and I fill her with my release. My teeth extend and I strike her neck. My fangs dig deep, and I taste her blood in my mouth.

It's not my little bitch's blood I taste, though. This is different. Her scent isn't that of roses and jasmine. My eyes flicker open, and I rip my mouth away, her skin still between my teeth. Blood sprays across the mattress as my fangs sever her artery. Spitting out the lump of flesh, I let go of the woman's body. She gurgles as she chokes on her own blood and collapses on the mattress.

My cock goes soft and slips from her hole. She might not be my little bitch, but for now, she sated my hunger and lust. I push to my feet and leave the tent and body behind. Her blood coats my body. I'll need to wash up before I head to town and find somewhere to stay for the night.

Chapter Thirteen

Lila

I've been in the cabin for a week now. Hunter has been diligently changing the dressing on my leg every other day. Cayden even went to town and got more medical supplies including a leg brace. The wound itself feels much better. Hunter thinks it will only be a few more days before he can remove the stitches.

He's no longer sure the crack I heard was a bone breaking. Instead, he thinks it was the sound of the wolf's tooth as it broke off. It hit a nerve, and that is what caused the pain. I still have a slight limp, and he insists I wear the brace he gave me for a little longer.

I can move a lot more freely around the cabin and only need help up and down the stairs. Hunter is more than happy to assist with that. Since we kissed in the bathroom, he's hardly left my side.

I thought his presence would feel stifling, but it isn't. We are happy to sit in relative silence at the dining table with me reading a book from the huge bookcase behind it and him working on his laptop. We've fallen into a sort of routine.

Hunter has been waking me in the morning with a cup of coffee in the loft bedroom, a bedroom I'm still not sure who the owner is. My bet is on Cayden; he seems like the leader of this little rat pack group. After I've drank my coffee, Hunter carries me down the stairs and straight to the dining room table.

Either Hunter or Cayden cooks us a full breakfast of pancakes, eggs, and bacon. Of course, I add a huge helping of maple syrup to my entire plate and enjoy my food with another helping of coffee. After that, Cayden disappears and leaves Hunter and me together for the day.

He and Grayson only reappear for meals in the evening. Apart from that, Grayson is out in the woods doing God knows what. I still get mostly just grunts and the odd word from him when he is in the same room as me.

Picking up the cup of tea that Hunter has left for me on the kitchen counter, I take a sip and hobble over to the door, opening it. The brisk, cold air hits me full in the face and I shiver. Wrapping my hands around the cup, I attempt to steal any warmth I can from it.

With a tug, the blanket from the back of the chair by the door falls. I pull it over my shoulders before I step over the threshold and out onto the deck. The surrounding ground is still white, though now I see the footprints that lead around the side of the cabin and into the forest. Moving to the rocking chair on the deck, I take a seat and bring the cup to my lips and sip my tea.

A movement in front of me draws my attention, and that's when I spot him. The black and gray wolf, with liquid silver eyes. The one that was in the cabin. He's sitting at the edge of the forest. Those eerie eyes watch my movements, but he doesn't move any closer. I've seen him a few times this last week through the windows, although he's come no closer than the tree line.

"I told you he didn't want to hurt you." Hunter strides up the stairs, his arms loaded with logs that he stacks with the rest just outside the door. He takes a seat beside me. "He wants to make sure you're safe."

"Who does it belong to?" I watch the wolf cautiously, ready to bolt back into the cabin if he moves even an inch.

"He doesn't belong to anyone, really. He's been here as long as we have," Hunter responds, leaning back into the chair.

There are a few types of wolves I've met, and for the most, it was a displeasure. The nice ones have been hard to find. Between the wolf that attacked me in the woods after I crashed my car, the handsy shifters at the balls, and those in the cave, this one is like none of them.

When I first met him, his muzzle was covered in blood and he was the biggest wolf I'd ever seen which terrified me. After that incident he hasn't come closer than the tree line.

I bet he could smell my fear of him, even behind a thick sheet of glass and huge wooden door. Seeing him on the edge of the woods still sends shivers through me, but they lessen the more I see him.

"Are you sure he won't hurt me?" I question. I'm still unsure of the large animal.

"He won't touch a single hair on your body, unless you let him, of course." At Hunter's words, I think I spot the wolf's ear twitching in our direction, as if he is listening to us.

Placing my cup on the floor by my feet, I push myself up and limp closer to the edge of the wrap-around. The wolf lifts a paw from the ground, moving it forward as if to ask for permission. With a small nod from me, the paw hits the ground again and he walks one step closer to me.

Arms wrap around me from behind and Hunter leans his chin on my shoulder. His warmth envelops me, holding me against his hard body. The wolf takes another small step forward, and then another, until he's only a few feet away from the edge of the deck. With Hunter wrapped around me, I feel like I could take on the world, or in this case, a wolf.

"Why don't we move a little closer?" Hunter coaxes, moving around to my side and offering me his hand.

I place my hand in his. He leads me to the steps and I move down the first one. I stay there, not wanting to get my sock-clad feet wet. The wolf moves closer until he is at the bottom of the steps. He looks up at me with huge silver eyes, his tongue lolling out the side of his mouth.

Crouching down, my ass hits the top step and I sit. Hunter takes a seat next to me and the wolf moves toward Hunter, who reaches a hand out to the huge beast. Instead of lunging for him, the wolf nudges his head into Hunter's outstretched hand, nuzzling against it.

My fingers twitch, wanting to reach out and stroke the wolf. Lifting a shaky hand, I bring it close to its head while it's distracted getting an ear scratch from Hunter. It jerks sharply in my direction and I let out a yelp at the sudden movement. The wolf lowers its head and lets out a soft whine.

"She's scared. Don't move so quickly." It takes me a moment to realize that Hunter is talking to the wolf and not me.

The wolf moves at a snail's pace and leans its head towards my still outstretched hand. The first feel of its fur grazing my palm has me shivering, but not in fear. I want to sink my fingers into its soft fur and feel it in my grasp.

I lean closer, my face almost level with the wolf. Without warning, a long, wet tongue licks straight up the middle of my face, almost knocking me off balance. A chuckle bursts from my lips as the tongue takes another swipe at me. My fingers sink deeper into the fur of the wolf as I let it cover me in slobber.

"Try not to drown her." Hunter's laughter comes from beside me.

The wolf draws back from me, its tongue lolling from the side of its mouth again as it watches me once more. I don't let my fingers pull from its fur once.

"He's only giving me kisses. Is that right, boy? Don't get so jealous, Hunter." I laugh out loud, cocking my head toward Hunter.

"What if I'm the one who wants the kisses?" Hunter quips, and I drop my hands to my lap. Does he mean he wants kisses from me or the wolf?

I'm not sure how to answer him. His touch should repulse me but he and Cayden are the first men in a long time that haven't made me run screaming. I've even fantasized about Grayson touching me, too. The nightmares are still happening, but now I also imagine myself in a forest with these men. Their heated kisses and touches set my body on fire.

"It's...he isn't too bad. He's showing he's a good boy, aren't you?" My eyes trail up to the wolf as he snuggles his head into my lap. "A very big boy."

The wolf before me is absolutely huge. At least double the size of the wolf that attacked me in the woods after my accident. But right now he's being nothing but playful, and I can't stop myself from reaching for his fur and running my fingers through it again.

"Told you. He won't hurt you, Lila." Hunter smiles. Sidling closer to me, he rests an arm around my shoulders.

"Does he have a name?" I question.

"Gr...whatever you want to call him," Hunter answers.

A million names rush through my head, but none of them seemed to suit the stunning beast at my feet with his head in my lap.

"Fluffy?" Hunter cackles at my suggestion, and the wolf cocks his head to the side as he stares at me before he shakes his head. "Okay, not Fluffy."

"Mr Slobbers?" Hunter raises an eyebrow at me. "What, he's practically drooled all over me." I eye the wolf, but he doesn't look taken with the name.

"Wolfie?" The wolf lifts his head and licks up the side of my face, and I let out a giggle. "Seems he likes that name. I guess it works. He definitely has some wolf in him."

"He's a hybrid—we think," Hunter cuts in.

Wolfie definitely isn't a normal wolf, that's for sure. Not with his size. But what he is, I'm not sure.

Chapter Fourteen

Lila

Hands grab at my flesh, ripping and tearing as they fight to pull my legs apart. I can't see who it is, but I know it's him. Alaric is the main monster who features in my nightmares. Fingers poke and probe in places I don't want them, and I attempt to push my legs closed, but I can't fight against the ropes that are now bound around me and hold my legs apart.

Wrestling my way out of the nightmare, I sit up suddenly in bed. I clutch the cover around me like a security blanket, my body damp with cold sweat. The magic born tried to help me with the nightmares, but no matter what I let them do, it didn't help. The thoughts of Alaric, Rufus, and the other wolves were too strong.

The nights here have been different, though. Since that moment on the porch with Wolfie, he's started coming inside the cabin and insists on sleeping next to me on the bed. The first night, Cayden tried to drag him away, but Wolfie nipped at his arm until he let go. Cayden looked my way to see how I would react, but I patted the bed, allowing Wolfie to climb up beside me.

During the day, he sits with me at the dining table, or on the couch while I read. Hunter has even given me a little more space, telling me it's fine if Wolfie is here protecting me. He doesn't believe there is any way that the hybrid wolf will let me get hurt by anyone or anything. I've been trying to teach Wolfie a few tricks, and he's picked up on them pretty quickly.

At night I snuggle up against Wolfie's warmth. The nightmares of *him* have become less and even when they drag me under, it's easier to fight my way out of them. A shadowed man wraps his arms around me and chases the terror away.

Soft humming always filters through my dreams until the darkness is gone. I'm left with light leading me to a bed, the forest, and three shadowy figures that stand above me keeping watch.

Wolfie isn't here now, though. That's the only reason I can think of as to why the nightmare dug its claws into me and woke me in such a panic. I push myself to the edge of the mattress and stand slowly. I wrap the blanket from the end of the bed around me to fight off the morning chill that nips in the air.

Padding over to the edge of the loft, I look over the railing, but the lower floor is empty of any life. Hunter isn't sitting at the table reading, which is where I usually find him, and the couch is empty of Cayden. There is only a coffee cup on the table in front of it to tell me at some point between falling asleep and now he's been sitting there.

My body still feels horrible, with sweat clinging to me. It's nothing a cup of the tea Hunter's been making me won't cure. Running my hand down the banister, I shuffle down the steps from the loft the best I can without Hunter's help. The bottom step creaks as I drop my weight onto it and I wince at the sound, but none of the guys appear. Not even Wolfie. It's the first time I've really felt alone in the cabin.

Looking around the living room and kitchen, I spot an open book on the table. There are dirty dishes next to the sink, and the cup on the table by the counter is half full of coffee.

I limp to the kitchen, fill the kettle with water, and ignite the burner, placing the metal container over the flames. With a hobble, I search the cupboards. I know Hunter has made me tea, but I have no idea where the bags are.

As I'm about to close the cupboard I've just finished searching, I hear grunting from somewhere within the cabin. Curiosity gets the better of me. Leaving the kitchen behind, I move to the corridor I'd only ever been down to use the bathroom. I pause and wait to see if I hear the sound again. The sound comes again from the opposite end of the hallway.

There are two more doors in the hall, and I move cautiously down it. Leaning against the wall so as not to put too much weight on my healing leg, my ears perk up. The grunting sounds louder as I get nearer to the door at the end. The wood isn't flush with the frame and I see light coming from the crack.

Moving closer, I lean against the door frame and glimpse inside. It's darker than the rest of the cabin, but I see two figures silhouetted next to the bed. One of them is on their knees in front of the other. It can only be the guys, but I can't see who.

As my eyes adjust to the dim light, I notice that whoever is standing is completely naked. The one who is kneeling has their mouth wrapped around the other's cock. I want to move away, give them their privacy but I can't bring myself to.

Grunts come from the one standing, his fingers lacing with the other man's hair. He uses his hands to obtain control of the other's movements as he thrusts into his mouth.

"That's it, use your tongue." The sultry words are almost whispered, but I know that voice.

It's Grayson. The man who I only see once a day, otherwise, he seems absent. Where he goes, I'm not even sure. Wolfie is here more than he is. Hunter told me that the town is at least twenty miles away, so he could go there. Hands skim up the back of Grayson's legs, gripping at his ass.

"Take it all," Grayson grunts as he slams his length into the other man's mouth repeatedly.

My legs tremble as I continue to watch. I should leave. Walk away now. Rubbing my legs together, I nibble at my lip to suppress the moan that is trying to escape. I shouldn't be feeling this way, not with the horrors of what happened in the caves plaguing me. But I can't tear my eyes away from the two men.

Absent-mindedly, one of my hands loosens its death grip on the blanket and glides down my stomach. It slips underneath the boxers I'm wearing until my fingers brush against my clit. As I drift my hand lower, I'm already wet, and I'm startled at the fact. I feel dirty for feeling this way, but at the same time, I desire nothing more than to sink my fingers into my pussy and get off as I watch the two men.

"Enjoying the show, Lila," Cayden's voice whispers next to my ear and I can't stop the small scream that rushes between my lips as I pull my hand from within the boxers.

Hands plant themselves on my hips to hold me steady and pull me back against solid warmth. My whole body shudders before I relax against his warmth. My thoughts jump back to the kiss we shared. They don't know my history, but they have been respectful of my space since I freaked out on Hunter in the bathroom.

"I was... I... tea," I stutter out the words and go to step away, but Cayden doesn't let me go.

"You don't need to explain yourself. I enjoy watching them too." Cayden's words leave me shivering, but it's all I need to shift my eyes back to the room. "We all enjoy each other's company from time to time. We'd have no issues adding another."

Removing one hand from my side, Cayden reaches past me and nudges the door open further. Grayson's head is already turned in our direction but he continues to thrust into what I assume is Hunter's mouth. Grayson strokes his hands through Hunter's hair and Hunter moans around his cock.

I shouldn't be so turned on by seeing these two men being intimate with each other, but I can't help it. The fact that Hunter came onto me in the bathroom doesn't even cross my mind.

"He's getting close, can you tell?" Cayden whispers, and I shakily nod my head. "He feels so good when he swells in your throat just before he comes."

Cayden's words drift through my mind and I lick my dry lips as I watch. Grayson's movements are getting more frantic now, but his eyes remain on me and Cayden. With a final stutter, he slams his cock all the way down Hunter's throat and roars. His stomach is flush with Hunter's nose and his hips jerk as he comes.

"Is that what you crave, Lila? To feel his cock as he chokes you with it before spilling down your throat? Or would you prefer him to shove your legs apart and ram his cock deep inside your dripping pussy?"

Dizziness crashes over me, and my eyes slam shut. All I see is my legs being ripped apart as Alaric rapes me repeatedly. Him making me watch, chained against the wall, as he fucks another of the women. Their screams and cries ring in my ears. Struggling in Cayden's hold, I turn on him, pushing against him, but it's like trying to push against a brick wall.

"Lila, what the hell?" Cayden shouts, but I hardly hear him over the screams in my mind.

My knees buckle and I drop. Before I hit the floor, arms reach under my back and legs, lifting me. But I'm pulled into the flashback now. I fight against the one holding me and scream, clawing at their flesh with my nails. I hardly even notice as I'm placed on the couch and Cayden calls for Grayson.

Curling into a ball, I screech again when I feel a weight jump up beside me. Something brushes against my bare legs and I throw out my arms. My hands brush against a furry, warm body that lies over me. A rough tongue licks up the side of my face and I take in a shuddering breath. My fingers burrow into the fur beneath my hands and a soft growl sounds.

The heat of Wolfie laying over me soothes my nerves. The trembling in my body subsides as I stroke my fingers through his fur. Repositioning myself, I lay flatter, with my spine against the back of the couch. Wolfie lies beside me and I wrap my arms around him, pressing my face into the fur at his neck.

He feels safe, like he would protect me from the world. With the smell of damp pine infiltrating my nostrils, I let the exhaustion from my panic attack take me under. I know right here I'm protected; I don't even think of the three men in the cabin as I drift off to sleep.

Chapter Fifteen

Hunter

I pull my pants back up my legs and jog out of the bedroom after Grayson. It doesn't take him long before he shifts into his wolf form and jumps onto the couch with Lila. At first, she tries to fight him and I can't stop myself from stepping forward, but Cayden's arm across my chest stalls me.

"Wait," Cayden snaps.

We watch as Lila runs a hand over Grayson's fur and lets out a shaky breath. I see the exact moment her body relaxes. She shifts her arms in an attempt to wrap them around his huge frame. Her breathing settles and I can tell the exact moment she slips into sleep. It's always the same way when she's with him. In wolf form he soothes her anxiety. She seems calmer and less scared.

Cayden drops his hand and I move closer to the couch. Grabbing a blanket off the back, I lay it over her so she doesn't get cold. Grayson looks up at me with silver eyes. He lets out a huff before he closes them and settles his head onto the cushions. Lila looks so small curled up against him.

Turning my back on them, I spot Cayden already stalking to the kitchen and follow behind him on silent feet.

"Cayden, what the hell did you do?" I glare at my alpha. He quickly raises a finger to his lips to quieten me and I see a flash of confusion marring his features.

"I have no idea." He looks over to Lila and Grayson and my eyes track in the same direction as his.

One minute Grayson's cock was down my throat as he fucked my throat. I had fisted myself, knowing full well that Lila was at the door watching us, her scent permeating the air. When Cayden appeared in the hallway, I was too distracted. The next minute, I heard her screams as Grayson ripped himself away from me having just hit his own release.

"Lila was enjoying watching the two of you. I could smell it on her." He brushes his fingers through his hair, tugging at the ends. "I asked her if that was what she wanted to have done to her and she freaked. She was like a feral beast." Moving his hand from his hair, he runs his fingers over the already healing scratches on the right side of his face. I hadn't noticed them until now.

"I don't think she would have done that if she'd realized it was you. It was like in the bathroom, she wasn't there anymore, she was somewhere else."

I know all too well about Lila's freakouts. She's had a few of them since being here, but we are no closer to knowing what is causing them. She's gradually getting calmer around us but is only a fraction better compared to when she first arrived. It's why Cayden has been keeping his distance since their kiss. Well, until now, that is.

I'm not sure why she was in the hallway, or why Cayden felt the need to approach her the way he did. The mating bond is pulling on all of us, but we've distracted ourselves with each other. It's why Grayson and I were in my room. He'd gone for a run after Lila said she loved him. Or rather that she loves Wolfie.

He'd barged into my room as naked as the day he was born, shoved me to my knees, and rammed his weeping cock between my lips. That's how it always is with Grayson and me. His wolf loves dominance. The only person he is submissive to is Cayden, but even then his beta fights against our alpha.

But his wolf is different with Lila; he's calmer and seems to do the same for her. Cayden can only presume that Gray's wolf knows she's his mate, which lessens both man and beasts struggle with the darkness trying to consume them.

"I meant to tell you. I was doing some research. I was trying to see if Lila may have had contact with any others of our kind." I lower my voice a little. "Grayson went back to where he found Lila. He found her bag. I found her ID in there."

"What else?" Cayden implores.

"Her full name is Lila Moore. I did a quick search on the internet. I found an article about a missing girl in Portland from a few weeks ago. It's her." I nod toward Lila.

"Well, she obviously isn't missing anymore," Cayden responds. His voice is laced with confusion.

"No, she isn't, but along with this article, it mentioned other women that went missing in that state. They found some of their bodies in the woods, or along the roads beside them. Animal attack."

"So, it was a supernatural then?" Cayden scrubs a hand down his face. "But that's vampire territory. You don't think...?" Cayden doesn't finish his sentence.

"That maybe it was rogue wolves? It could have been. But until she tells us herself, I don't want to pry." The terror I've felt from her during her panic attacks is enough to make me cautious about how I approach the subject with her. "There is more to it than just the fact a wolf attacked her outside the compound, though. Her words when she first saw Wolfie in the cabin. She said they take what isn't theirs." I call Grayson by the name Lila has given him just in case she can hear me.

"And she's not opened up to you at all?" Cayden questions and I shake my head.

"Nope. She has not said a great deal at all. Usually, when I'm working, she just comes and steals a few paperbacks and curls up on the couch or sits outside on the porch with Wolfie."

"She's the same when I'm around. She doesn't say a lot. I think she prefers to avoid me after I kissed her." Cayden's shoulders slump.

"She'll let you get closer if you weren't so...you." That gets Cayden's attention, and he glares at me. "What? I'm a lot softer around the edges than you are." Cayden lets out a huff before speaking.

"What about Gray? She's been around him a lot, even if she doesn't realize it. She doesn't seem to stop talking to him. Has he said anything?"

"As far as I know, he doesn't know anything, either. But you know what he's like, Cay. He's not exactly the most forthcoming at the best of times." Cayden gives a nod, agreeing with me. Even before the curse, Grayson wasn't the most chatty. As beta and enforcer of the pack, he prefers to talk with his fists than his words.

"Do you think she suspects what we are?"

"If what I presume happened to her is true, I don't reckon she'd have stayed if she did." I move to the cabinet under the sink and pull out one of our smaller medical kits. Removing a saline solution and cotton gauze, I twist off the cap on the small plastic bottle.

"We'll get to the bottom of it. I think she just needs more time," Cayden suggests.

Even if she opens up to us eventually, would we ever be able to tell her what we are? I'm thinking she will just hightail it out of here. If one of the rogue wolves took her, she has every right to be afraid of us.

Too many are succumbing to the curse and forcing themselves on females who aren't even their mates in a last-ditch attempt to try to turn back time and return to how they were. Most ignore the fact that all a blood mate will do is pause the curse for a little while before dragging them quicker into the shadows.

Wetting the gauze, I approach Cayden once more. I wipe the cotton over his cheek, the nicks from Lila's nails are all but gone, but blood still mars his skin.

With a few swipes, the red is completely gone and only pink lines are left. Hurling the stained wipe into the trash, I lean back on the counter, letting out a sigh. My thoughts rush to Lila and what might have happened to her if she had been captured by a rogue.

Cayden steps closer to me and wraps his arms around my waist. I rest my head on his shoulder. He must have felt that my mind is whirling with images of what could have happened to Lila, which causes my hackles to rise. The arms banded around me tighten and I breathe in his scent of cinnamon with hints of vanilla.

If Lila would just speak to all of us, or even just one of us, then maybe we could help her. We might not be the sanest men out there anymore, but we are all drawn to her. My wolf wants to protect her. He'd happily lay his life down for hers if it meant that she was safe from whatever is haunting her.

Cayden pushes back from me and his hand trails down to mine. He leads me from the kitchen and through the lounge. My feet stumble as I attempt to get closer to the couch to see her.

"She'll be fine with Wolfie." Cayden squeezes my hand as he speaks. "Let me take care of you."

I'm reluctant to leave her, but Cayden speaks the truth. With Gray in his wolf form, he's the best to protect her right now. I allow Cayden to drag me down the hallway and back to my bedroom.

Once we're inside, he slams the door behind us and we quickly shed our clothes. Falling together on the bed in a tangled mess, Cayden lets me take the lead. As I sink deep inside him I envision the woman lying on the couch and how much she is going to change our lives.

Chapter Sixteen

Lila

Cayden, Hunter, and Grayson stand around the bed in the middle of the forest. Naked and standing proud, each man grips their length, tugging up and down their shafts as they look down at me.

My hands trail over my body, tweaking at my nipples before I slide them lower. When I'm almost where I want to be, Cayden launches himself onto the bed and pulls my hands away from where I crave them the most.

He places both of my hands above my head, holding them in place on the pillow above me with one hand. His other hand takes over from where I was before he stopped me.

My eyes shift to Grayson and Hunter. Their lips lock together, and they stroke each other's cocks, letting out deep moans. Cayden's fingers brush over my pubic bone and my attention is dragged back to him. He nudges my thighs wider and slips a finger between my folds.

"You're so wet for us. Are you enjoying the show?" Cayden rasps and I nod. A moan slips from my lips as he pushes a thick digit inside me.

Cayden braces his shoulders between my thighs and uses his hand to push my legs apart. His tongue darts out as he licks from my hole to my clit. A shudder runs through me as he thrusts his finger in and out of my pussy. His tongue attacks my clit, leaving the odd nip on my flesh, making my back arch up on the bed.

A grunt sounds from the direction of Hunter and Grayson, and I twist my head toward them. Hunter is on his knees, his hands braced on Grayson's thighs as the larger man thrusts in and out of his mouth in time with Cayden fingering me.

"She just got so much wetter." Cayden pauses his assault on my clit for just a moment before resuming.

Cayden adds another finger, stretching me as my walls tighten around the intrusion. My back lifts from the bed again and I keep my eyes on Grayson and Hunter. It's not long before I'm crying out, my leg quaking as Cayden propels me over the edge. He removes his fingers from me and lifts them to his mouth, licking them clean.

Cayden's hand fists his cock as he moves closer to me, lining up the huge, mushroomed head with my entrance. He brushes the tip against my core, using his hand to cover himself with my wetness. Leaning over me, Cayden braces himself with one arm beside my head. He brings his body in line with mine before pushing himself inside my pulsing walls.

He fucks me with abandon, drilling me into the bed. The moans and grunts from Grayson get louder as he slips his fingers through Hunter's hair and fucks his mouth. Both Grayson and Cayden's thrusts are perfectly in time with each other and soon I feel another orgasm threatening to drag me over the edge.

A roar pulls my attention back to Grayson as he whips his cock from Hunter's mouth. He drags the smaller male to his feet and shoves him down onto the bed so Hunter's head is close to mine. Hunter's lips are on mine, devouring me. I swallow his moan as Grayson pushes his body forward and thrusts inside Hunter's ass.

"Fuck, yes," Grayson growls. "Squeeze Cayden as hard as Hunter is squeezing me, Lila." His words make my pussy clench and Cayden lets out a grunt.

Hunter breaks our kiss and he looks into my eyes. His pupils threaten to make all the color disappear from his irises. He kisses down the side of my neck until his lips brush against my ear.

My orgasm crashes over me hard. I cry out and Cayden's cum fills me. I swear I see stars as Grayson cries out his own release.

"You're ours, Lila." Hunter nips at my neck and I grab the back of his head, dragging his lips back to mine.

Something warm and wet runs up the side of my face, dragging me from the high I'd hit in my dream. When it comes again, I let out a shriek. Peeling my eyes open, Wolfie is sitting on the floor in front of the couch, his tongue lolled out to one side as he blinks down at me and I giggle.

"Not exactly how I was expecting to be woken up, Wolfie." Laughter sounds from behind me.

"She's got you there, buddy." Hunter sniggers. "Note to self, licking Lila's face is not the best way to wake her up." He lets out another chuckle and my thighs clench together as I remember the words he spoke to me in my dream.

Ours.

Wiping the slobber off my face, I stretch out. Everything is stiff and I'm feeling a little flushed from my dream. I expected the stiffness at least from sleeping on the couch. I push myself up and swing my legs over the side until my feet reach the floor. I'm about to stand, but Wolfie drops his head onto my thighs and whimpers.

"I'm okay, I promise." He kept me safe and pulled me back from the brink of my panic attack before the terror of what happened to me could pull me further under. "Thank you." I lean down and kiss the top of his head before straightening once more. His gaze follows me and he has those puppy dog eyes that melt everyone's hearts.

"You don't play fair." I ruffle the fur on the top of his head and he lets out a yip as I scratch behind his left ear. He seems satisfied that I'm okay.

"He's a sucker for that. He wants you to fall madly in love with him." Hunter rounds the side of the couch, a cup of coffee in his hands. He passes it to me and as I grab it, our fingers briefly touch before I pull them away and take a sip of the scalding black liquid.

"Thanks." I take another drink, still running my hand absentmindedly through Wolfie's fur. "He doesn't really have to try. What's not to love about him?"

Wolfie lifts his head and looks at Hunter. If he were human, I'd have said he was grinning at him. I let out a snort and shook my head.

"Don't say that, he's already got a big enough ego," Hunter quips and I watch as he heads towards the dining table and sits down on the pulled-out chair. He lifts a book and starts reading, taking sips from his own mug.

"He's a dog, Hunter. I'm not sure dogs have egos." I look back to Wolfie and pat him on the head before I stand and follow Hunter to the table.

Wolfie sits by my side, leaning his warm body against my legs, and I smile down at him. I stifle a yawn and down the rest of my coffee. My body and mind feel beyond exhausted. I know I had another meltdown. Only this time it was like all the oxygen was stolen from my lungs until I couldn't stay upright any more. I assumed Cayden was the one to catch me but after that everything was a little hazy until I felt Wolfie lying beside me.

"What happened?" I can't stop the question as it slips from my lips.

"Another panic attack. You just dropped. Cayden took you to the couch." Hunter takes another sip of his drink, resting the book upside down on the table. "He called

Wolfie in. When he jumped on the couch with you at first, we thought you were going to attack him as well."

My eyes flicker to the hybrid beside me. "I'm sorry." I wrap my arms around his neck and give him a squeeze. When I release him, he licks up the side of my face. I guess he accepts my apology, or at least whatever he thinks I said. It's not like he can understand me. "Wait, what do you mean 'as well'?"

"Cayden tried to hold you but you attacked him." Hunter is far too blunt sometimes, but I did ask the question.

"Oh, shit." I quickly look around the cabin, looking for Cayden. "Is he okay?"

"He's fine. Nothing he can't handle, he's been in worse situations." Hunter tries to reassure me but I'm not sure if I can relax until I see Cayden in the flesh.

As if my thoughts have beckoned him, Cayden strides through the cabin's front door. He looks a little ruffled from being outside in the wind, but otherwise, he seems okay. I trace my eyes over his face as he gets closer to Hunter and me and he gives me a soft smile.

"I'm sorry," we both blurt out. Cayden stops in his tracks and Hunter lets out a chuckle.

There is an awkward silence as Cayden and I stare at each other, neither one of us sure who should talk next. I take a moment to brush a loose strand of hair out of my face, and Cayden takes another step towards me. Rising from my chair, Wolfie backs away from me and I pat him on the head. I close the gap between me and Cayden.

I assess his face closer, lifting a hand to rest my fingers under his chin. I turn his head this way and that, looking for any marks I may have left.

"If you want to check him out properly, Lila, you only need to ask. I'm sure Cay will take all his clothes off for you." Hunter lets out another snigger.

Cayden snarls in Hunter's direction, but I feel my heart rate kick up a notch. The dream comes flooding back to me. Of all three of them naked before me, Cayden worshipping my body while Grayson dominates Hunter. I have to stop myself from clenching my thighs together.

"Hunter, you're scaring her," Cayden barks out. But I'm not scared. I'm horny. Something I've not felt in a very long time, not since long before *him*.

"I'm good... I'm okay." I rush the words out. "I'm not scared. I just—I need to go for a shower." Spinning on my heel, I speed away from them and straight into the bathroom.

Chapter Seventeen

Lila

Even with a door between us, I struggle to calm my racing heart. There's something about all three men that draws me to them. I couldn't explain it if I tried. This is the first time in a long period that a nightmare of *him* hasn't claimed the prime spot while I've slept.

I'm attracted to all of them. I've already kissed Cayden and Hunter, as well as letting him get close to me. And it was only a short time ago that I watched Grayson getting a blow job.

My head's a mess. When Cayden whispered those words to me about craving the same thing, the fear took over, but a small part of me desired to be on the receiving end of Grayson's cock. It's the only thing I can think of that would explain that dream.

Thank God it was only a dream, though. I'm not sure I'm ready for something like that right now. Not if certain comments are going to set me off into a panic. I need to open up to them and try to explain what happened to me. But what if they kick me out? I'm not sure I want to leave just yet.

Hunter has said they will all protect me, but what if it's not enough? What if they think I'm damaged goods and kick me to the curb?

Come on, Lila. Pull yourself together. I scold myself as I lean my forehead against the coolness of the wooden door. Shaking out my shoulders and straightening my spine, I take a few deep inhales and exhales as Hunter taught me.

I move to the sink and splash my face with cold water. Grabbing the towel off the rail, I dry off and look at myself in the mirror. I look different. Even with the nightmares sometimes trickling in, the marks under my eyes have lessened and my face seems fuller. Three stable meals a day could do that to a girl.

When my hands are dry, I open the door only to find Wolfie sitting like a guard dog right outside. Cayden and Hunter stand at the end of the hallway, but the warning growls coming from Wolfie keep them from taking another step forward. I lay my hand on his head and he swivels it around to look at me.

I step out of the bathroom. Wolfie is on his feet, keeping pace with me as I brush past both Cayden and Hunter, and head for the dining room table. I take the seat at the head of the table, the place where Cayden usually sits if we are all together, but he'll get over it. I need to talk to them; I need to feel like I'm in charge, and this is the only way I can do it.

The two men take a seat on the chairs closest to me and Wolfie sits on the floor to the side of me. I place my hand on his head and steel my spine once more.

"What happened, Lila?" Hunter questions and I peer up at him.

I go to open my mouth, but nothing comes out except a squeak. Wolfie nudges his huge head against my thigh and I look down at him once more. His snout pushes into my lap and under my other hand. I reach for the top of his head. It's like he's encouraging me to talk to the guys about what happened to me.

Even though I told myself I would, with them both around me now, I'm not sure I can. But with Wolfie's presence calming me, maybe he will give me the strength to tell them about the horrors I endured.

"What I need to tell you isn't a nice story. Are you sure you want to know?"

"Lila, please try for us. We are trying to give you the space you need. But we need to know what's triggering you so we can avoid it." Hunter reaches a hand across the table, gently laying his fingers over the top of mine.

"He's right, Lila." Cayden's voice grabs my attention. "We all care about you. We want to protect you even if it's only from the nightmares."

I swallow hard. My mouth suddenly feels way too dry. Even when I was with the magic born, I didn't tell them what happened to me. They only worked some things out from what the other women had told them.

"I used to live right here, in the wolf sector," I start. "I was forced to go to those stupid balls. My mother found my father at a young age, but she loved dressing me up all pretty and telling me fantastical tales about friends who had found their mates and how much she wanted the same to happen to me."

I think about the sleazy men, some old enough to be my dad, grabbing at me those first few years until I worked out where to hide.

"I hated them. The shifters there were vile. Too many fondling me even when I said no." Wolfie tenses beneath me and a growl rumbles in his chest. "I attended but knew someone on the wait staff who let me hide in one of the side rooms by the ballroom for a few hours till I could go home and tell my parents I hadn't found the one. My mom was so disappointed, but she didn't see these men. I'm sure she would have thought otherwise if she had been there."

I take a deep breath, and Wolfie settles somewhat. Hunter squeezes my hand, encouraging me to go on.

"When my parents died, I'd had enough. After their funeral, I left. I had a job offer in Portland, so I sold my parent's house and went West. I thought I was finally safe from wolves. But I was wrong." This part of the story is easy.

"I remember that night well. I'd gone to celebrate getting the job and I was so excited to start. There was this guy in the club. He seemed off but I couldn't put my finger on it. I ignored him and after a few drinks, I left." A shudder races through my body as I remember what happened next.

"They kidnapped me from outside the club. It was the guy who'd tried to talk to me earlier in the night. He was weird, but I told him I had a boyfriend and he seemed to back off." I pull my hand away from Wolfie and brush a strand of hair from in front of my face. Letting out a breath, I continue, "Clearly, he didn't because as I was walking back to the hotel, I was staying in he grabbed me. That's all I remembered until I woke up naked in a cage surrounded by other women in the same situation."

"Who took you?" Cayden lets out with a growl.

"It was wolf shifters. I didn't know that at first, though. Not until one of them shifted. One woman tried to escape after he assaulted her. She didn't get far." I remember how she'd barely even made it a few feet before the wolf had taken her down, closing his massive jaws over her neck and biting. I look down at the table. I don't want to see how my words affect them.

Wolfie pushes his head into my chest, and I wrap my arms around him, holding him close. With my head on top of his, I inhale deeply and drag his woody scent in. A sense of relief washes over me.

"They were all crazy, feral. Worse than the ones at the balls. They fought a few times both as men and wolves until one of them won. The winner got to claim his pick of women."

"Did they..." Hunter can't seem to finish the sentence and I look over to where he's sitting. He's no longer holding my hand. Instead, his are fisted together on top of the wood.

I nod and close my eyes. A bang echoes through the cabin. My eyes shoot open again and Wolfie bares his fangs at Cayden. The large man is now standing, his hands laid flat on the table as he leans against it.

"Those fucking savages," he shouts, his voice gruff. I see the anger rising in him. If steam could come from someone's ears, that's exactly what would happen with Cayden right now.

"Cayden." Hunter shifts his attention from me to his friend, reaching across the table and lays his hand on top of Cayden's.

"I'm sorry, Lila. I'm not angry at you." Cayden's tone softens.

"I know." And I do. But the power this man possesses scares me, even when it's not directed at me.

Cayden shoves away from the table and paces a few lengths before coming back and resting his hands on the back of the chair. His knuckles are almost white from how tight his grip is. "Is there more?"

"Yes." My voice is quiet now. I should tell them about *him*. The fact I can almost feel *his* eyes on me, even after we were rescued.

"There was this one wolf, his name was—" I struggle to get his real name past my lips. "Alaric. He's the one who has been stalking my nightmares. He wasn't the wolf in charge, but the guy who was let him do whatever he desired."

I take a moment to wring my hands together and compose myself. I glance around at the men. Hunter is sitting in silence, but I can see the darkness in his eyes. No longer do I see the sweet, joking medic. Instead, I see someone who is ready to murder—for me.

"He was utterly obsessed with me from the start. First, he beat me." A growl erupts from Wolfie, and I pet his head, whether it's to calm him or myself I don't know. I look over to Cayden; his face is red and flushed. The wood is straining under his grip. If he tightens it anymore, he is going to snap the top off of the chair.

"Then it turned to more." I blink back the tears that are trying to form. "He assaulted me repeatedly. Let a few others do it too. He loved to hear me beg. He didn't care if I was conscious or not, I'd wake up back in my cage and everything hurt." I all but choke on the words, but I need to get them out.

Hunter mutters something under his breath. My eyes focus on him but he doesn't repeat whatever he said. A growl rumbles in Wolfie's chest, he doesn't direct it at me. Instead, he keeps his head against my breasts.

"I wanted to die. They wouldn't let me." Every day in that cave, I hoped that one of his beatings would go too far, that he'd kill me. I was never so lucky. "He told me I was to be his blood mate. To make him how he used to be. He tried to tell me he was nice before the curse. He said that once I was officially his, everything would change. Then she came..." I trail off, and I think of Demi.

"Who came, Lila?" Hunter's question startles me a little and I almost jump out of my skin.

"They brought a new woman back to the caves. The leader announced she was to be his blood mate. That no one was to handle her but him. Demi was different. She gave me a little hope in a time when everything was shrouded in darkness."

"Lila, I need to know something," Cayden asks. "Did they go through with it? The blood moon ritual?" There is something written on his face, but I can't quite work it out.

"They never got the chance to. The night of the blood moon, Demi's vampires came for her. They killed those bastards. Or at least, I was told they did." I remember waking up on a cold slab of stone. My body had ached all over and I started screaming.

"The vampires freed us. I was terrified at first. All I saw was this man covered in blood and I couldn't stop myself from screaming. Then Demi was there, soothing me. She said they'd come and they did." Rufus, the leader of the wolves, had tried to get away from the vampire that was holding him, but Demi went straight over to him and plunged a knife into him over and over again until she was covered in blood too. I only wished I'd gotten the same opportunity with *him*.

"What do you mean, you were told they're all dead?" Of course Cayden picked up on that.

"Alaric...I'm not sure he's dead. Something in my gut is telling me he's still after me." A shudder races up my spine, and I can't stop my body's reaction to the mention of his name.

Wolfie brushes up against me and I sink my fingers into the fur on his back. I use him as my anchor, so I don't slip into the nightmares that the thoughts of Alaric usually bring.

"*He's* coming for me. I can feel it. I can feel *him*." It's almost like he's there, on the edge of my mind. The last week in the sanctuary had been the worst. I had to get out of there, to leave the other women and the magic born behind. All I wanted was to keep them safe.

"We won't let him near you, Lila." Hunter reaches a hand under the table and grasps mine within his.

"I don't know if you can stop him. He's a monster." Even though I thought these men could stop Alaric, I'm not so sure it wasn't just hope. How do these three men face a monster like him? I don't want their death on my conscience. "He'll kill you to get to me."

"You are more protected here than you know," Cayden announces, pulling my attention to him. "We won't let anyone near you. Please, believe us when I say that." And I do. I believe every word he says.

"Everything makes sense now," Hunter blurts out. "Your freakouts, the fact I found an article about you on the internet. It said you were missing. There was even a picture of you."

"Sorry, what?" I pull my hand from him. How did he manage that?

"I was worried about you, after your freakout with Wolfie." He looks over to the wolf hybrid, who has his head curled up in my lap. "Then again when, well, you know. When you came across me and Gray, and Cay was talking to you. I knew it wasn't nothing and I wanted to help you. I wanted to protect you."

Hunter's admission makes my heart flutter, but how can he protect me from what is coming for me?

"I found your ID in the bag Grayson collected from where he found you." Hunter is talking about the new ID the magic born had gotten for me before I left. "I looked you up and that was when I found the article. I saw it had happened in the vampire sector, but I never realized it was wolves that did this to you."

Hunter pushes to his feet and I shrink back from him. He kneels beside my seat and engulfs me in his arms. "I'm so sorry about what happened to you, Lila. I promise you, we will protect you. I'll die for you if it comes to it. But if he's really coming, I won't let him anywhere near you."

The sheer relief his words cause me is enough to shove me over the edge. My whole body shudders and the tears I'd subconsciously been holding back fall. We sit there for God knows how long as he holds me.

Wolfie is pressed up against my side, and I feel the heat of his body seeping into me. But Cayden hasn't come near me since my panic attack. Giving me space he thinks I need, part of me agrees with his assessment, but another wants him to come close to me again.

They are nothing like the monsters I've met in the past; they are more caring and gentle than any wolf I have met before. Yes, they have rough edges, but they made me feel safe and more at home than I have in a long time.

Chapter Eighteen

Cayden

I leave Hunter and Grayson with Lila. Her tears rip my heart apart and my wolf demands I go back to her and comfort her, but I can't. Not right now. Her story has rocked me to the core.

My own kind are the ones who have caused her nightmares. They are the reason that the first week she was here all she did was toss and turn in her sleep. They are why there were the mornings when she woke up screaming.

Hunter went to calm her each time; he's softer than me. He is still vicious when he wants to be, but right now, the darkness hasn't sunk its claws into him as much as it has for me. With Grayson in his wolf form, she's been calmer too.

I stomp through the tree line. My anger is getting the best of me. Without warning, I slash out at the tree closest to me. My claws explode from my fingertips before I'm even close to the wood, and as soon as they strike, they leave huge gouges in the trunk. I feel a growl building in my chest; my wolf is demanding to be let free.

The minute he bursts from me, I take off into the forest, leaving my shredded clothing behind. I wind through the trees and leap over fallen logs. I keep running until my chest is heaving and my breathing comes out in pants. Even then, I don't stop. I keep going until I hit the very edge of the compound.

I want to tear down the fence and hunt for the wolf that Lila believes is still after her. I want to rip him limb from limb. But first, I would beat him as a man, and let him feel what it is like to be on the receiving end. There is no way I could give him the full retribution that he deserves. I wouldn't lower myself enough to touch him in the same way he touched my mate.

His death won't be quick, though. I want to give Lila a chance to get revenge, even if I don't wish for her to be anywhere near him. I raise my head into the air and let out a thundering howl. The leaves on the trees shiver and everything for miles goes silent at the sound of my angry beast.

I track around the edge of the compound's perimeter. If Lila thinks this wolf or even something else might come for her, I need to make sure they can't get in. I run for miles, following the metal fence until I'm halfway around. There are no breaks so far.

A branch snaps behind me and I whip around with a snarl. A black and silver wolf stalks out of the bushes. Grayson. He approaches me slowly; his head lowered to show me he isn't a threat. I stand tall and look down at him. He rubs his cheek against mine and I reciprocate the gesture.

We can't tell her. Grayson's voice echoes in my mind. *She'll leave us.*

We don't know that, Gray, I answer.

She hates our kind, even if she tolerates 'Wolfie'. I'm not sure she will ever be able to accept us if she finds out the truth. Grayson pads around me in a circle as he communicates in my mind. I sit back on my haunches.

Gray's words swirl around my head. We need to tell her. This is not something we can keep from her if she's our true mate. But maybe, for now, he is right. We need to show her we aren't the same as the men that took her. Then she might accept the fact we are shifters.

Fine. For now, we don't tell her. But we have to eventually, Gray. I look over at the darker wolf, and he nods in agreement. *I'm going to check the rest of the fence. Go back to the cabin. Stay with her. She's going to need 'Wolfie'.*

With a quick goodbye, he takes off back into the woods toward the cabin, leaving me to my thoughts. I rise back up from the forest floor and continue my run around the rest of the perimeter. When I make it back to the same area I started, I keep a mental list of some of the weakened areas. Hunter and I will have to come out in the morning with tools so we can make the much-needed repairs.

I'll do whatever it takes to keep Lila safe. With that thought in my mind, I loop back to the cabin. As I approach, I shed my wolf skin and rise on two feet. The wind nips at my skin. It's colder than it's been in a while, and even with my increased temperature, I still feel the bite.

I move around the back of the cabin to the small storage box we've kept stocked with clothes since Lila arrived. I lift the lid and pull out some sweatpants and a hoodie, pulling them on before shoving my feet into the work boots I left inside. If Lila is still awake I hope she doesn't notice that I'm not wearing the same clothes I had on when I left.

Retracing my footsteps back to the front of the cabin, I trudge up the steps. I hear the sounds of laughter inside from both Lila and Hunter. I shove through the door to find Hunter in the corner of the couch. Lila is laid across it, her body pushed against Hunter and his arm is around her shoulder. Wolfie covers her feet and his head rests on her thighs. Hunter's laptop sits on the coffee table in front of them as they watch a movie.

Hunter barely glances in my direction, but nods to let me know that she's okay. Or, at least for now, she is. Heading down the hallway to the shower, I lock myself inside. I strip off my clothes and turn the water on warm. When I step inside, the water hasn't quite heated, but I shake it off and grab the soap to scrub my body clean.

If only there was a way for the dirt and grime to disappear with our fur when we shifted back to human form, but no such luck. I think of my mate, how strong she is. She survived what many people wouldn't, and if I ever get to meet Demi, I will have to thank her for making sure Lila made it out.

Another giggle sounds and I hear Hunter's raucous laugh from outside the door. I wish she would laugh like that with me, but then again, it's not like I've given it much of a chance. I always stress that my presence will set off another panic attack. I imagine her smile and her laughing at something I have said.

My cock hardens and I don't restrain myself from wrapping my fist around it. I'm rock hard and my balls ache. As much as spending time with Grayson and Hunter helps to take the edge off, it is nothing in comparison with what I could feel with Lila. She's made for me, for us. The other half of our souls that are dark and tarnished. She's the only one who can bring us back from the brink.

I run my hand up and down my steely length and I envision her. Her luscious blonde hair and those sparkling blue eyes that pull you in. The way her voice sounds and the way she smells. My toes curl and I tighten my grip on my cock. I brace my other hand on the shower wall and lie my forehead against the cool tiles.

Lila's pink lips cross my mind, only this time, she opens her mouth for me and I push inside as I fuck my cock into my fist. Her tongue licks the underside of my veiny length and as I draw back my hips, she tongues my slit. A moan slips from between my lips, and I bite down hard on it to cut off the sound. Hunter and Grayson are sure to have heard me. As long as Lila didn't, it doesn't matter.

I increase the thrusts in and out of my fist as I imagine it's her mouth back on me. Lila licks every inch of my cock. She takes me deeper until the head bumps against the back of her throat and even then I don't stop. I fuck her mouth with abandon until my hips falter and I lose the rough pace I had. My balls draw up and I bite down hard on my tongue until I taste the blood that floods my mouth.

With one last thrust, I empty my load all over the side of the shower. My movements still and I struggle to draw in a deep breath. My heart races within my chest. I wash my release away and finish my shower. When I'm done, I turn off the water and wrap a fluffy towel around my waist.

Unlatching the door, I step into the hallway and glance back to the main room. The three of them are still on the couch, but I decide to leave them to it. I head straight for Grayson's room and flop down on the bed before I roll onto my back and stare up at the ceiling.

Chapter Nineteen

Lila

A blissful heat warms my palm as my fingers trail up and down something hard until I hit what feels like a small batch of fur and I sigh. As my hand glides lower, I bump something large, soft, and a little damp, and a groan hits my ears.

I keep my eyes closed. I know if I open them, I will be in another of my dreams with one of the men I've been staying with in the cabin. Which one doesn't matter to me, because in my dreams, everything is perfect.

My fingers wrap around the steely warmth and as more of my senses come back, I feel the hard body half lying under me. I give his cock a squeeze and he jolts in my hand. Thickening in my grasp, I run my hand up and down the length.

Another groan sounds beside me and it makes me smile. I can't stop myself from grinding my core against the thigh resting between my legs. The sound encourages me to keep moving and I pump the cock faster.

The skin beneath my palm is silky and I feel every vein on its length. If I were awake, I wouldn't dare do this, the underlying fear of what happened with him would send me straight into a panic. But here in my dreams, anything is possible.

A hand wraps around mine, tightening my grip and increasing my speed. Without warning, the same hand pulls me from their cock and I let out a whimper. I wanted to make them cum. The hand trails up my arm and presses on my shoulder until I'm on my back.

A warm, very naked body lies over the top of me. Their cock nudges against my clothed core and I drop my legs further open. Slowly opening my eyes, Grayson is above me. His huge body dwarfs mine and blocks out my surroundings. He holds my wrists beneath his hands on the bed and descends on my neck. He licks and sucks my skin, giving me the occasional nip which has my hips jerking up. All I crave is some friction.

My head lolls to the side, baring my neck to him. I spot the wood walls of the cabin. That's strange. Usually, in my dreams, the bed is in the middle of the forest. Grayson doesn't give me much of a chance to contemplate it further as his lips brush against mine and my eyes flutter closed.

Tingles tickle my lips as he kisses me. His tongue sweeps across the seam until I open and he shoves his tongue inside my mouth in time with his cock which thrusts against my thigh. Grayson tastes amazing, like coffee and chocolate, and I crave more of him. I pull one hand from his hold and tangle my fingers in his hair to hold his mouth to mine, letting my tongue do its own exploration.

A rough, calloused hand wraps around my chin as Grayson breaks his lips from mine and tips my head back. He trails his lips down my neck and I let out a whimper when he runs his teeth against my pulse. My body shudders with desire as he nips at my skin and I release a breathy moan.

With the sound, Grayson thrusts his cock against me again. The hard length brushes over the top of my swollen clit and I let out another moan. I want—no, I need—him to strip me down and fill me with his hard cock. I want to feel him as he pushes inside me and claims me as his own.

Grayson's lips continue their journey south, and his lips reach my collarbone. He grabs the strap of my top and slides it off my shoulder until my left breast comes free. He leans back slightly. His silver eyes are almost black with lust when they connect with mine. It's like he wants my permission and I give him a small nod.

His mouth is straight back on me, his lips wrap around my nipple. His tongue laps at my hardened peak. My hands tangle in his hair, pulling at the strands, and he groans against my skin. Grayson fastens his teeth over my nipple and my back arches off the bed. He pulls the other side of my top down and he tugs on my other nipple, sending heat straight to my core.

Grayson releases it and treats the other with the same care. His other hand moves my top down to my waist and he leaves it bunched there. When his mouth leaves my nipple this time, he trails his lips down the middle of my stomach all the way to where my top rests at the waistline of my shorts.

My shorts are already soaked with my arousal, but they are in the way of my getting what I desire. I'm almost panting now, wanting him to go further, but Grayson just kisses along the top of my shorts. My hips thrust up, begging him to give me attention where I need it the most, but a hand presses me back down to the bed.

"Please, Grayson," I beg. His hand cups my mound and I groan.

"You're so wet for me." Grayson rubs his hand against me and I push against his palm.

He lifts his body away from mine and I finally get a glimpse of his hardened length. I never thought a man's cock could be gorgeous, but Grayson's is. It's steel wrapped in velvet skin. There is a light spattering of dark and light hair around the base, but his balls are completely bare.

I notice a single drop of pre-cum at the tip and my tongue darts out to dampen my dry lips as I take all of him in. Every time I have seen him he's always been in sweatpants and a t-shirt, but now I can observe him in all of his glory. His golden skin shimmers in the sunlight streaming through the window, and I see the faint scars that spatter his chest.

Grayson's fingers loop around the waistband of my shorts and he pulls them down until I'm bare from the waist down. He pushes my knees apart and runs his hands up the inside of my thighs until he reaches the apex. With a single finger, he traces it between my lips and I shudder at the touch. Flashing a wolfish grin, he lowers his head and licks up my slit.

"Fuck, Lila. You taste like heaven." A moan rushes from my lips as he does it again and I clench my fingers tightly around the bed sheet. "I need more."

With a finger on either side, he brushes my lips open and delves his tongue inside me, making my legs jerk. I almost close them on his head to hold him in place, but I do my best to resist the temptation. A finger presses against my clit as he thrusts his tongue in and out.

My hips jerk up off the bed once more, and my fingers tangle in his hair, holding him against my dripping core as he tastes me. His hips thrust against the bed, and I imagine his cock as he rubs his length against the sheets.

Grayson's finger continues to thrum against my clit and I feel myself getting closer to the edge. I need just a little more from him. As if he read my thoughts, he thrust two thick fingers inside me and I detonated. My walls clamp down on his digits and I come with a moan. My heart beats hard against my chest and I sink back into the bed as I ride out my release.

"Grayson, the fuck are you doing?" Hunter's voice bellows and I hear footsteps as he races up the stairs.

Grayson's movements still and he pulls his fingers from my core. Blinking up at him, my eyes widen and it suddenly hits me that I wasn't in a dream as I initially thought. Reality crashes down around me and I scramble back on the bed as I clumsily attempt to pull my shorts and top back into place.

Grayson wipes his mouth with the back of his hand to clean my juices away and I gape at him. I'm not sure what to say, or even what to do. I wasn't in a dream, and Grayson really is up here in the buff with his cock dripping pre-cum after going down on me. My heart races, but it's not from fear. Instead, there is excitement running through my veins. What could have happened if Hunter hadn't shouted upstairs?

Hunter stands at the top of the stairs, his arms folded over his chest. He glares at Grayson before he switches his eyes over to where I'm curled up on the bed.

"Are you okay, Lila?" Hunter moves to the side of the bed and kneels next to it.

"I don't even—what the hell is he doing up here?" I focus my glare on Grayson before my eyes flicker around the loft space and notice the lack of my hybrid companion. "And where's Wolfie?" Hunter clears his throat, and Grayson lets out a chuckle that I don't understand.

"Wolfie had to take care of business, didn't he, Gray?" Hunter looks up to Grayson, who is still very naked at the end of the bed. "And Grayson here, he sometimes sleepwalks." He pauses for a moment. "And sleeps naked, obviously." Yanking the blanket from the bed, he hurls it at Grayson, who catches it. "Dude, cover yourself up."

Grayson snorts. "She didn't want me to cover up five minutes ago, did you, Lila?" He makes no move to cover himself with the blanket in his hand.

My cheeks heat, and I'm sure they are glowing red. Grayson isn't wrong, but it's not like I'm going to say it out loud.

"She was so close to opening those sexy legs and taking my cock." Grayson smirks. "And she tastes absolutely delicious. Try her, Hunter. I know you want to." He lets out another laugh.

Hunter lets out a growl and jumps to his feet. He storms down the side of the bed until he reaches Grayson. He wraps his arms around the bigger man's neck and yanks him backwards, away from the bed. Grayson doesn't even try to fight him; he just laughs harder as he's dragged across the wooden floor.

"Get the fuck outta here. Go take a cold shower and leave Lila alone," Hunter demands.

When he reaches the stairs, he doesn't even stop before he lets go of Grayson's neck and shoves him. Grayson quickly stops himself from falling headfirst down the stairs. His laughter echoes around the cabin as he swaggers down the steps, dropping the blanket at the top.

Hunter spins back to me. There's a look of horror on his face. Shame suddenly fills me. He caught me and Grayson together even after I've spent so much time with him.

What the hell is wrong with me?

Between these three men, I've kissed two, gotten close to one of those, and let the other go down on me and nearly fuck me. I really do have issues.

"I'm so sorry about him. After everything you told us yesterday, he shouldn't have done that." Hunter's voice stalls my spiraling thoughts.

"You're not mad at me?" I whisper.

Hunter storms straight back over to the bed and sits beside me. His arms are around me in a second and he holds me close. "I could never be mad at you, pretty Lila." He strokes a hand down my hair. "I can't say we don't all have feelings for you 'cause that would be a lie."

My heart stutters at his admission and my arms slip around his waist as I rest my head on his chest. I can hear his heartbeat in his chest and it soothes my frazzled nerves. They all have feelings for me and I can't deny how they make me feel, too.

Hunter is sweet and kind, always placing my needs first. Cayden is a little rough around the edges, but he sure can kiss. And Grayson, well, he might have been scarce since I've been here. Even as he broods on the other side of the table during dinner and then rushes away as soon as his plate is empty, I still miss him when he's not around.

My hand traces up Hunter's side and I give him a small push until he leans away from me. He locks his amethyst gaze with mine and his pupils dilate. A rush of air pushes through his slightly open lips. I tangle my hand in the back of his hair and draw his lips down to mine.

Hunter's lips brush softly against mine and I let out a soft moan. I might have just come but I'm still horny as hell. His arms tighten around my back and he pulls me closer. We kiss for what feels like an eternity, his tongue delving inside my mouth as he explores every inch of me.

When Hunter breaks the kiss, we are both breathless. We stare at each other and I smile. He returns it with one of his own. I nestle into Hunter's arms and close my eyes. He shifts a little in the bed and lies beside me. His fingers stroke through my hair as he hums close to my ear.

If Hunter hadn't shouted up the stairs and made me realize it wasn't a dream, would I have let Grayson fuck me? A part of me fights against letting another man have his way with me, but my belly flutters with butterflies.

Chapter Twenty

Cayden

I only caught the end of whatever was going on upstairs, but then Grayson swaggers down the stairs. He's completely naked and his cock is swinging in the breeze. There's a huge grin on his face.

As soon as he sees me, he winks, and I lose my shit. I storm across from the main door, grabbing him around the back of his neck. His legs flail as I drag him down the corridor, into his bedroom. The door slams behind us and as soon as it does, I let him go.

"What the hell just happened?" I demand.

"I got a taste of her and my God, Cayden, that pussy tastes just like heaven." Grayson swoons a little as he speaks and licks his lips. "I was this close to shoving my cock inside her." He holds his fingers barely an inch away from each other to give me an idea of how close he was.

"You did what?" I roar as I launch myself at him. I knock him clear off his feet and straight onto the bed. My legs are on either side of his thighs and I hold his arms against the mattress.

My fangs and claws ache to make an appearance as I glare down at him. He's talking about Lila like she's his plaything. After everything she told us yesterday, he should handle her with care. She's been through enough already without him terrorizing her.

"I can't believe you, Grayson," I snarl. "You heard what she told us. She was kidnapped and repeatedly raped, used against her will. And you do this." My anger gets the better of me and the darkness tunnels its claws into me.

That's it. Show him what you think of him touching what's ours, the voice in my head growls.

My claws dig into his wrists and sink beneath his flesh. The tang of blood hits the air making the darkness within me growl. My fangs splinter through my gums and another snarl rises from my chest.

Make him hurt, the darkness calls. *Make him bleed.*

There's a shift in Grayson as he takes in my appearance. It's like the cockiness drains from him. He lowers his gaze and bares his neck at me, an act of submission to his alpha. I propel myself away from him and back across the room until my back collides with the wall. The darkness claws at my chest. It thirsts to sink deeper, but I can't let it.

My eyes slam shut and I picture her, beautiful Lila. Her pale skin, and her bright blue eyes that take in all the details around her with only a quick look. The image of her in my mind shoves back against the darkness and it loosens its hold on me. My claws and fangs disappear. I sag against the wall and slip down it until I'm sitting on the floor.

"Cayden..." Grayson actually sounds scared.

I slowly open my eyes and look up to where he's perched on the edge of the bed. He looks like he wants to come closer and flee all at the same time. This is the first time since we've been in the cabin that I've really let the darkness get a hold of me. I've fought against it for so long, but the way he was talking set me off.

"I'm sorry. I shouldn't have..." He trails off. "My wolf hungered for her. He wanted to claim her. To protect her," he continues. "If we claim her, if that other wolf is around like she believes, he won't be able to touch her again." He fiddles with the blanket on the bed. "I don't know what I was thinking."

I do. I know exactly what he was thinking. Lila is the one thing that has been keeping his darkness at bay. If there is another wolf after her, if he can take her, it will be the end for all three of us. Grayson, in his own special way, was trying to protect his brothers and himself. But most of all, if he claimed her then another wolf wouldn't be able to blood bond with her.

That wouldn't stop the other wolf from taking her though. If what Lila told us is true, then he wouldn't care who had claimed her. He wouldn't be able to form a blood bond, but if he's as crazy as he sounds, he may kill her out of spite.

"We'll talk about this later. Get dressed." I push up from my feet and rush out of the door.

I take the steps two at a time until my head peeks high enough to see over the top step. Lila and Hunter are tangled together on the bed, their lips connected and totally consumed by each other. At least I know she's okay.

I make my way back down the steps and straight out of the front door. I strip down and leave my clothes under the porch before I wheel around, shift, and take off into the woods. It doesn't take me long until I make it to the lake and I drop onto my belly.

I can't believe I let the darkness take over so much. I could have killed Grayson, and what if I'd hurt Lila? My chest aches as I envision what could have happened, but she pulled me back from the brink even if she didn't realize it.

The wind ruffles my fur and I inhale. There's a tang of something putrid in the air, but I can't quite place it. I rise to my feet and circle until I can make sense of where it's coming from and then I dart deeper into the woods. I follow the trail all the way to the boundary, where it gets stronger right next to the fence.

My hackles rise and a growl bursts from my chest as I take in another deep inhale. A putrid smell invades my nostrils, one I've smelled before. My father began to attain the same scent a few weeks before he went feral and as the weeks passed it got stronger until he snapped.

At the time I didn't take much notice of the scent. But the rogues that we have come across recently smell even worse. They must be inches from being completely feral.

I finally noticed the underlying tones of wolves, not real wolves, shifters. I snap my jaws and snuffle around the area to see if I can identify where else they have been.

There are at least three different scents in the area, but one of them is more overpowering than the others. I breathe it in; I need to remember this one in case it comes any closer. It's not uncommon for passing rogues to catch our scent and check out the perimeter, but they usually lose interest quickly enough.

There's the scent of wolves at the boundary. I speak to Grayson directly across the pack link, and I feel him bristle. My enforcer is the best for this matter.

I'll be right there, Grayson responds before the link snaps closed. He'll follow the pack bond to find me.

I continue to pace up and down the perimeter, waiting for my packmate. It isn't long before he bounds through the trees and skids to a stop beside me. He lowers his gaze once more before he approaches the fence and puts his nose to the ground.

A growl thunders from his chest as he catches the same scent I have. He paws at the ground, digging to get under the fence.

Grayson, stop, I speak in his mind. *We don't know if it's who Lila was talking about.* I nudge his side and he pauses. *She said there was only one, but there is more than one scent here.*

Then we keep checking the boundary. Grayson turns to me. *We have to keep her safe.*

Chapter Twenty One

Alaric

My wolves have been staying in the town closest to where we found my little bitch's abandoned car. I have warned them to keep a low profile, though some got a little wild. Not that I blame them. The pickings in town may be slim, but there are some stunning bitches ripe for the taking.

I slip through the quiet streets on the hunt for my beta, Ryan. I know his scent well enough to be able to find him and when I do, he's balls deep inside a woman. Her arms are braced against the brick wall at the back of the bar and I chuckle. His head swivels in my direction and we both grin.

I lean against the wall and watch in fascination as he thrusts in and out of her body. The scent of sex and sweat permeates the air and I inhale sharply. It's enough to make my cock harden. The brunette's head tilts to look at me with glazed eyes and pink cheeks. A loud moan slips from between her lips.

With my hand on my zipper, I lower it and pull out my hard length. I fist my cock and pump my hips. Her eyes fall on my cock as she licks her lips. I stride forward and without pause; I shove between her lips. She wraps around my length and I fuck her mouth with brutal thrusts. I feel the vibrations of her moans against my cock; it spurs me on.

Saliva drips down the side of her mouth as she soaks my length. The head of my cock hits the back of her throat with every flex. My fingers tangle in her hair, ripping strands straight from the root. I pull her mouth onto my cock with every forward motion of my hips. My eyes close and I relish in the feel of her hot, wet mouth.

Ryan grunts and his hips falter as he comes inside her. And with a few more pumps I'm not far behind him. My cock is deep in her throat, cutting off her airway as pulse after pulse of my cum is released. She coughs and chokes, her throat muscles making my orgasm that much richer as she tightens further around me.

We both pull free at the same time and her body crumples to the floor.

Bathe in her blood, the voice in my mind prompts, but I shake my head to knock it away.

We must keep a low profile, or my little bitch will bolt again. As much as I enjoy the hunt, I grow tired of having to chase her. I need to feel her pussy around me. I take pleasure in others, but it's never enough to sate my real hunger.

She's ours. I nod in agreement with the voice.

I tuck my soft length back into my jeans and saunter away from the bar. Ryan follows behind me. "Where to, boss?"

"Have the others arrived?"

Between Portland and here, I've been in search of other rogues. I need to rebuild what we had there, which means I need a new pack. I need more bodies to stop them taking my little bitch. There are those out there like the vampires that will try and steal her from me. We are stronger together.

She's ours. Don't let them take her, the voice echoes in my head.

Ryan nods. "Most arrived this morning. I've given them the rules."

"Good. I need one more wolf. We need to find out exactly where my mate is hiding. Safety in numbers." My thoughts aren't even entirely coherent. "Meet at the car."

I stride into the quiet streets and leave my beta behind to fulfill my request. Heading straight out of the town, I move down the eerily quiet road until I hit the border of the forest. I strip off my clothes and leave them in the bushes. My body shifts and I land on powerful paws, taking off across the snow. I keep going until I find the car once more.

Her scent is even weaker now, but without the other wolves there, I can smell the sweet aroma of her blood. I pace the ground, waiting for Ryan to join me. I know she was alone when she left the sanctuary and when she crashed the car. Someone must have stopped to help her. The fact she's in wolf territory, it could be another of my kind.

Ryan pads up beside me. He's brought Martin—Matthew—Mitch. I have no idea what the other wolf's name is, and I don't even care. I give them both a nod and move toward the scent of her blood.

How dare she spill her precious blood. She will have to pay for that.

Her blood is mine.

Her body is mine.

She. Is. Mine.

A growl settles low in my throat. I can't wait to get my hands on my little bitch. She has a lot of punishment to look forward to. I will keep her chained and fuck her day and night, filling all of her holes over and over. Would she like my animal to claim her? The wicked thought crosses my mind and I chuff, the closest sound my wolf can make to a laugh.

The smell of her blood gets stronger the closer we get to a small patch of grass and I take several deep breaths. I come to a sudden stop a few feet away from a huge metal fence. Pressing my nose into the snow, I nudge away the white powder. It's the strongest here. My paws clear more of the snow away and then I see it. A dark patch of red frozen in the ice under the fresh snow.

My tongue darts out and I lick the frozen water until it melts beneath my hot tongue. I can taste her. My cock gets hard again, this time in my wolf form. The two wolves beside me shuffle around. The shift takes over again and Ryan follows suit.

There is no pack bond between us. We are rogues, after all.

"It's her blood. She's here." I look closely at the fence. It has been repaired recently. I glance beyond the linked metal, but all I can see are trees beyond it.

"What now? We can't get over it." Ryan interjects.

"We check the entire fence. Find any weak spots." Ryan nods. I look at the remaining wolf and he nods too.

Ryan and I both shift back and I take the lead. I can smell other shifters in the area. They must have her. They took my little bitch and I will get her back. I'll rip them all apart. Vampires already took her once. I won't let it happen again.

She's mine.

We keep our distance from the fence, eyes shifting up and down, checking every inch of the metal structure. While the top isn't made to keep anything out, it's too high to clear, even for us. We keep a steady pace as we round the entire fence; it goes for miles, with only a singular locked opening before curving gently until it joins up where we began.

A growl of frustration rips from my throat and my claws burrow deep into the ground. They scratch against the hard soil and I keep going, leaving the snow disturbed in my wake.

I need to get to her.

A howl pierces the quiet and I growl. My eyes fixate on the darkness beyond the fence. Ryan nudges my hind leg and I turn on him. My teeth are on full display and he lowers his head before he and the other wolf take off into the woods. With one last look at the fence separating me from my little bitch, I follow the others.

I lead us straight back to where I left my clothes and quickly shift. I put on my now damp clothes and huff out a breath.

"They took her. They fucking took her. They have my mate."

"Don't worry, Alaric. We'll get her back." Ryan pulls on his jeans and t-shirt.

"Yeah, we will. Then we'll fuck them up." The other man laughs as he dons his own clothes.

"Michael is right. We'll destroy them for taking your mate," Ryan grunts.

"Now, we plan."

We set off back toward the town. Before we reach the streets, Michael peels away and heads into the forest. Ryan keeps pace with me but I stay silent. My anger is writhing just below the surface of my skin.

They took her, and she let them. *Fucking bitch.* I growl low in my throat.

Claim her, mark her, fuck her, make her bleed, that voice in my head calls

The darkness claws at my insides and it threatens to rip me apart from the inside. It won't stop until I have her back.

She's mine.

"I'm going hunting," I say. Ryan grunts in response before he heads away from me.

People stumble out of the bar where I found Ryan earlier. It must be kick-out time. The group disperses and one lone man ambles down the street, his hands pushed deep inside his pockets as he whistles. I follow behind him, keeping to the shadows. He passes a small motel and a convenience store before he hangs a right down a deserted side street.

I've already scoped out the town and the only thing down this way is more forest and a truck stop for weary drivers to grab a nap. The lights of the diner are dimmed and the lighted sign in the window reads closed. The man freezes for a moment and looks over his shoulder. I step deeper into the shadows.

He shakes his head when he sees nothing and resumes his walk. He enters the truck stop and drifts toward a lone logging truck. I don't sense another person nearby.

I'm the hunter and he's the prey.

My claws extend and my fangs sharpen as a partial shift takes over. The pebbles under my feet move as I run at him. I launch myself forward and force him to the ground mid-turn. My hand goes over his mouth as I shove my claws deep into his side and his blood spills over my fingers. The scent of copper fills my lungs and I laugh.

Chapter Twenty Two

Lila

Hunter's arms wrap around me. After he kisses me for what feels like an eternity, we settle back on the bed as I lie in his embrace. My head is on his chest, and I listen to his steady heartbeat beneath my ear.

"None of us wants to hurt you, Lila," Hunter whispers as he runs his fingers through my hair. "Please, give us a chance." He's so sincere that I believe him. None of these men would hurt me. They are safety. I am safe.

I want to stay, but at the same time something is still telling me to escape. Not that I can with no car, no cash, and a healing leg.

I can feel *him*. It's like *he's* under my skin and getting closer. Even in the safety of Hunter's arms, there is still something pushing me.

"What are you thinking about?" Hunter murmurs.

"Nothing. I just don't understand how the three of you can desire me." I want to curl up further. "Especially after what I told you. I'm broken—damaged."

Hunter sits straighter and pushes me back slightly. "You are anything but broken, Lila." He cups my face and I lean into his hand. "You are one of the strongest women I've ever met. To go through what you have and come out the other side, it's amazing."

"Barely..." I don't feel strong. I'm still the scared woman who got out of that cave.

"You don't see what we see. You might be injured, but that won't ever stop you." Hunter smiles down at me, his fingers caress my jawline.

I want to believe his words, but my past still haunts me. I close my eyes and take a deep breath. I made it out the other side, though. I'm still here. And I'll fight to get back to where I used to be.

I push up on my knees and straddle Hunter; he gasps in surprise. His hands fall to my thighs as I roll my hips. His cock hardens beneath me, but I don't stop my movements against him as his hands guide me back and forth.

"We don't have to." Hunter breathes out between moans.

"I know. Thank you." I press against him. My body heats as my clit rubs against his hardened length.

Hunter doesn't wish to push me, but I want to know how far I can go. I got pretty close with Grayson, but I didn't realize that wasn't actually a dream. Now that I'm fully conscious, just how far can I take it with Hunter?

My fingers dig into his chest as I rub up and down his length. The fabric of my shorts catches on the overly sensitive skin. I shimmy down his legs and reach for the top of his jeans. My hands tremble as I grasp the button and pull it undone.

I move to the zipper next and my body quivers. Hunter lays his hand over the top of mine. My trembling slowly abates as he helps to guide my hand down, taking his zipper with it. His hard bulge pushes out of the gap in the material against the fabric of his boxers.

Slowly he guides both of my hands to the waistline of his clothes. He lifts his hips and helps me pull the fabric down his thighs. His cock springs free and I startle. He's huge. A piece of metal pierces through its head and pre-cum beads at the tip.

Each vein stands prominently down the entire length and he's completely hairless. Hunter doesn't move a single inch as I marvel at him. When my hands come loose from the fabric of his clothes, I reach for his cock. My fingers brush against his steely flesh and he shudders.

I wrap my fist around him, but even then, I can't close my hand all the way around his girth. For a moment, I just hold him, feeling the heat seeping through my hand.

"We don't have to go any further if you don't want to." Hunter lifts my chin so my eyes meet him.

"I want to." With that, I raise my hand up his length and back down to the root until Hunter groans. My eyes flicker to him and I find his closed.

My fingers tighten on Hunter's length and I work him up and down. His mouth drops open as he lets out another groan.

"Lila..." His voice is breathy.

I release him and fumble with the waistband of my shorts. I need to feel him against me. When the fabric is down to my knees, I remove them from my legs and resume my position above him. The bite that's healing on my leg sends a small shock up past my knee, but I ignore it.

Hunter's eyes snap open as I lower myself back into his lap. His cock nudges against my folds, but I don't allow him entry. I rub myself against his length and lubricate his cock. We both moan as I rock my hips back and forth, his cock pulsing beneath me. Hunter's hands grasp my hips and help guide my movements.

I feel myself convulse as my movements become more rapid. I'm almost there. I just need a little more. Hunter fulfills my need as he presses a finger against my clit. I detonate, the orgasm overtaking my body. With a groan, Hunter follows me over the edge. His cum splatters all over his stomach and his hips jolt. The head of his cock slips inside me but he stills his movements.

Hunter is barely penetrating me, not as far as I crave him, but enough to make me squeeze around him. Hunter chokes out another groan. His nails bite into my skin and I know he wants more but he stops himself.

"Fuck, Lila. I want to be buried so deep inside you." His hips twitch and his cock pushes a little further into me, making me moan. Even though he's only just come, his length is still hard.

I brace for the terror to hit, but it doesn't. There isn't even an ounce of fear as I raise my hips. I wrap my hand around the base of Hunter's length and sink down. I feel his girth as he stretches me. The base of his cock feels wider than the rest. The mixture of pleasure and pain makes me wince, but I don't stop.

Once he's nearly seated fully inside me, I pause for a moment to adjust to his huge size. Hunter's fingers hold my hips down and he flexes, tearing a moan from me.

Hunter lets me take the lead and I raise myself until his mushroomed head is the only thing inside me. I drop straight back down on him, my hips rising and falling until I hit a steady rhythm. After that one flex of his hips, Hunter lets me claim control. He doesn't force me to do what he desires. He lets me take pleasure from his body at my pace.

Our grunts and moans fill the loft space. A fine layer of perspiration covers my body, but Hunter hasn't even broken a sweat. I close my eyes as I take him whole, my body tightening around his length. It doesn't take me long until I'm reaching my peak once more. My walls clamp down on Hunter's cock and squeeze him hard.

With a shuddering moan, I come again. Stars flash behind my eyes and my vision narrows until it's almost black. Sex has never felt like this with anyone before. Hunter suddenly grasps my waist and pulls me from his cock. He wraps his hand around himself and pumps until his cum splashes all over my pubic bone.

Part of me wants to question why he didn't come inside me, but I'm still too high from my orgasm to bother. Hunter curls up at my side and wraps his arms around me. The cum on his stomach and my pelvis slips from our bodies to the bedsheets and Hunter chuckles.

"Guess that means we should both get cleaned up? Maybe even get Cayden's bed sorted before he gets back." Hunter smirks. It's the first time someone has confirmed whose bed I have been sleeping in.

Hunter kisses me then leaps from the bed and tugs up his boxers and jeans. He grabs a used towel off the floor and hands it to me to let me clean up. Once I'm done, I pass it back to him and he wipes his stomach off before he drops it to the floor. He reaches down and lifts me straight off the bed. A squeal of surprise leaves my lips as he holds me against his chest, and I wrap my legs around his waist.

His softening cock rubs against me and I let out a moan, followed by a wince as he nudges against my sore flesh. Hunter locks his lips with mine and kisses me softly. He loosens his grip and lets me slip down his body until my feet graze across the floor and I stand. With a quick movement, he grabs my shorts and hands them back to me along with a kiss and I quickly put them on.

When I'm dressed, Hunter makes quick work of stripping the sheets from the bed and bunches them up into a ball under his arm. He grabs my hand and leads me to the stairs.

"First the sheets, then we need to get cleaned up." With a grin, he makes his way downstairs, taking it slow and at my snail's pace.

At the bottom, he releases my hand and heads straight for the kitchen. Tossing the dirty sheets into the washer that's fitted under the counter, he turns back to me and smiles again once it's running. He's the smiler of the group, but I'm not sure I've seen him this happy the entire time I've been here. It must be contagious as the corners of my lips turn up.

Hunter comes straight back to me and wraps his arms around my waist as he pulls me close to him. "Thank you for having so much faith in me. You've made my dreams come true."

I feel his smile against my cheek as he leans down and holds the side of my face to his.

The door opens and we both spring back from each other like small children being caught doing something wrong. Cayden stomps through the door, followed by Grayson. The latter stops and stares straight at us both. His nostrils flare and his eyes darken as we lock gazes.

Does Grayson know what just happened between Hunter and me? As much as Hunter has said already that all three of them desire me, it's hard to believe that any of them would let the other one touch me.

"Hunter, we need to talk." Cayden's voice pulls me from my staring match with Grayson and I quickly look away.

"Sure. Lila, why don't you go grab a shower while I find out what's going on?" I give Hunter a nod and stare after the three men as they walk away from me and toward the kitchen.

With a sigh, I head for the bathroom, letting the door close behind me. I turn on the shower, Hunter's warning about allowing it time for the water to get through the pipes echoes in my mind.

While I wait, I look at myself in the mirror. My appearance is so much better than when they first found me. The color is back in my cheeks and now my skin glows. I quickly strip off my clothes and check the waterproof dressing on my leg to make sure it's secure before I step into the shower enclosure.

The water is heaven and I close my eyes as it cascades down over my body. My muscles relax as I think of the time I spent with Hunter. Not once did my fear or nightmares hit me. Not once did a panic attack seem to be on the verge of happening.

Maybe I could be happy here.

Chapter Twenty Three

Cayden

Lila heads for the bathroom and I beckon for Grayson and Hunter to follow me to the kitchen. As soon as Hunter is close enough, I smell her all over him and the darkness rears its ugly head again.

He took what's yours. Kill him. A growl slips from my lips and Grayson wraps his arms around my waist as I snap my teeth in Hunter's direction.

"Cayden, stop. He's our brother," Grayson's voice whispers in my ear. My teeth snap again and I push against Grayson's arms, but he tightens his grip. "You love him, Cay. Remember that." Grayson is in my ear again.

I think of my two brothers, my packmates. Of everything we have been through together. Actively shoving the darkness away, I remember our fights and struggles with our pack. Their love for me pushes through our pack bond and my shoulders drop.

I sense Hunter's excitement through the bond. The pull he has toward Lila is strengthened after being with her. As a glow of light pulsates from my soul, it thrusts back at the darkness until its grip on me is only a few wisps.

"I'd never betray you, brother." Hunter takes a step closer and Grayson's grip on me loosens until his arms fall back at his sides. He remains close, though. "She was curious. I assume even if she doesn't realize it, Lila feels this connection, too." His smile increases as he speaks.

"She wants us all?" Grayson questions over my shoulder.

"I think she does. She doesn't understand it, but I think she wants to see where it goes."

My heart feels lighter. Lila hasn't chosen only Hunter, by the sounds of it, she's chosen all of us. My mind pulls back to the real reason I asked Hunter to talk to me. "We have a problem. Well, two."

"What is it?" Hunter exclaims. His eyes flicker over to the bathroom door and then back to me. Dividing his attention between me and what Lila is doing.

"As you just saw, the darkness. It's getting worse." I can still feel it, the tiny hooks piercing through me. They want to expand again but surrounded by my pack mates, it's overpowered—for now.

Hunter places a hand on my shoulder and squeezes. "She is the one, Cay. Lila's the one we have been looking for, I'm sure of it." He's so confident in his words and I can't disagree with him.

"But how do we tell her? As soon as she finds out we're shifters, she'll run."

We can't expect her to stay. She doesn't trust our kind. The rogues took her and defiled her body for their own needs. They didn't once care for the women they kept captive.

"I don't want her to bolt. My wolf thinks she's already his." Hunter's hand traces down my arm. "I caught Grayson with her. I thought she'd be scared but I could smell her. She wanted him as much as he wanted her."

"We have another problem," Grayson cuts in. Hunter shifts his gaze to him. "Cayden found new scents at the perimeter."

Hunter bristles and clenches his fists. "Whose?"

"They could just be rogues passing by. They smelled us and came to check it out. It wouldn't be the first time it's happened." I make my way over to the sink and fill a glass with water. I take a sip while I think.

"I don't know. Doesn't it seem like too much of a coincidence to you? Lila said that the wolf was still coming for her." Hunter quips.

"We're going to make sure someone is with Lila at all times. The others will run the fence daily. We'll check for breaks. No excuses for taking too long to repair a breach anymore." It's not much of a plan, but it's a start.

I shift my attention to Grayson, and he nods before he speaks. "I'll take Hunter to where you found the scents so he can familiarize himself with them."

"Okay. Do that. Check every inch of the fence while you're out there." With my order, the two turn and head out the front door.

I lean on the counter, my fingers going white as I grip the edge. I inhale deeply before I let it out and repeat. The sound of the shower cuts out and I turn towards it. The door opens and Lila scurries out with only a towel around her damp body, another wrapped around her golden hair.

She lets out a squeak when she sees me. "Sorry, I heard the door. I thought no one was out here. I was gonna get upstairs while no one was around."

"Our home is your home, Lila." She inhales sharply and looks to the floor. "I mean it. While you're here, treat it like you own the place."

"Thank you." Her voice is quiet, but I hear her. Pushing off the counter, I make my way over to her.

"There's no need for your apologies or your thanks." I pause for a moment. "I enjoy having you here, Lila." Her eyes flicker up to mine and a small smile graces her lips.

My hand rises and my fingers reach for her face, but I stop them when I'm barely an inch away. I silently beg for her permission and Lila gives me a nod. The pads of my fingers connect with the soft skin of her cheek, and she leans her head into the palm of my hand. My thumb traces over her cheekbone.

Lila's eyes lock with mine and her breath hitches. I hear her heart rate increase and the skin pinks on her chest and cheeks from only a simple caress. I don't even feel myself shift closer, but then she's right in front of me. Her breasts press up against the thin fabric of my Henley and the heat of her body seeps through. Our lips are barely a hair's breadth away.

My wolf wants to consume her, to claim her. But I won't take anything from her without permission again. "May I kiss you?"

Lila nods and then I'm on her. My lips brush against hers and she instantly opens for me. My tongue delves into her mouth and her taste explodes on my taste buds. A moan falls from her lips and I swallow it down. Her small hands grip my shoulders. My arms wrap around her waist as I pull her against me.

My body is wrapped in jasmine and roses and it's like a drug to me. My hands trail down her sides and grip her backside before I glide them under her thighs. Lifting her until she wraps her legs around my hips, I push her against the wall in the hallway. Another moan escapes from her mouth as I grind myself against her. The nails in my shoulders dig deeper as she holds onto me for dear life.

After a few minutes, I break the kiss. Both our chests heave and her cheeks are bright red . Her eyes are glazed over with lust; she looks beautiful. "You're everything, Lila."

"But Hunter?" she mumbles.

"What about him?" My eyebrows knit together as I frown. Is she rejecting me?

"I... we..." She gulps. "We had sex."

"I know." Lila's face blanches and the red of her cheeks disappears until she's as white as a sheet. "I still want you. My friends and I are close, as you've seen." I remember her watching Hunter and Grayson together. "But all three of us still desire you equally."

"I don't want to get between you all."

I laugh at her comment. "Nothing can fracture the bond we have with each other. But you, beautiful, you could make it so much stronger." As true mate to all three of us, we'd be a bonded pack, with Lila as our sun.

"Okay," Lila agrees and my wolf howls.

Chapter Twenty Four

Lila

A yawn stretches my mouth wide as my eyes slowly blink open. The loft is already light, even with the curtains closed. Sunshine flooding in from the living room below makes it bright, even up here. I roll onto my side and straight into Wolfie. After his disappearance yesterday, he finally came back shortly after we'd had dinner.

I run my hand through his fur and he lets out a snuffle. His tongue lolls out of the side of his mouth and I let out a soft laugh. One of his silver eyes flickers open and moves to me. I smile at him and laugh a little harder.

"I'm sorry. You're so cute when you're asleep."

Wolfie snorts at me and clamps his mouth shut before he lunges forward and runs his tongue up the side of my face. A squeal peals out of my mouth and I hold my hands in front of him to stave off his licks.

"Mercy, truce, parley, whichever of those you understand." The licks stop, and Wolfie jumps to his feet. He bounds off the bed and straight over to the drawers. Snagging a blanket in his huge jaws, he drags it over the floor to me, and places it on the edge of the bed. "Thanks."

I grab the blanket and wrap it around my shoulders to stave off the chill in the air and then Wolfie is off again. This time he goes to the drawers and uses his jaws to pull open the top one. Rearing on his hind legs, he rests his paws on the edge of the drawer and sticks his head inside. When he moves back and falls to the floor again, he has socks bunched up in his mouth.

Wolfie trots over to me and places two pairs on the bed before he nudges them to me with his nose. I rub his head before I shove both pairs on my feet. When I'm ready, I clamber out of the bed and stand.

The blanket pools around me like a waterfall and helps to cover my legs. Wolfie nudges the back of my calves and I make my way to the stairs. When I reach the top, Cayden is lounging on the couch with a cup of coffee already in his hands. As if he heard me, he twists to look at me and smiles. I offer him a small wave before I make my way down the steps.

Once I reach the bottom, Wolfie comes galloping down behind me and heads straight for the front door. Cayden places down his coffee cup and goes to let him out.

"Morning," Cayden offers as he turns back to me. "Hunter will be back soon. Then he's going to make you some breakfast. Grayson and I need to head into town. We'll be gone most of the day."

Cayden stalks toward me and pulls me into his arms. I let him, shivering at the feel of his mouth as his lips brush against mine. I taste the coffee he's been drinking and moan. His tongue brushes against my lips before he devours me fully.

I'm barely even aware of the door as it opens and closes again as Cayden kisses me.

"Don't mind me. I'll start breakfast," Hunter says and I break the kiss between me and Cayden.

My hand reaches out and I snag Hunter's sleeve before he can get past me. I pull him toward me and move from Cayden's embrace to his. Hunter is quick to wrap his arms around my waist and I beam up at him. I press my lips against his and he tightens his grip on me.

At dinner last night, we all talked. I told all three of them I wanted to give whatever this was a chance...for now. Though I kept the last bit to myself. Every time they are close, I feel something that tugs me closer to them. They make me feel safe; I can't deny the fact I revel in that feeling.

"If this is how I'm going to be greeted every morning, I'm going to have to give you mind-blowing sex more often." Hunter snickers and Cayden shakes his head at him. "What, you never greet me like this the morning after."

I know that all three of them are close. I've seen it for myself with Hunter and Grayson, but I never realized that the intimacy moved to Cayden and Hunter. The thought of them together makes my skin flush and both men turn to stare at me.

"Does that turn you on, beautiful?" Cayden grins as he asks. "The thought of me and Hunter together. I know how hot you were for Grayson and Hunter."

I swallow hard but don't answer. My eyes move to Hunter's chest and I let out a shuddering breath.

"Don't you have places to be, Cay?" Hunter quips. "Leave me to make my girl breakfast."

Cayden's deep laughter rings through the cabin. "That means you have to actually make food, not literally make *her* breakfast." With that last comment, Cayden spins and strides out of the cabin.

Hunter laughs and pulls me back to him, kissing my forehead gently. I curl up against his chest and listen to his heartbeat. We stay like that for a long time before he pushes me away and looks down at me. Those amethyst eyes of his bore into mine and I shiver at the look.

"Breakfast?" I mumble and he nods. His hand drifts down the side of mine until he interlocks our fingers together and leads me to the kitchen.

After a hearty breakfast, Hunter lets me help him clean up and put everything away. My calf feels better than it has since I first woke up here. It still twinges, but I can get around the cabin with a lot more ease. I survey the books on the shelves; there's all sorts and they can't be all the guys' choices.

I pick out a random story and the blurb tells me it's a Beauty and the Beast retelling. The cover is black with bold, gold writing, a black spiked collar, a golden rose and chains, cobwebs, and a death head moth.

The entire thing draws me in and I can't wait to get it started. Hunter walks behind me. His hand trails around my waist as he heads to grab his laptop from the dining table. He makes his way over to the couch and takes a seat. I follow behind him and curl up in the corner with the book in hand.

As soon as I get myself settled, I open the first page and dig into the story of a kidnapped princess and a cruel mage. I devour page after page as Hunter works beside me. After a few hours, he jumps up from his seat and heads for the kitchen, but I don't look up from the tale I'm entwined in.

A plate is placed down on the coffee table in front of me full of sandwiches and chips, and I pick at them as I read. Hunter leans over the back of the couch and kisses my cheek gently. I feel the heat rush to the surface of my skin.

"I have to go, but Wolfie will stay with you till Cayden gets back." I glance up from the pages and around the room. There is no sign of the wolf hybrid.

Hunter shrugs on a coat, opens the door and heads outside. Wolfie charges through the open door and straight over to the couch. He jumps into Hunter's empty seat and flops down beside me. His huge head leans on my thigh. It's enough to stop me from reading and I lay the book down. My fingers sink into his fur and I scratch behind his ears, eliciting a soft whine.

"So, what are we gonna do now, Wolfie?" I look around the cabin. There's not much here to do other than read, but that's all I've done for weeks. Boredom is kicking in and I need to do something different before cabin fever sets in. "How about we head outside?"

That gets Wolfie's attention. He shrugs my hands away and lifts his head to look straight at me. He shakes his head a few times as if he wants to tell me he disagrees with my decision.

"Please," I whine. "I'm so bored. I've only seen the inside of these walls for weeks. I'm going mad. Plus my leg feels better, I need to stretch it out a bit." Wolfie's ears flicker back and forth before he climbs off the couch and tugs on my sleeve.

I guess he's agreeing with me after all. I head for the stairs and up into the loft. The guys have left me an assortment of clothes on top of the drawers and I dig through the pile. I bring each item to my nose and give it a sniff. When I smell coffee and books, I know they are Hunter's.

With the sweatpants and long-sleeved top in hand, I shrug off the things I'm wearing and throw them in the wash basket before I pull on Hunter's clothes. I could ask the guys if they can get me some of my own items when they head to the store, but I enjoy being wrapped up in clothes that smell like them.

When I'm ready, I head back downstairs and find my boots, one of the few possessions I have here, sitting by the door. I shove my feet into them and lace them up. Wolfie comes and sits beside me as he waits patiently for me to be ready. As soon as I'm done, he trots over to the coat rack and pulls a large fur-lined coat from the hooks.

Wolfie drags it back over to me and raises his head until I grab it and put it on. This has to be the warmest item of clothing I've seen these guys own. It's not until I push my hand through the sleeve that I notice the sales tag still attached to the cuff. With a snort, I tear it off and leave it on the shelf of the rack.

Opening the door, I step outside onto the porch. The moment I do the bitter wind hits me square in the face and I quickly do the coat up and shove my hands in the pockets. I feel something soft and wooly under my fingers on both hands and pull them back out. A woolen hat and matching gloves are grasped in my fingers.

"They're one step ahead of me, apparently." I let out a small laugh and quickly donned the hat and gloves. They are thick enough to stave off the cold. "Okay, can we just take a quick stroll around the cabin?" I look at Wolfie and he gives me a nod.

With my hand on his back, we descend the steps together and begin our walk. The snow isn't thick, but it doesn't take me long to find a few patches of ice beneath the white powder. I'm fine at first, as I use the railing to make my way along the front of the cabin. As we reach the side, it's an entirely different matter.

On one bad patch, I feel my legs go from under me, but Wolfie is straight there. His huge body is under me to catch me as I fall forward. I let out a laugh and wrap my arms around his body as far as they will go to give him a hug before I release him.

When I'm upright again, we set off down the side of the cabin once more. With one hand on the timber logs that form the sides, and Wolfie on the other, it's a little better going.

"The guys say they all want me. And I don't know what to do, Wolfie." He shifts his gaze to me and I shrug. "I know you can't answer me, but I need to tell someone." I give him a weak smile. "The thing is, I want them all." Wolfie lets out a yip that startles me. "I can't describe it. Since I've been here, it's like my body has been pulled toward them, even when I was afraid of them."

This is it. I really have gone mad. I'm talking to a wolf hybrid who only a few weeks ago scared the crap out of me. But better out than in, I say.

"I was dreaming about them before anything really happened, and they weren't exactly PG in content. I can't even tell you the amount of cold showers I've had to have." I look down at my hybrid and he nods his head as if he's agreeing with me.

"I want to see what this thing is with all of them, even if that makes me a hussy." I laugh. "Now, just to convince Grayson that he doesn't have to sleepwalk naked and crawl in bed with me to get my attention."

Wolfie yips in response and bounces on his feet as if he's delighted by my words. I shake my head at the craziness of it, but my whole life is crazy right now. I had left the sanctuary because I thought he was after me, crashed my car, and ended up in a cabin surrounded by three men. I should probably have run from them, but now all I want to do is have sex with them all.

We reach the back of the cabin and I take in the forest behind us. We are surrounded by it. Even if I wished to leave, which I don't, I wouldn't know which way to go. I take a step closer to the trees and then another. There's blackness beyond them, the sun barely even piercing through the foliage to light what's beyond the tree line.

Wolfie is suddenly in front of me. His hackles are raised, and his ears are pressed back against his head. The hairs on my arms rise and goose pimples erupt over my skin. A shiver quakes down my spine and I take a tentative step back. Growls push through Wolfie's fangs as he keeps his eyes trained on the woods beyond us.

It's that feeling again, the one of being watched. With a howl, Wolfie takes off into the trees and I'm frozen to the spot. I'm on the wrong side of the cabin and there's no door on this side. Turning on my heel, I do the only thing I can do—run.

The snow kicks up under my feet as I skid around the side of the cabin. A twinge in my leg almost sends me to the ground but I keep going. Using the pillar of the porch, I pull myself around the corner, along the front, and straight up the steps. I didn't lock the door when we left and I sprint straight inside, slamming it behind me.

With trembling hands, I slide the heavy bolt into place and sink down to the floor with my back against the door. I left Wolfie out there, but I had to get away. If it's him, he'll tear the hybrid apart. My heart clenches as I wonder what fate I've left Wolfie to. I need to contact the guys, but it's not like I've seen a phone in the cabin to use.

I race to the dining table and grab a chair, bracing it behind the door. If he really wants to get in I don't think there will be any stopping him, but it makes me feel a little better. Throwing off my coat, I search the kitchen and living room for any sort of phone, but I come up empty-handed and let out a groan of frustration.

A knock on the door has me jumping out of my skin and I let out a scream. "Lila, it's me." Grayson's gravely voice comes from the other side of the door and I race over to it.

Chapter Twenty Five

Grayson

Lila and I haven't been out in the snow for long, but I listen to every word she says. When she tells me she thought she needed to convince me that I didn't need an excuse of sleepwalking to crawl into bed with her, I almost shift and drag her back to the cabin.

Even my wolf wants me to transform onto two legs and say I'll take her straight to bed if that's what she desires from me. It would have been a complete disaster, though. If anything, she would have run away screaming and never looked back. She hates wolf shifters too much for me to just spring that on her.

We get closer to the trees that line the back of the cabin and that's when I smell them. Another wolf is close by, and I don't think I am the only one who could tell. Fear spikes in Lila's scent and it freezes her to the spot.

I take off into the woods, hoping that my mate would get back to the cabin without me. As soon as I burst through the tree line, I hear them rather than see them. The sound of twigs cracking underfoot and heavy panting assaults my ears. The darkness is close on my tail, making demands to end the intruder's life.

As I run, I think I am gaining ground, but the sound of footfalls gets fainter as my paws eat up the distance. I leap over a small stream and hit rockier ground but keep going. When I hit the fence a few miles from the cabin, the paw prints stop abruptly and become human feet. There's no way anyone, or anything, can jump the fence from this side.

With a quick look up and down the length of the metal, I spot a gap. This one isn't from general wear and tear. Someone has snipped straight through the links and pried them apart.

Someone has come through the fence. A shifter, for sure. I send my message through the pack link. *I'm southeast of the rear of the cabin.* I rein back my need to track them down. *Lila's on her own.*

I'll be right there. Go back to Lila, Cayden's voice echoes.

I heed my alpha's command and head straight for the cabin. I hear Lila inside when I get close. Her footfalls shift around the cabin as she tracks from the kitchen to the living room, slamming cupboard doors as she goes. I stop at the storage where we all keep clothes and slip into the same clothes I was wearing when I left this morning.

Once I'm dressed, I make my way around the side of the cabin and up the steps onto the porch. A quick knock has Lila screaming, and I take a deep breath. "Lila, it's me."

I hear her on the other side as she hurries for the door and pulls back the bolt. She flings the door open and runs into my arms. "Grayson! Oh my God. I was so scared." Her voice trembles. "I was out with Wolfie, and then he was in front of me and growling, then he took off. I came straight back here. It was *him*. I'm telling you it was *him*. My nightmare. *He's* here for me." She barely takes a breath.

My arms wrap around her shoulders and I back her into the cabin. I give the door a kick until it shuts behind us. "Shhh, it's okay. No one is going to get you."

"You don't understand. *He'll* kill you. *He's* going to kill Wolfie." Panic laces her voice.

"Everything will be okay. Cayden rang me on the way back." The lie rolls off my tongue. "He said someone had stumbled through the fence, he's showing them out. Wolfie is with him."

"You're sure?" Lila looks up at me with pleading eyes.

"I am." The lies come far too easily, but I don't want to scare her away. "Come on, I'll make you some of that funky tea Hunter uses to calm your nerves."

Lila pulls away and nods quickly at me. I engulf her hand in mine and tingles spread through my fingers as I lead her to the kitchen. I don't want to let go, but I need both hands. Quickly, I gather the things I need. When the hot water is on the stove, I drop a tea bag into the cup and wait.

Lila edges closer to me and I wrap an arm around her shoulders, pulling her close. Her hand rests against my chest and I can't suppress a groan at her touch. She lets out a light giggle and smiles up at me. My body leans down to her and my mouth grazes hers. The kettle whistles and I quickly pull away. I don't miss the look of disappointment on Lila's face.

With one arm firmly around her, I turn off the gas and fill the cup to the top. The smell of chamomile rises from the tea and I put the kettle back on the stove. Wrapping my hand around the cup, I pass it to Lila and she takes it before she pulls herself from under my arm and moves to the couch.

The book she was reading earlier lies forgotten on the coffee table as she places the cup beside it. Lila lowers herself down to the thick cushion and I stand awkwardly for a moment. Not sure if I should stand guard or sit down, the decision is taken from me as Lila grabs my hand and pulls me down beside her.

With a humph, I land beside Lila before she grabs the steaming cup, curling up against me. She's already calmer and she hasn't even drunk any of the tea yet. I watch her every movement as she takes small sips of the liquid. A small moan escapes her lips and I groan. My blood rushes south and my jeans grow tight.

Lila might look innocent, but I reckon she knows exactly what she does to me if the brief glances at my crotch have anything to say about it. The next time she takes a sip, she moans again causing me to shift in my seat. A small smile breaks across her lips against the cup. I want to snatch it out of her hands and really make her moan.

As a distraction, I turn the television on and stop on a movie that is halfway through. Lila has her entire body pressed against mine. Her heat seeps through my clothes, her closeness too much of a temptation. But by the end of the movie, my arm is around her shoulders and her head is laid against my chest. Her hand strokes up and down my abs.

The things this woman does to me. To distract myself, I've had to spend more time than usual with Hunter. Apart from the night I was in her bed in my wolf form, I'd forgone my visit to Hunter's room before bed. Her moans and arousal had caressed my senses and forced my body back into its human form.

That morning when she'd touched me, I'd thought we were getting somewhere. We kept going and not once did she flinch. Not until Hunter had ruined my fun. And later I'd ruined his ass for cock blocking me so spectacularly.

The thoughts of that morning have my cock twitching and hardening. I lay my head against the back of the couch and let out a groan.

"Do you need some help with that?" Lila's voice has my head snapping up. Her gaze is on the bulge in my jeans.

"No," I groan. "I'm good."

"It's not like I haven't seen it already, Gray." The way she uses my shortened name has me twitching again. "I want you. I don't fully understand it, but I do."

Lila's hand drops onto my leg and her fingers creep closer to the apex of my thighs. I should stop her, but I can't. When she reaches my cock, she rubs her palm against me making my hips rise involuntarily from the seat cushion.

"Fuck..." I rasp.

Lila takes that as some sort of permission, and she pops the button of my jeans before she pulls the zipper down. The metal rubs against the head of my cock and I let out a groan. I watch her hands as they move. When the zipper is all the way down, she reaches inside the gap and wraps her fingers around my length.

The feel of her skin against mine is pure heaven. She slides her hand up and down a few times before she lets go and grabs the top of my jeans. I lift my hips and she pulls the pants down my thighs until my throbbing hard-on is on full display to her gaze.

"Christ, Lila. You don't know what you do to me." Her hand wraps around me as I speak and my hips rock.

My stunning mate lowers herself until she has her head above my crotch. Her tongue darts out and licks at the pre-cum forming at the tip. My fingers dig into the couch to stop myself from taking hold of her hair and shoving her down onto my length. When she opens her mouth further, she envelops the mushroomed head in the wet heat of her mouth. Her tongue continues to lick around the top as she engulfs more of my cock.

A moan travels up her throat and vibrates against me. My hips buck up off the seat, pushing more of me inside her mouth. I assume for a moment she might pull away, but she doesn't falter as she glides up and down. Her hand moves to my balls as she caresses my sack and she sucks me.

My claws threaten to erupt and shred straight through the fabric of the couch as she teases and kneads my balls. I'm barely even aware of the cabin door opening as Hunter saunters inside. He looks at both of us and grins.

"If I knew this was the party I was coming back to, I'd have gotten here sooner." Hunter laughs.

Lila pulls her mouth from my cock, a trail of saliva from the head to her lips. She wipes her mouth with the back of her hand and goes to pull away, but I hold her in place.

"Ignore him. Pretend he's not even here," I suggest. Lila looks at me with questioning eyes and I give her a nod.

The fact Hunter is here doesn't bother me in the slightest. "You don't mind if he watches?"

Lila shakes her head and looks over to Hunter, who gives her a nod of approval as he kicks off his boots and takes up a seat on the other end of the couch. My mate moves back to where she was. I let out another groan as her hand wraps around the base of my cock and her mouth descends back over me.

Out of the corner of my eye, I see Hunter rubbing his own hardening cock. As she sucks my length, the scent of Lila's arousal fills the room, which has both me and Hunter groaning. He moves closer to us. His hand reaches below Lila's head and he wraps his fingers around my balls.

"Do you really want to make him purr, Lila?" Hunter questions.

Wolves don't purr, asshole, I blast over to his mind and Hunter laughs out loud.

Lila moves away from my cock again and I groan in frustration. Hunter jumps to his feet and pads down the hallway to his bedroom. When he comes back, he has a bottle of lube in his hand. I raise an eyebrow, wondering exactly where he plans on taking this.

"Take off his boots and jeans," Hunter commands.

Lila works deftly to undo the laces on my boots and pulls them from my feet, depositing them on the floor before she yanks my jeans the rest of the way down.

"Gray, lie down with your head at the end of the couch." I do exactly as Hunter asks. Lila watches with fascination. "Now, Lila, get on top of him. Get your pussy right over his face."

Lila looks unsure for a moment, but she complies with Hunter's demand. She shucks off her clothes entirely. With a leg on either side of me, her sweet scent is within reach. I inhale deeply and draw her in; she smells divine. I can already see the wetness on her lips.

"Suck his cock like you were when I came in." Lila doesn't hesitate this time. Instead, she leans forward. Her hair bruises against my thighs, sending tremors through my body. Her tongue circles the head of my cock before she devours me. With my hands on her hips, I lower her body until her pussy is right above my mouth.

My tongue darts out and I lick her slit from her clit to her ass. A moan echoes from her mouth and the vibrations go straight to my balls. I lap at her slit, her juices dripping down my chin, and I lick up every drop I can. The couch by my feet depresses and Hunter opens my legs. He lifts one onto the back of the couch and the other off the side.

There is a squirt of the lube bottle and then the coldness hits the bottom of my balls and drips to my hole. A finger probes my entrance as it smears the lube around the puckered skin. Lila rocks back against my tongue, but I still don't enter her.

The finger at my ass presses inside me slowly and I groan. The tip of my tongue presses between Lila's lips and we both let out a sigh. Hunter's finger moves out a little before pushing back in deeper. I follow his actions with my tongue. As he increases his thrusts into me, I do the same with my tongue in Lila's pussy.

Chapter Twenty Six

Lila

A moan spills from my lips as they wrap around Grayson's cock. He thrusts his tongue in and out of my pussy like he's fucking me. My attention is drawn to Hunter, though, as his finger disappears beneath Grayson's balls and into his ass. Hunter is painfully dressed still compared to me and Grayson, and I want him to strip, too.

My mouth bobs up and down Grayson's length as he attacks me with his tongue. A very talented tongue. Hunter pulls out his finger and Grayson whines; the sound makes me tingle. It doesn't take long before Hunter thrusts two fingers back inside Grayson and the man below me groans.

I can't stop my body as I push back on Grayson's face, craving for him to go deeper. Hunter fumbles with his pants and my eyes move up to watch him as I continue to lick and suck on Grayson's cock. Hunter pulls his hard length free and wraps his fist around himself, pumping rhythmically.

With one hand holding me up on the couch and I reach out the other. I slip my fingers around the base of Hunter's cock, where he isn't holding himself. He removes his hand

and lets me take over as he reaches for my hair and laces his fingers in the strands, tugging on them slightly. The pleasure with a side of pain—pain that should have me jumping away—but I want this.

"That's it. Suck him while he eats you out." Hunter's voice is raspy and his hips jolt as he fucks himself into my fist.

Grayson and I increase our pace at exactly the same time. I ride his face as his hips lift for me to take more of him into my mouth. His length brushes the back of my throat and I resist the urge to gag. I breathe through my nose as he blocks my airway with his huge cock. All three of us are moaning as we move together.

"I need to taste you, Lila." Hunter flexes his hips as he pulls his fingers from Grayson.

Hunter lifts me off Grayson's erection and the loss of his tongue from my pussy makes me whine as my walls clench. Hunter pulls me down Grayson's body and as his wet cock slides across my clit I let out another whine.

With me in his arms, Hunter stands. He lets me slide down his body and his length pushes into my stomach. "Don't worry, we'll be getting right back to it."

Hunter steps back from me and takes off the rest of his clothes so he's standing gloriously naked in front of me. I take in every detail of his body and smile. His shaft bobs at my appraisal. He turns me so I'm facing Grayson, who shrugs off his top until he, too, is completely naked.

"Grayson, fucking move and let our woman lie down." Grayson jumps up and stands beside me. He leans down and kisses me. I can taste myself on his lips.

Hunter runs his fingers around my side and grasps my hand in his. He leads me to the couch and gently pushes me down. When my butt hits the seat, he grabs my ankles and pulls me so my ass is up against the arm. He spreads my legs and moves around the edge. He's standing over me and I look up at him.

With a hand braced on the arm of the couch, he bends over at the waist and licks straight up my slit. I shudder and moan at the contact, sparks of pleasure shooting to my core. Without words, he looks up at Grayson, who nods. Grayson grabs the lube and covers his cock from root to tip with the slippery liquid.

Grayson moves around behind Hunter. With a hand on Hunter's back, he propels his face straight into my crotch. I can't see exactly what is happening behind Hunter, but I can imagine. Grayson shifts forward, his hand disappearing behind Hunter. The man in question jolts forward and sighs against my clit.

Hunter's hips rock back and forth slowly as he attacks my pussy with his tongue. A groan comes from Grayson as he pulls his hips back and thrusts, the action making Hunter jerk forward. The groan that vibrates against my clit tells me that Grayson just pushed his cock inside Hunter's ass.

Grayson begins slowly, but gradually increases his tempo. Hunter's tongue is deep inside me. He shifts slightly and a finger nudges against my pussy alongside his tongue. I shudder as he attacks me with both, thrusting inside me in time with Grayson's thrusts. I watch the expressions on Grayson's face, from a smile to a slight grimace, and he pumps his hips faster and faster.

I'm shocked I've lasted this long, but I can't hold out for much longer. The sounds and smells of sex fill the room and I'm spiraling. Hunter presses another finger between my folds as his tongue laps at my clit.

My hips lift from the couch and my legs snap closed around Hunter's head. Grayson lets out a roar and his hips jolt forward, shoving Hunter's face into my pelvic bone. With his tongue on my clit and his fingers inside me, I explode. My walls clench down and Hunter moans against me. All three of us reach our climax together.

My head spins and my chest heaves as Hunter licks me through my orgasm. My legs weaken, falling back to the sides. A fine layer of sweat covers my body and I feel hot and clammy.

Hunter lifts his head from between my thighs and straightens, his lips glistening with my juices. Standing behind him, Grayson pulls Hunter back against him, making Hunter's fingers slip from my pussy, leaving me empty.

Twisting his head, Hunter kisses Grayson hard, before he licks around Hunter's mouth. They both groan into each other's mouths and it sends a shiver down my spine. I never thought watching two men together would be such a turn on.

They break apart and both their cocks are still semi-hard. Gazing down at me, the lust is clear in their eyes. Hunter leans forward and grabs me around the back. He pulls me into his arms and stands back up straight.

"We'll have to do that again, and soon. Maybe one of us at each end," Hunter murmurs against my ear. "But for now, you need to shower. We all do."

The visual of me together with both of them in the shower fills my mind and I sigh. I curl up against Hunter as he carries me to the bathroom and deposits me on the bench seat. He turns on the water and adjusts the temperature.

"I'd love to stay, but if I do, I'm just going to end up with you against the tiles." He kisses me quickly and all but runs out of the bathroom, closing the door behind him.

My laughter fills the room as he leaves and I shake my head. I rise slowly and stand on quivering legs as I move under the blast of water from the shower head. The water feels amazing against my overheated skin and I soak in the warmth as I let it soothe my body. When I'm thoroughly relaxed, I quickly wash my hair and body.

Even though Hunter and Grayson are only outside the door, my body craves to be near them again. I wrap a towel around my chest and another around my hair. My gaze shifts around the room and I realize the clothes I was wearing are still in the living room.

I pad out of the bathroom and spot all three guys spread around the room. Hunter and Grayson are dressed again and they are having a heated conversation. One that pauses the minute they realize I'm there.

"I didn't mean to interrupt." All attention turns to me and I almost shrink back. Instead, I stand a little straighter.

"Don't worry about it. We were discussing keeping a closer eye on the fence. We don't want people trespassing and getting hurt." There's a glint in Cayden's eyes as he speaks, but I don't know what it means.

"I'm gonna go get dressed." I step out of the hallway and quickly ascend the steps to the loft room. I dig through the pile of clothes and grab another pair of sweatpants and a t-shirt that's far too big for my tiny frame.

The voices downstairs can be heard from up here, but I can't hear exactly what they are saying. I use the towel to dry my hair to the best of my ability and leave it down to air dry. When I get back downstairs, Cayden is lounging on the couch inspecting the book I was reading earlier, and Grayson and Hunter are both in the kitchen making food.

It's the first time I've seen Grayson doing anything that requires being in the kitchen and it's a pleasant surprise. The two men laugh and joke together as they chop vegetables and toss the ingredients into a pan.

When I reach the couch, I sit beside Cayden and smile. He returns with a grin of his own and hands me the book he's been reading the back cover on. I blush slightly, knowing full well the contents of the story.

"Interesting read?" Cayden asks as I hold the book close to me.

"It's great. You guys have an amazing collection."

"That's all on Hunter. Grayson told me about earlier." My eyes widen at what Grayson has told Cayden about our time together with Hunter. "Your fright out back." A rush of air leaves my lips. Not what I was thinking then.

"That was totally on me. I thought *he* was here." I pick at a loose thread on the t-shirt, not wanting to look at Cayden. "It's fine though. It was a trespasser and you dealt with it. The woods must have freaked me out."

"You're allowed to be scared sometimes, Lila. You're only human." The way Cayden says 'only human' catches my attention, but only for a second before he continues. "With everything you have been through, it's a natural reaction. But don't fret, we'll keep you safe."

Cayden places his hand over mine and he squeezes the top of my fingers. I turn my hand and lace our fingers together. I believe his words. He's not the first of these men to tell me they will protect me. I can only hope it never comes to the day when they have to because I'm sure my nightmare will destroy them, and then me.

Chapter Twenty Seven

Hunter

The fire roars in the log burning stove the following day when Cayden stalks back into the cabin as I brew coffee. He's covered head to toe in fat flakes of snow which are gradually melting into his clothes. He shakes off his hair, sending water droplets all over. A snort escapes my lips and he pins me with a glare.

"It was cold out there, even for me," Cayden says as he kicks off his boots.

The temperatures have been gradually dropping for the last few days and we are hearing more reports of snow storms hitting. It's not the most ideal for tracking the wolves that have been breaching the fence, but we'll have to make do.

With a cup in each hand, I take one over to Cayden and he snatches it with a grunt before he goes and takes up his spot on the couch. The stairs squeak as Grayson pads down the steps in his wolf form. With the grace of many years of shifting, he's on two legs before he even hits the bottom step.

Seriously, you're doing that shit in the house? I snark through the bond.

Grayson ignores me as he passes by, grabs the cup of coffee straight out of my hands, and finishes it in a few gulps before handing the empty cup back to me.

"I'll be back later." Grayson opens the door and lets it close behind him. His black tail swishes through the crack as he transforms straight back into his wolf form.

With my cup in hand, I go back to the kitchen and refill it before I head over to the couch and sit on the edge.

"I was thinking maybe we could do something fun today," I say between sips of the delicious coffee. "Lila hates being cooped up. I bought some things last time I went to town, so we can take her outside for a while and have some fun."

"You know how that went yesterday, Hunter."

"But there's two of us this time. No one is going to come close." I shrug. "They'd be stupid to."

"Fine, go do whatever you're planning. I'm going to catch a few hours' sleep." Cayden finishes his coffee and takes the cup back to the kitchen before he heads down the corridor and straight into Grayson's room. With one of us always on patrol, there's a bed free for him whenever he needs it.

The door closes and I finish my drink before I rest the cup on the coffee table. It'll be a few hours before Lila wakes up and I need to get started. I grab a coat from the rack and pull it up my arms. If it's as cold as Cayden implies, there's no way I'm not putting on an extra layer if I'm not going out there covered in fur.

It's still dark outside. The days are getting shorter and there's still time before the sun will wake up to make its way up into the sky. I grab the shovel I left on the porch and move down the steps, walking until I find what I know is level ground. I dig the shovel into the thick snow, clearing away a large circle of powder and ice and flatten a larger area around it.

In no time at all, I've done my first task. I grab some of the wood we have stocked for the stove and build a small fire in the middle of my circle, compressing the snow at the sides to give it a wall. When I'm happy with my work, I dig the lighter out of my pocket and get the fire started.

I have this whole thing planned out. The last time I was in town, I bought all the ingredients we needed for s'mores and hot cocoa. I even got Lila some warmer clothes, which she had found yesterday.

Fire built, now I just need some bigger logs that we can sit on. With that in mind, I head for the storage at the back of the cabin where we usually keep our clothes for after we've shifted. Inside, I've left a few larger logs that are thick enough to be used as seats. With one under each arm, I carry them back to where I've built the fire pit and add them to either side of the fire.

It's an hour later when I reenter the cabin and shrug off my coat. Hues of orange dance across the sky and the air temperature is increasing, albeit slowly. I pause inside the door and listen for movement. All I can hear is Cayden and Lila's steady breathing as they sleep.

There's not much else for me to do until Lila is awake, apart from starting breakfast. I check the cupboards and fridge and opt to make scrambled eggs and toast. With a few eggs cracked in a jug and a splash of milk, salt, and pepper added, I put the mixture into the fridge so it's ready.

"Please tell me it's not another day of lounging around doing nothing but read?" Lila's voice pierces the silence as she makes her way down from the loft.

"Nope." As soon as she is at the bottom, I wrap a blanket over her shoulders and press a cup of coffee into her hands. She smiles up at me and I kiss her gently on the cheek. "I have what I'm hoping will be a fun-filled day planned."

"Do I get to know what it is?"

"No, ma'am. I'm keeping it to myself for now."

"Meanie." Lila laughs and I grin back.

"Come and sit down. I'll get breakfast going. Cay's still in bed, but you are more than welcome to dump a bucket of water over his head after we've eaten to get him up."

I head for the kitchen and Lila grabs a seat at the dining table, the blanket pulled tightly around her shoulders and her coffee cup grasped between her hands.

Flicking on the gas for the burner, I heat some oil in a pan. The bread goes in the toaster next before I retrieve the pre-done mixture and butter from the fridge and add the mix to the pan.

As the toast is popping up the eggs are done. I serve it out onto two plates, adding a generous helping of butter to the freshly toasted bread. I place one down in front of Lila and she gives me a small thank you. Taking the seat next to her, I shuffle closer so our shoulders are almost touching.

We dig in, keeping the conversation light. Even though Lila keeps trying to get me to tell her what my plans are for the day, I refuse to tell her. Once we are done, I grab her a glass of water. "For Cayden."

With a giggle, Lila jumps from her seat and takes off down the hallway. Her footsteps are light on the wooden floorboards. A minute later, there is a roar and a slew of curses as Lila hurtles back down the hallway and straight into my arms.

"Lila!" Cayden bellows and she flinches against me at the same time as laughing.

My alpha stomps out of the bedroom and down the hall, his muscles flexing as he leans an arm on each wall. He's surprisingly dry on his head, but then I notice the wet patch on his gray shorts.

"I bet you put her up to this, didn't you?" Cayden snarls, his eyes boring into me.

"Me? Never." I try to hold it in but I can't stop the laughter that bursts through my lips.

"I'm surrounded by children," Cayden mutters as he heads for the kitchen to grab himself a coffee.

Lila stays wrapped around me as I lean my head on top of hers. "Don't worry, I'll protect you from the grumpy asshole."

"It's not me I'm worried about." Lila sniggers. "You're the one who gave me the water." She looks up at me innocently, but I know otherwise.

"That's it, blame me." I look over at Cayden and for once he's actually smiling. It's a genuine smile too. "Head upstairs and check the bottom drawer in the dresser. I left some things there for you."

Chapter Twenty Eight

Lila

After we are all ready, Hunter grabs my hand and drags me outside, with Cayden following us. They both have mischievous grins on their faces. I narrow my eyes at them as we wander out into the sun. Flames draw my attention and I stare at the fire that's already lit. It wasn't here the last time I came outside. My gaze shifts to Hunter and he smiles back.

He leads me over to one of the large logs beside the fire. The heat warms my cheeks as soon as I'm close enough.

"Sit. I'll be back in a moment." Hunter kisses my cheek and races back inside as I sit down.

Cayden takes a seat opposite me and watches me through the flickering flames. Even from here, I see his heated gaze. I quickly turn to look at the cabin door as Hunter comes bounding out, his arms laden with marshmallows, bars of chocolate, and Graham crackers.

"We're making s'mores," Hunter announces as he stops beside me and drops the items to the floor at my feet.

A smile lifts the corners of my lips and I let out a giggle. Hunter drops onto the log beside me and rips open the marshmallows. He hands whittled sticks to Cayden and me, shoving a few marshmallows onto his own.

"You know you're going to burn them like that?" I say as Hunter holds the stick over the fire.

"I got this." Hunter smirks and turns the marshmallows slowly.

The fire catches the edge of the chewy goodness and it's not long before the flames lick up the sides. A roar of laughter barks from across the fire. My eyes swivel to Cayden as he shakes his head.

"Fuck," Hunter curses. He pulls the stick back out, blowing on the blackened, sticky mess.

"You're meant to wait till the fire dies down first. More embers, less fire." I signal to the flames, which are still burning brightly.

"She's right." Cayden sounds smug as hell, and I can't stop the smile caused by his praise.

Hunter drops the stick and flaming marshmallows into the snow beside the log. It sizzles as the flames die down to nothing.

"What? I've never made s'mores before. How was I meant to know?" Hunter says.

"You're saying the computer guy doesn't know how to do a simple Google search?" I gasp and cover my mouth to quell my giggles.

Hunter bounces to his feet and hops over the log. He moves away from me and I swivel my gaze back to Cayden. He's still watching me from across the fire. I stand and make my way over to him, plopping down beside him. I snuggle closer to him and he stiffens momentarily before he rests an arm around my shoulders.

"He really hasn't had s'mores before, but he's good at other stuff." There is a suggestion in his tone. He knows I've already slept with Hunter, but has seemed distant since.

I open my mouth to speak but I'm cut off when a snowball hits the side of Cayden's head, sprinkling me in snow. I shriek and glare at Hunter. He already has another one in his hand, ready to throw at us.

Cayden jumps up from where he's sitting and tackles me. His weight pushes me backwards off the log, taking me down with him. His huge body covers mine and he grunts.

"This means war," Hunter bellows, his voice muffled by Cayden's body over mine.

"A war he ain't gonna win." Cayden smirks down at me and winks.

Cayden's body rolls off mine and a snowball soars over the top of us, hitting the ground a few feet away. "Stay down," he orders as he jumps to his feet, a fistful of snow already in his grasp.

Cayden's hand whips over his head as he launches the snowball away from him. There's a smack and a grunt, and I assume Hunter takes a hit. Another ball hits Cayden in the chest and he grins as he gathers more snow in his fists.

"Make me some more snowballs, beautiful." Cayden flashes me a smile and I do as he requests.

Each time he hurls a ball, I have another one ready to pass to him. We work well together and there are several grunts from behind where I'm pressed with my back against the log.

"That's not fair. It's two against one," Hunter shouts.

I peek over the top of the log and find Hunter standing behind a tree not that far away. He keeps leaning out to look our way, but Cayden launches snowball after snowball at him. Most of them hit the trunk of the tree, but on his next shot Cayden times it perfectly and it smacks Hunter square in the face.

"Motherfucker." Hunter snarls and rushes around the tree. He covers the distance in only a few strides between where he was and where we are.

Hunter jumps the log I'm hiding behind and launches himself straight at Cayden. He takes the bigger man to the ground and they scrap on the floor, neither one of them able to get the upper hand. The leftover snowballs lie at my feet and I grab one in each hand.

I push to my feet and move quietly over to the two men who fight and laugh all at the same time. "Hey, boys."

My voice stops them moving and they both look up at me just as I let go of the snowballs and hit them both in the face. They both gasp and spit out some of the tighter packed-together chunks of snow.

"Lila," Hunter whines. He reaches up and brushes the snow out of his face, the remnants falling on Cayden, who shoves him away.

"You better run, beautiful." Cayden curls his lips and grins.

Laughter filters from my mouth and I pivot and bolt. I round the fire and head for the cabin. Arms wrap around me and I spin as I'm pulled to the ground. I land with my back to a hard body. Cayden walks toward me and Hunter as we're sprawled on the floor.

"You're in for it now, pretty," Hunter whispers in my ear and shivers tingle down my spine.

Cayden drops to his knees in front of me and Hunter's legs slip between mine. He pulls them apart to give Cayden the space he needs to get closer to me. Hunter's arms come around my sides and hold my arms close to my body. Moving in, Cayden leans over me, his nose running up my neck as he inhales. His tongue snakes up my skin before he blows out onto my wet skin.

"You're ours now, Lila. You know that, right?" Cayden looks into my eyes and my teeth sink into my lip before I nod.

Cayden's lips descend on mine and Hunter's move against my neck as he nips at my skin. Their lips are so warm, contrasting with the cold air around us. Rocking his body against mine, Cayden's hard length presses against the apex of my thighs.

Cayden swallows my moan as Hunter skims his hands between mine and Cayden's bodies, running his palms over my breasts. The many layers I'm wearing dampen the feeling. I should feel cold, but I'm cocooned in their warmth between their bodies.

"Gods, you're so beautiful," Cayden mutters against my mouth before he swipes his tongue over my lips.

Suddenly his body tenses as he drags himself away from me and glances behind us. Hunter sits up with me in his arms and it's like they are having a silent conversation.

"I have to go." Cayden propels himself to his feet. "Sorry." He looks back at me before he takes off at a jog towards the trees and disappears from view.

"What just happened?" I question, and Hunter tightens his arms around me.

"He probably wanted to go check on Grayson. He's been gone all morning." There's a hint of dishonesty in his tone and I want to question it, but Hunter cuts me off. "Let's go see how the fire is doing."

Without another word, Hunter pulls me to my feet and laces his fingers with mine as he walks to the fire where the flames have died down to embers. He readies a few marshmallows on the two sticks that Cayden and I dropped to the ground before our snowball fight.

"Come on then, my s'mores guru. Show me how it's done." Hunter hands me one stick and I hold it above the fire.

Teaching Hunter how to melt the perfect marshmallows for s'mores is enough to distract me from Cayden's sudden disappearance.

Chapter Twenty Nine

Cayden

Cayden, come quick. I found their scents again. Grayson's voice makes me stiffen and I pull my lips from the sweet taste that is Lila.

I peer over my shoulder into the trees and beyond. Whatever lust I was feeling quickly evaporates. Hunter sits slowly with Lila still in his lap.

Go, don't worry. I got her, Hunter responds in my mind.

Are you sure? I question.

Yeah, I got this.

If you smell them even anywhere close, get inside and call for us.

"I have to go." I drag myself to my feet and look down at Lila. I see the hurt on her face as she pouts with creased brows. "Sorry." I take one last look at her before I jog into the trees.

I ensure I'm far enough away before I shed my clothes and transform into my wolf.

Where are you exactly? I send it directly to Grayson. While I can use the bond to find him, a specific location will make it quicker.

Southwest side of the lake. I adjust my direction and move toward the open span of water.

I only make it to the North side when I'm hit with the putrid scent I associate with wolves who are almost completely taken by the darkness. Slowing my speed, I crouch low to the ground and keep myself downwind. Three shadows creep out of the bushes next to the lake and I watch as they smell the ground. They're coming in my direction.

A low growl rumbles in my chest and two of them stop. Their ears twitch as they try to work out where the sound came from. The third continues to come my way, his fangs bared as he snarls. I lift to my full height and step out of the tree line. Their hackles rise as they feel the alpha in me step forward.

The two that stopped both take a step back, but the third refuses to back down. My blazing amber eyes turn on him and narrow as I return his snarl with my own. He's feral, beyond help at this point, but if I can get him to transform back to human, I can question him. My fangs gnash together as my claws dig into the ground.

With a growl, the third male launches himself at me. I take a swipe at him with my paw and smack him straight across the muzzle. It knocks his head to the side and he gives it a shake before he whips his focus back to me. The two other wolves squirm away, not wanting to get between us.

Grayson. North side.

He rushes at me again, his jaws aiming for my neck. I rear back away from him. My claws come down on the side of his face and he lets out a howl as they cleave deep. Blood drips into his eye from the wounds I give him, but he doesn't back down.

The wolf circles me. I match him step for step, making sure he is never out of my line of vision. He feigns to the left, but instantly veers and barrels into me. My paws scramble on the icy ground and I lose my balance as his head knocks into my shoulder and he forces me to the ground.

A lesser wolf shouldn't be able to overpower me but rogues can be an entirely different ballgame. The darkness fuels them to be more unpredictable and feral. I snarl up at the male as he hovers above me and I snap my jaws at him but I can't get the angle I need to latch onto his neck and take him down.

The need to keep him alive stops me from simply ripping his throat out. Grayson's scent hits my nostrils as he rushes into the side of the wolf above me. His growl echoes around the lake and there is a crunching sound as a bone is broken. I push to my feet and look over to the mass of fur as Grayson and the male fight.

Don't kill him, Gray. But I'm met with silence.

The two trade blows and blood splatters on the rocks. I want to jump in and help my brother, but if he isn't responding to me he's too far gone for me to interfere. He could easily turn on me as well.

The wolf transforms back into a man and Grayson hovers over him just like the male had me only a moment ago. He whimpers as he mutters apologies and begs Grayson not to kill him. A scream exits his mouth before there is a sickening crunch. Grayson's jaws close on the male's throat, snapping his neck.

My brother holds the limp body of the dead man in his jaws and shakes his head violently. The corpse is covered in claw marks and bites dealt by Grayson and his blood stains the rocky ground. I quickly scan the area for the other two wolves but they're already gone.

Grayson, let him go. I reach for Gray.

Feral eyes turn on me, but Grayson doesn't let go of his kill.

My kill, he snarls around the dead man's throat.

Yes, he's yours, Gray. I take a tentative step forward but freeze when Grayson snarls again.

Mine. Mine. Mine. Grayson's voice echoes across the bond.

Yours. I modify my tactics. *Thank you for saving me.* I bow my head to my friend. It's something an alpha would never normally do but these aren't normal circumstances.

When I next catch Grayson's eyes, he looks a little less feral. His jaws open and he drops the dead body to the floor, pawing at the man's side.

Saved you.

Yes, you did. I move toward Grayson again, this time he doesn't snarl at me. When I'm close enough, I nudge my head against his and he leans against me.

Gray's wolf slumps down to the ground and I stand over him. I keep at least one part of us in contact as his mind swirls with so many thoughts. I slide down beside him and rest my body on his. We stay like that for a while.

Cay? Grayson's voice in my head is a little clearer now. He looks from me to the dead man's body.

It's me, Gray. Don't worry. I got you. I press our noses together. The dead man's blood transfers from Grayson to me, but I don't care. Not as long as my brother comes out of this intact.

I'm sorry, Cay. I didn't mean to kill him. But I saw him about to hurt you. I couldn't stop myself.

The darkness embeds itself in wolves in different ways. Each wolf tells a different story, and it's no different for me, Grayson, and Hunter. Though we've never spoken about what it does to us out loud.

It's fine. Let's get cleaned up. I shift and Grayson does the same.

I hold my hand out to him and pull him to his feet. We both head for the edge of the lake and step into the frigid water to clean the blood from our bodies. We'll dispose of the corpse later. For now, I just want to get back to Lila and take my brother away from the death.

Chapter Thirty

Alaric

The fact that other wolves have my bitch is enough to drive me to madness. A cackle bursts from my lips. Madness has nothing on me. I crave her. I want her. And I'll do anything to get her. That includes ripping those three wolves limb from limb for touching what is mine.

Mine.

Mine.

Mine.

I pace the alley behind the bar, my long strides eating up the distance as I march from end to end. My gums itch with the need for my fangs to drop. Claws extend and retract from my fingers repeatedly, digging into my flesh when I ball my hands. The sting of pain distracts me but only for a moment before the wounds close again.

You shouldn't have let her go.

I had no choice, though. They'd snatched all the women including my mate. The vampires would have killed me. When I went back to the caves, I found parts of the pack's bodies scattered around. But other means killed my alpha, Rufus. His body had been covered in stab marks.

They've taken what's yours again.

A growl rumbles deep in my throat. My fist shoots out and shatters the brick at the end of the building. The pieces scatter on the floor like their bodies will when I kill them.

Kill them.

"Boss." Ryan rounds the corner and stares at me.

"What is it?" I spit out between fanged teeth and I notice his slight flinch.

"They killed Steven." I hear the pain in his voice. Ryan was quick to join my cause, to be part of a pack again. "Me and Drew had to scatter. We heard his screams as they murdered him."

Kill them.

These three wolves are the only thing that stands between me and my bitch. We need a plan and quick. The blood moon is fast approaching once more. I need her away from them so I can claim her.

Claim her. She's ours.

"Bring the men together." I bark out the order, and Ryan scurries away.

I head for the fully paid-up motel room I've taken over from some loser who was staying for a week. With a swipe of the keycard, I'm inside. There's blood on the carpet, but a 'do not disturb' sign keeps out any nosey cleaners.

Leaving the door slightly open, I wait for the others to arrive. When I have them all gathered, I lay out the plan.

"We get in. We take her. Then we desecrate them like my pack was." My heart rate increases as I imagine bathing in their blood, covering me and my bitch in it as I fuck her over their dead bodies.

What joy it will bring me to revel in their deaths and her body at the same time. I will strike them all down and fuck her till her blood joins theirs. Then I'll take her away from this place, bond under the blood moon, and she'll be mine.

My cock jerks as I imagine her with my fangs buried in her neck and my length deep inside her as the red glow of the moon bathes our bodies. A cackle leaves my mouth and some wolves around me shift uncomfortably from foot to foot.

"What?" I demand and stare them down, but not one mutters a word in response.

"Where do we get in?" Ryan questions. "They're going to be keeping a closer eye on the fence now."

"I don't care how we get past them, as long as she's mine once more."

My mind is pulled back to my bitch. My cock fucking her mouth as tears spill down her dirty cheeks. Her gagging on my length as I shove it down her throat and leave a bulge in her thin neck. I'll trace my fingers over the lump in her throat and be able to feel my cock as I choke off her airway.

Oh, she'll love to feel me spill down her throat again. She'll swallow every drop. My hips jerk involuntarily.

"...sure we have the bolt cutters. They'll seal the fence again," Ryan orders Drew, who slips out of the door.

I don't hear the full sentence, but I nod in agreement to whatever my beta said. I pace the room again. I'm so close to getting her back.

She'll be ours again. I hear the excitement in the voice in my head and I grin as I wring my hands together.

"Ryan makes the plans. Now get out." A lot of the wolves look puzzled, but they heed my order and Ryan ushers them out of the door.

My beta looks over his shoulder at me. "You all good, boss?"

"Perfect." I smirk at him as he closes the hotel room door.

I stalk to the bathroom door and push inside. The beaten man in the bath looks up at me and screams against the gag in his mouth. But no one is coming for him.

"Did you hear that? My little bitch is coming home." My voice is almost gleeful, and the man's eyes widen. "I can't wait to fuck her over their bleeding bodies. Maybe I'll let them watch as I fuck her first. She loves an audience."

The man ignores my words and thrashes around in the bathtub, the soles of his feet unable to get a grip on the slippery surface. Stomping forward, I reach for him and wrap my hand around his neck. My nails lengthen and dig into his flesh.

"You should listen to your betters when they're talking to you." A snarl leaves my lips. I yank the gag from his mouth. "Apologize, now."

The man opens his mouth to scream and I grab his tongue, using one of my sharp nails to sever it from his mouth. He gurgles, choking on his own blood, and I shove the gag back into his mouth.

The cloth is quickly covered in red, and the scent of blood fills the small room, along with his whimpers. My mouth breaks into a smile and I drop the man's body back into the bathtub. The mixture of scents and sounds makes my cock painfully hard. I pull open the button of my jeans, shove the zipper down, and yank it out.

My bloody hand wraps around my length, the viscous red fluid making my fingers glide up and down as I jerk my cock. I fall back into the memories of her blood when it covered my cock as I ripped her open. Remembering us together, I imagine ramming myself balls deep, my cum filling her as I wish for my knot to expand and lock us together.

No matter how many times I fucked her, it never happened. Rufus promised as soon as I bonded with her my knot would swell and keep her close. I'll fuck her even with my knot enlarged. Watch as it pulls back out of her holes, stretching and tearing her delicate skin.

She'll love every minute.

My balls tighten and I come back to reality as I release ropes of cum all over the man in the tub. He pushes back as he tries to get away from each splatter, but it's no use. He sobs and I lean down over him.

"My cum isn't meant for you." I lift him from the tub and lick up the side of his face. The taste of his blood and my cum explodes over my tongue as I shove my clawed hand through his chest and rip out his heart. "It's for her, and only her."

I drop his limp body back into the bath and marvel at the warm organ in my hand before I sink my teeth into it. I rip a chunk out of it and chew slowly, moaning at the taste. Blood drips down my chin and I smile. Casually, I wander back into the main room and jump on the bed to enjoy the rest of my snack.

Chapter Thirty One

Lila

The sky is getting darker as the sun disappears behind the trees and the temperature drops. We've been outside for hours eating s'mores and now I'm sitting on the log between Hunter's legs as he curls around me. His arms wrap around my waist and I lean back into him. Heat envelops me, from him behind and the fire in front of me, which he stoked before sitting down.

I lay my hand on my churning stomach. It's aching from the sheer amount of sugar we consumed between us in the last few hours. Even the break to build a snowman wasn't enough to settle my stomach.

A snowflake lands on my nose and I shake my head. When I look up, more hits my face. A small laugh that slips through my lips as I marvel at the sight.

"Is it always like this in winter?" I stretch out my hand to let the snowflakes fall into my open palm. The cold liquid tingles in my hand as they melt. I don't even know how long the guys have lived out here. It's not something that crossed my mind to ask.

"We pretty much got snowed in when we first arrived. It's a good thing Cayden likes to make sure we're stocked up on food and wood." My thoughts stray to Cayden, the man who got me hot all over and then left when the fun was just beginning. "Can you imagine what would happen with Grayson if we ran out of food?"

"The dining table would be less messy, for one." I don't stop the unfiltered comment and Hunter barks out a laugh.

"You're not wrong."

"It's beautiful." I look back at the snowflakes falling around us. They land on my coat and gradually melt from my body heat.

I marvel at the sight before me. It's been so long since I wasn't running from something, I've not had the chance to sit back and take it all in. Running from the balls, running from this sector to another, and running from the sanctuary.

Hunter's arms tighten around my waist and his lips brush against my cheek. "Not as beautiful as you are."

"Such a charmer." I giggle and lean my face into him.

Hunter abruptly pulls his lips away and looks to our left. My head turns in the same direction. Grayson and Cayden trudge out from between the trees. Their clothes are a little disheveled and wet. There's something else there. While they look like they normally do, ignoring the rumpled clothes, Cayden is holding his side with a slight limp to his gait.

"Everything okay?" Hunter asks as he unwraps his arms from around me and stands. He offers me his hand and pulls me to my feet. I shake off the snow that has settled on my jacket and stand beside him.

"We're good. Just a little problem at the fence," Cayden responds, and I raise an eyebrow at him.

I'm left in silence as the three men look between each other. Another silent conversation I'm not privy to seems to go on.

"You know you can tell me what's going on," I encourage. "I'm not that fragile."

Grayson whips his eyes to mine and stalks towards me. His arms wrap around my waist as he pulls me close. He buries his nose in my hair and inhales, humming as he does. "You're not fragile. Not ever."

My arms reach for his shoulders and I lean back in his embrace. He smiles down at me but I see a flash of something in his silvery eyes. I feel a need to be close to him, like he needs me. I lean back into him and let him gather me in his arms.

"Thanks, Gray. But I mean it. Please don't shut me out." My words are muffled against his chest, but I feel Grayson nod.

"It was just some hunters." Cayden's voice sounds close. "They sometimes break through the fence and kill the deer."

"Ever thought about electrifying it?" I turn my head to find Cayden a few steps away from where Grayson is holding me.

"She's got a point, Cay. Might keep out the nasties," Hunter responds. "Especially unwanted pests. A quick zap would solve a few issues."

"If we turn it up high enough, they'd be extra crispy." Grayson laughs, and his chest rumbles against my cheek.

"Enough," Cayden snaps. "Let's get inside. It's getting cold." He stomps off toward the cabin.

Grayson lifts me into his arms curling me against him. Hunter falls into step beside us as Grayson carries me bridal style over the threshold. I've never been one for being carried by a man but I love being in their arms.

"I'll make dinner." Hunter heads for the kitchen, and I look around the cabin, wondering where Cayden has gone.

Grayson tumbles down onto the couch and I let out a yelp as we bounce onto the seats. He doesn't let me go as he repositions me on his lap. I feel the bulge in his pants, but ignore it and let my body drape over his, too tired to even bother to remove my outdoor clothes.

Pots and pans clink in the kitchen as Hunter gets food ready. I let my eyes drift closed as I sit and relish in the comfort that is Grayson's arms. It's been a long day and now we are in the cabin's warmth, tiredness pulls on me. I let it take me as I listen to the soft thuds of Grayson's heartbeat beneath my ear.

"Lila," Hunter's voice whispers close to my ear and I let out a yawn.

My eyes slowly blink open and I look at him. I'm still on the couch in my clothes, but someone has removed my boots. My feet are still toasty and warm, with a firm weight over them. I lift my head to find Wolfie curled up at the end of the couch and my lips raise into a smile at the sight.

I haven't seen him all day. I went to bed with him last night and curled against his warm fur, but he was already gone by the time I woke up this morning.

"I didn't want to wake you, so I kept a plate of food warm for you." Hunter kneels beside me and brushes a few locks of my hair out of my face as I turn my smile to him.

"Thank you. Now, if you can just get the dead weight off my feet, I'll grab it." I shift my gaze back to Wolfie and shrug.

Hunter smirks and reaches for the wolf hybrid on my feet and nudges his huge body. "Hey, Wolfie. Get up."

Wolfie is suddenly alert. He jumps from my feet and turns to snarl at Hunter. I sit up quickly and pat Wolfie's head. His teeth are on show for a moment before his eyes take me in and his lips drop. He licks my hand and nuzzles against it.

"Sorry." My stomach grumbles. "But I need to eat."

Hunter pulls me up off the couch and the blood rushes back to my feet. Pins and needles tingle through my soles and I hop on the spot for a moment. Wolfie barks and copies my movements, his front paws lifting and falling in time with my feet. Laughter bubbles through my lips as I take in his crazy antics.

I let Hunter lead me to the kitchen. He pulls out a steaming plate of meat and mashed potatoes with gravy.

"Go sit. I'll bring it over." I listen to his order and make my way to the dining table, taking off my coat and hanging it over the back of the chair before I sit.

Hunter places the plate in front of me and the delicious aroma hits my nostrils. With a grateful sigh, I dig in as Hunter kisses my forehead and makes his way over to the cabin door. He opens it and the cold air from outside wafts in causing a shiver.

When the fork is halfway to my mouth, a long tongue licks up the side of my face. I glance at Wolfie out of the corner of my eye before he turns tail and takes off.

With a bang of the door, Hunter makes his way back to the kitchen and comes back with a glass of water. He places it on the table and sits next to me while I eat. It doesn't take me long before my plate is cleared.

"Where's Wolfie off to?" I place the fork on the plate and take a sip of my water.

"He decided I could have you for the night," Hunter quips.

"He did, did he?" I laugh at the thought of the hybrid somehow giving his permission for Hunter to have me for the night. "And what if I wanted him, not you?"

Hunter feigns shock and hurt. "Your words wound me." But he can't stop the snort and laughter that follows.

A yawn stretches my lips wide and I hold my hand over my mouth. "I guess you'll do." I wink at Hunter as he clears my plate away and places it into the sink in the kitchen.

"Good to know. Why don't you head up? I'm gonna grab a quick shower and I'll be straight in."

I rise to my feet and head past the coffee table, swiping the book I've been reading, and head for the stairs. Hunter slaps my ass as he passes, but doesn't stop his stride as I pause on the first step and watch his retreating form.

When he disappears into the bathroom, I carry on up the steps and head straight for the bed. I perch on the edge of the mattress and let my fingers push into the covers. I take a deep breath before letting it rush out of my lips.

Bar the morning I woke up with a very naked Grayson, it's been a long time since I've slept in a bed with a man. I had a few flings before I left for the vampire sector, but they were one-night stands. A quickie and then I kicked them out. But it's different with Hunter. I want to curl up with him and fall to sleep in his arms.

I absentmindedly pull off my socks, and then my hoodie. Soon my clothes are in a pile on the floor, leaving me in a tank top and panties. I slip under the comforter and relax back into the bed. I can't stop myself from fidgeting, though. After a few minutes of shifting, I sit up and pummel my pillow before I flop onto it.

"What did that pillow ever do to you?"

I glare up at Hunter as he appears at the top of the stairs. "It was being an asshole." My eyebrows pull together as I finally take him in.

Hunter stands at the top of the stairs with a white towel slung low on his hips. His muscles flex as he uses a small blue towel to dry his sandy blond hair. I dampen my lips with my tongue and my thighs rub together involuntarily.

The man before me is stunning, all golden skin and delicious muscle. He throws the small towel on the floor and grins up at me when he spots me checking him out.

"See something you like, Lila?" My mouth goes dry at his words and I wish I'd brought up the water I'd left downstairs.

"No," I lie.

"Is that so?" Hunter asks, and I nod my head. "We'll see." With a flick of his wrist, the white towel around his waist falls to the floor and my eyes zero in on his length. Even soft, he's huge.

The metal at the end of his cock glistens in the lamp light. Hunter stalks toward the bed and kneels on top of the comforter. He crawls closer to me and I grab the covers to stop myself from reaching out to him.

When Hunter's next to my body, he flings a leg over my waist and rests a knee on either side of me. His hardening cock lies on my stomach and my eyes fall to it. I see the drop of pre-cum at the tip and I lick my lips.

"Are you sure there isn't something you can see that you like?" My eyes cut to Hunter's and I see the amusement in his eyes.

"Maybe," I squeak.

Hunter wraps his hand around his cock and slides it up and down his length. I feel his knuckles as they rub against my stomach through the comforter and my top. A soft moan slips through his lips and I look up at his face. His teeth dig into his bottom lip as I squirm, but his body over mine blocks me from moving too much.

"Wrong answer." Hunter pumps his hand faster and pre-cum coats the head. My eyes settle on his movements. I can't help but watch as he pleasures himself.

I feel my wetness as it dampens my panties. I want to touch myself, or even better have him touch me. Hunter's nostrils flare and he lifts enough to pull the comforter down and away from my body. With one hand on his cock, he slides the other into my panties and straight to where I need him to touch me the most.

Hunter runs his fingers through my slick before he pushes two inside me. "Fuck, Lila. You're so wet and tight." His hips jolt and he fucks his hand, his fingers pumping inside me with vigor. My moans split the air.

"Please..." I say between whimpers.

"Please what, pretty?" Hunter's eyes fill with lust as he stares down at me.

"I need you."

"What do you need? Use your words." Hunter adds another finger and my walls clench around him as I moan.

"I need..." Hunter nods his encouragement. "I need you to fuck me," I whisper.

"Thank God." Hunter releases his cock and rips my panties from my legs.

With Hunter's cock lined up at my hole, he pushes through my folds and his piercing rubs that special spot inside me. I thrash when it moves back and forth over it as he presses deeper.

My teeth dig into my bottom lip and I try to hold back my scream when he sheaths himself all the way inside me. The root of his cock feels thicker than it did before, stretching and widening me.

"You feel so good, Lila. And you're all mine." Hunter pulls back to the tip before he thrusts back inside me. "For tonight at least." His arms fall on either side of my head.

I'm so wound up already it will not take me long to cum. When Hunter's finger thrums against my clit, it's game over and I scream his name. Even after my release, he continues to thrust wildly in and out of my body, propelling me toward a second orgasm.

Hunter buries his head into my neck as he nips and licks at my skin. "I need you to cum again, Lila." He pants down my ear. "Squeeze me dry."

Hunter's words are too much. He flicks my clit and scrapes his teeth over my neck. With the combined sensations, I spiral over the edge again and my walls clamp down on him hard. With one last thrust, Hunter pulls from me without coming. His hand wraps around his cock as he holds himself up above me, he rubs the head against my sensitive clit as he pumps his length.

With a groan, Hunter's cum splatters over my stomach and pubic bone. My eyes flutter closed, not even opening as Hunter swipes a slightly damp towel over my skin.

When Hunter is done, he lies beside me and pulls my body into his so my back is to his chest. He's still naked as he pulls the comforter over the both of us and wraps his arms around me. He kisses the back of my neck and rests his head against mine.

"Good night, Lila."

Chapter Thirty Two

Grayson

Cayden fills Hunter in on what happened in the forest with the three wolves we found, as well as the body we got rid of. The cabin reeks of sex when we get back and my wolf pushes at my skin. He wants out. His need to claim his mate drives us both insane.

Lila is in the loft resting and the three of us are spread around the lower floor. My wolf pushes harder and the darkness calls to me.

Kill them all. Maim them.

The image of the dead man on the floor by the lake floods my mind. I vaguely remember Cayden calling out to me, begging me not to kill the man so he could question him. But he came for my mate, he had to die. There was no way he was walking out of there alive.

You should have made it hurt more, the voice calls to me and I struggle against it.

Cayden eyes me from the other side of the couch. I feel his gaze on me. After we cleaned up in the lake, we headed back to the cabin and used clothes from the box at the back before we came inside.

It's not your fault, Cayden's voice announces through the link and I glance over to him. He looks solemn, but I see the truth of his words in his eyes. *He was going to kill me; you did what you had to protect our pack.*

I did what I had to do to protect her. My eyes move to the stairs that lead up to the loft. I hear Lila's soft breathing from here as she sleeps.

Cay's right. You saved his life, Gray. Never think what you did was wrong. Hunter joins the conversation from the kitchen. He's busy making us breakfast.

We needed to question him. I should have waited, I bark over the link.

You should have gone after the others, ripped their spines from their bodies, and feasted on their flesh, the voice snaps back, but only I hear it.

The darkness digs it's hooks in deeper. My claws push through my skin and puncture the fabric of my jeans into the skin on my thighs. The couch dips beside me and Cayden's warmth is close to me. His hand rests on top of mine and my fingers flex, releasing their hold on my legs.

Cayden leans his head on my shoulder. "Whatever it's telling you, ignore it, Gray," he whispers near to my ear. "Don't let it win. Please, for me—for us. I can't lose you." His fingers lace through mine and he grips my hand tightly.

"I'm trying. My mate is so close, but I daren't claim her." I sigh. "We need to tell her."

"Not yet," Cayden implores. "She'll run."

Claim her. Make her ours, the voice in my mind calls out to me and I do my best to ignore it.

I need to tell her the truth before it's too late. Even if it's too late for me, I want to at least give my brothers a chance. She's the true mate to us all, all we need to do is claim her. My own thoughts are at odds, though.

If we don't tell her, we risk the chance we could hurt her. But if we tell her, she could run. She will run. Either way, we could lose, but I don't want to die with her not knowing what we really are. She deserves the truth.

"I'm going to tell her." I pull my fingers from Cayden's and go to stand, but he grips my arm.

"No." His alpha power hits me like a ton of bricks and I fall back onto the couch. I glare over at him.

"Tell me what?" Soft footfalls on the stairs have my eyes moving to where Lila is halfway down them already.

"It's nothing," Cayden cuts in, his alpha power strangles my voice and stops me from telling her the truth.

"Grayson said he was going to tell me something. I want to hear it," Lila scolds. Hunter sweeps out of the kitchen and wraps an arm around her shoulder.

"Cayden didn't want to worry you, that's all, pretty Lila," Hunter's voice soothes. "Some hunters got through the fence again." Even to me, his lies sound truthful.

Lila shrugs out from under Hunter's shoulder and rounds the couch. She stops in front of me and looks into my eyes. "Is that right, Grayson?"

Cayden's power batters against me and I give her a sharp nod. "Yes. Hunters. Fence. Everything's fine now." I push out the words through gritted teeth as her blue eyes watch me.

Take her. Fuck her. Knot her. Kill her.

The last one leaves me reeling. The darkness, while wanting me to claim Lila, still wants to drive me to the brink. A mated wolf losing their true mate is a death sentence. The loss would drive me insane. My brothers would still have to kill me before I killed them both.

My hand snaps around Lila's wrist. She squeals as I pull her down into my lap. Her arms lace around my neck and she rests her head on my shoulder. I breathe in her scent of roses and jasmine and the hooks loosen their hold on me a fraction.

"If you're sure?" Lila invites me to speak, but I can't. Not right now.

"Big, old Grayson sent them on their way. Tails between their legs," Hunter jokes, but I ignore him.

Instead, I relish in the feel of her as she sits in my lap. Her body curls around mine. Her hair tickles my neck and

I wrap my arms around her waist, pulling her tight against my chest.

I spend the entire night in bed with Lila, this time as a man instead of as a wolf. When she asked me where Wolfie was, I told her he hadn't wanted to come in last night. The others left us alone, knowing that after mine and Cayden's encounter in the forest I needed to spend time with my mate.

Lila stays in my arms, my body curled around hers. The skin-on-skin contact soothes my beast. As we both fall asleep, I expect images of the dead man to haunt me but I was wrong. Instead, my dreams are filled with Lila.

But morning is here now; I hear Cayden and Hunter downstairs moving around the first floor. I look down at Lila and smile. I kiss her forehead and untangle her limbs from mine before I climb out of the bed and pull my jeans and shirt back on.

As soon as I move, her hand reaches for where my body lay, feeling for me. When she can't find me, she snuggles her face against the pillow that still smells of me. She drags it down and wraps her arm around it as she holds it against her chest.

A smile splits my lips and the need to crawl back into bed with her pulls at me but I force myself to turn and amble down the stairs. Hunter is in the kitchen with Cayden making toast and coffee. I steal a plate straight off the counter and wolf it down before either of them can complain. I grab a steaming cup of coffee and down it without even bothering to add creamer or sugar.

Hunter stares at me with a raised eyebrow but doesn't comment before he shoves another two slices of bread into the toaster.

"Morning," Cayden talks past me and I turn to see Lila coming down the stairs.

Her hair is tousled from sleep and she's wearing one of Cayden's t-shirts and his boxers. She smiles down at all three of us, the conversation from last night having been forgotten.

"Hi," Lila utters as she hits the last step and shuffles over to the kitchen.

Hunter offers her a steaming cup and a plate stacked with freshly made toast. She heads straight for the couch and curls up on the seat. I make my way over and drop beside her, my body angled to hers.

"I'm heading out for supplies soon. What's everyone need?" Cayden speaks between bites of his own toast.

"More chocolate." Hunter is the first one to answer and Lila looks over at him with a smile. "What? I want to make more s'mores with you."

"Of course you do." I can't help the snort that escapes me. He had all the fun while Cayden and I were going after the rogue wolves.

Blood fills my vision for a moment before her voice cuts in.

"Aw, don't be jealous, Gray." Lila softly pushes my shoulder, with her half-drunk coffee in her hand. "You can join us this time. You too, Cayden."

"We'd love to, Lila." Cayden moves toward the coat rack and pushes his feet into his boots, he sits on the edge of the coffee table to tie the laces. "Anything else?" He looks between me and Lila. I shake my head.

"More of that tea that Hunter makes me would be great." Cayden nods at Lila's request and pushes to his feet before he walks out of the door.

Look after her, I won't be long. Cayden's words echo over the link.

"So, what are we up to today?" Lila places her cup and plate onto the coffee table and snuggles into my side as I swing my arm over her shoulders.

"Nothing for me. I was up most of the night working. I'm gonna grab some sleep." Hunter heads straight for Lila and kisses her forehead. He grabs her discarded crockery and takes it back to the kitchen before he heads down the hallway to his bedroom.

"Guess it's just you and me then?" Lila looks up at me and smiles.

I lean down and kiss her lips before I pull away. "Guess so. I can go find Wolfie if you'd rather spend the day with him?"

Lila blinks a few times before she pushes up on her knees and climbs into my lap. Her legs are on either side of my thighs and her arms loop around my neck.

"Drowned by Mr. Slobbers' saliva, or have you touching me?" I chuckle at the mention of one of the names she tried when I was Wolfie.

Lila ponders her answer for a moment before she sets her lips on mine and kisses me hard. Her body pushes up against me. She's given me her answer. I flip us over and lie her down on the couch. My body covers hers, yet we don't break our kiss.

My hands trace down her sides and under the hem of the t-shirt she's wearing. I lift it slowly up her body and only pull our lips apart so that I can raise it over her head and discard it on the floor.

Claim her. She's ours, my wolf whines.

Trailing my lips down her body, I leave small kisses against her skin as her fingers grip my hair and push me lower. When I reach the waistband of the boxers she's wearing, I can smell her and it's delicious. I want to taste her again.

I'm about to slip the material down her legs and feast on her when I pause, inhaling deeply. My hackles rise as the putrid smell of rogues hits my nostrils. I pull away from Lila and she stares at me with hooded eyes. With a quick kiss on her lips, I shove to my feet and rush for the door, leaving my discarded clothes behind.

Kill them, the darkness calls in my mind.

"Grayson, wait," Lila calls out from behind me but the need to kill takes over.

I ignore her as I jump down the steps. The snow batters me from all sides, though I don't feel it. My mind is solely focused on killing the wolves that are coming for what is mine. The shift takes over and my remaining clothes shred from my body as my beast bursts out of my skin. My paws hit the ground and I take off into the trees.

Chapter Thirty Three

Lila

Scrambling from the couch, I grab my discarded t-shirt and pull it over my head. I run after Grayson as he speeds out of the cabin, but he's already way ahead of me. Before he disappears fully into the blizzard his body shifts, switching from man to beast and I stop in my tracks.

My hands grip the edge of the doorway as my knees give out as my heart shatters into a million pieces. I fall to the floor, my knees smacking hard. A bite of pain jolts up my thighs.

He lied to me—they lied to me. If Grayson is a shifter, then the chances are that all three of them are. Even after everything I had told them, they kept it a secret. Nothing they have said is true.

Moving on silent feet, I grab the first hoodie and pair of sweatpants I can find and pull them on. Wiping the tears that are forming in the corner of my eyes away, I let out a sniffle, as I stuff my feet into the only pair of shoes I own.

I sneak out through the open door, hoping not to wake Hunter. The lack of clothing doesn't even occur to me. The need to get away from them is the only thing racing through my rapidly fracturing mind.

Snow crunches under my feet as they sink into the white powder. Fat flakes fall around me and settle over the tracks I leave behind. The blizzard swirls around me and my path is obscured by the snow as I make my way through the trees. I know there is a fence that goes all the way around the cabin. I need to find it before any of them can stop me. A shiver races down my spine.

When I've been trudging through the heavy snow for what feels like forever, I stop for a moment to wipe the snow from my eyelashes with the sleeve of the hoodie. It's already damp from doing it a dozen times, but I keep going.

The wind howls around me and it's bitter. Hunter said they get pretty bad winters here and I guess that's one thing he hadn't lied about. His words don't help stop the cold as it sinks into my bones and makes me shiver.

My foot collides with an exposed root and my arms windmill for a moment until I regain my balance again. I step closer to the tree nearest me in hopes it will protect me even a little from the bracing cold. I spot a gap in the trees ahead. I feel a pull in that direction, telling me it's the way I need to go.

Shifting course, I stumble through the snow until I reach the gap. The wind relents for a moment, just long enough for me to see the fence a few feet away. My fingers latch onto the entwined metal as I keep close to it as I move alongside it. The metal suddenly ends. The fence is split straight down the middle and bent slightly inwards.

I look back in the vague direction I came from, though I'm not sure if it's exactly the way my gaze falls. My footprints in the snow have already disappeared. I bring my focus back to the gap in the fence. It's barely big enough for me to squeeze through, but I need to take my chance.

With my left foot through the hole first, I shimmy the rest of my body through the gap, wincing as the fence claws my sides. The metal gouges into my side, ripping clean through the hoodie and t-shirt straight into my skin.

Another shove and I've made it through. That's all that matters. A quick glance at my sides shows the red spots forming on the light material. I need to find a road or something. I need to get as far away from these three men as possible before they can tell me any more lies.

My breath comes out in plumes of mist as I breathe heavily. I haven't been going fast, but the lack of exercise over the last few weeks and the added injury to my leg takes its toll. My chest heaves as I take a moment to slow down; my whole body aches, but I need to keep going.

After a short rest against the fence, I take off again and end up straight back in the trees. They are a little thicker here and it helps to keep some of the falling snow from reaching me but the wind hasn't let up and it whistles between the trunks. My body shivers with every step I take, each one taking me closer to getting away.

A howl splinters the air to my left and my head whips towards the sound. I don't even think before I set off at a run in the opposite direction. Another howl echoes, only this time it's in front of me. I skid to a stop and change direction.

The howls come again and ramp up in volume and proximity. I skid to a stop and change direction once more. I have no idea which way I'm going. The sound of the howls disorients me until I don't know which way is which anymore, but they don't stop and I feel them closing in on me.

Blurs race past every side of me. When one gets too close I switch direction. A shadow to my right pulls my gaze that way. I spin on the spot and collide with something directly behind me.

"Hello, my sweet little bitch. I finally found you." That voice. It's *him*. The wolf of my nightmares has found me.

I turn to flee, but a hand grabs my hair, pulling a shout from my lungs as he yanks me back. Arms tighten across my chest and pull me into his body. I flail in his grasp as I try to get away, but he's not letting go.

Alaric's tongue licks up the side of my face and he laughs in my ear. "I can taste your fear, little bitch. I love how you play our games," he coos before he bites down on the top of my ear. His teeth dig into my skin and a yelp bursts from my lips.

My upper body is immobilized, but it doesn't hinder me from slamming my foot down onto his. It takes him by surprise enough for his grip to loosen. I'm off again, but I only make it three steps before a large body falls on top of mine.

The ground comes up quick and fast, and I smack into it hard. I don't even have time to put my arms in front of me to save myself. They're trapped underneath me as the body on top of me holds me down.

Alaric straddles me. His hardness prods into my back from the confines of his jeans, and I let out a yelp. A rancid smell fills my nostrils as his hair drapes across the side of my face. I want to puke, but I swallow it back down. A hand moves my hair from the side of my neck and Alaric bends even closer, his nose running up against my skin.

"You've caused me a lot of trouble." A growl sounds next to me and my sight falls on the huge wolf shifter next to us. "They tried to take you, but you're mine. You've always been mine. They can't have what I've already claimed."

Alaric's body stiffens for a moment before that sadistic laugh echoes in my ear again.

"Mine. Mine. Mine." There's an edge to his tone which terrifies me.

Thoughts race through my mind. Would I have been better off staying with Hunter, Cayden, and Grayson? Could they have protected me from him?

"I'm not yours...Alaric." I stutter out his name but I need to say it out loud. I can't keep referring to my nightmare as *him*.

"That's where you're very wrong, little bitch." Alaric licks up the side of my neck and I try to pull away. "Those beasts may have left their scent on you, but I'm going to fuck it out of you."

The blade of a knife glances up my back as he pulls his body away and slices up the back of the thin material.

"You'd love that, wouldn't you? You crave me." Alaric chuckles and I buck my hips. The sharp edge digs into my back and I whimper. Alaric flips me onto my back, and shreds up the front of my clothes before he rips them away.

"Oh, how I've missed these beautiful breasts." Alaric traces the tip of the knife around my now erect nipple. The sharp edge nicks at the peak and I bite my lip to smother the whine that's lodged in my throat.

My nightmare simply grins as he sees the pain flash across my features. Alaric trails the blade over my skin, slicing as he moves to my other breast. Blood beads in the shallow cuts he leaves behind.

"We're going to have so much fun, my little blood mate." Alaric leans down and licks across the blood, lapping it up and moaning as he tastes me.

Alaric's hardness pulses between my legs and I attempt to close them, but he's too strong. Instead, it seems to encourage him, and he pushes into my crotch harder. Bile rises in my throat. I swallow it down as a scream claws at my chest, desperate to get out.

As soon as he realizes, Alaric shoves his hand over my mouth and quells the sound. My shout is only muffled. Now I'm on my back, I see the other wolves and men that surround us. A few of them take a tentative step forward before they pull back as they look from me to Alaric.

Alaric wraps a hand around my neck and lifts me from the floor as he stands. He lumbers through the trees and drags me beside him as the others follow. I can't even think of what he plans for me. I need to fight. I thrash in his hold, my hands clawing at his arm. I try to loosen his grip, but it's no use.

"I can't wait to have you again. My cock has been so hungry for you. I fucked others, but they aren't you. Never you. I made them bleed, just like I will you." Alaric laughs, but I'm not really listening. "I'm going to fuck every single one of your holes till you bleed, as well."

One of the wolves gets a little too close to me and I kick out my leg. My foot hits the wolf square in the jaw and it stumbles to the side. It growls and lunges straight for me as it rips me from Alaric's grip and shoves me to the floor.

Saliva drips on my face as the wolf holds my body to the ground. His huge paws rest on my shoulders, its claws digging into my naked flesh. A scream erupts from my mouth and the sound echoes through the forest. Alaric shoves into the wolf and knocks it straight off me before he straddles my waist.

"She's mine." Alaric's voice thunders and his eyes glow amber as he glares at the wolf. The wolf quickly lowers its head and backs away. "Once I've bonded with her, I'll let you all have your turns with her mouth and ass. It'll be a party. But her pussy is mine." He growls the last word and I scream again.

Alaric sniffs and shifts his gaze back to me, smiling down at me. "Why did you have to scream again, little bitch? You need my cock in your mouth to shut you up." His eyes shift around. "I can't wait till later. I'm going to fuck you and claim you right here." Alaric nips at my neck. "My cum is going to drip from every hole until everyone knows you are mine."

Another scream forces its way from between my lips, but Alaric quells it with his hand over my mouth once more. His other hand traces over my chest, pinching my nipple hard before he moves down to the top of my pants. He roughly shoves them down my legs. When he can't get them over my feet, he uses his knife to rip them in half before he stabs the blade into the ground.

Alaric shoves my legs open and licks his lips. My body is slowly going numb and not just from the cold. I need to block everything out; I don't want to feel anything as my nightmare forces himself on me. The sound of a zipper being pulled down reaches my ears as I squeeze my eyes closed.

A mournful howl sounds from far away as he rips my legs open and I let out another shriek. Alaric presses me down to the ground as my screams continue to echo around the forest.

Chapter Thirty Four

Cayden

She's gone, Hunter shouts through the bond. I slam my foot on the brakes. The truck skids on the ice before it settles and I'm out the door in a matter of seconds. Hunter's words echo in my mind.

I leave my truck at the edge of the road and rush through the trees as the branches whip against me. My wolf howls to be let out and I let him take over. My clothes shred around me as I land on all four paws. I eat up the ground, bounding over fallen logs and roots.

As I get closer to the fence, thoughts of Lila being gone push me forwards. My muscles bunch and I jump, clearing the obstacle as if it's not even there. My wolf screams at me to get back. I won't let anything get in my way.

Grayson's mournful howl echoes not only through the bond, but also through the forest. The cabin comes into view and I rush towards it, jumping up the steps and straight through the open door. Grayson is on his knees, his hands tearing at the strands.

"No, no, no, no," Hunter murmurs, and his body shakes.

"Where is she?" I demand as my body finishes its transformation back to its human self.

"I don't know. I woke up and found the cabin empty. Her boots are missing," Hunter responds. "I've looked around the cabin. She's not here. Her scent leads into the woods, but her tracks are gone."

Grayson jumps to his feet and shoves me out of the way as he makes for the door. "I smelled them. I went after them, but they left the compound as soon as they knew I was following. I came back but she was gone. She can't have gotten far." He stomps out of the door, with Hunter and me on his heels.

With his head to the sky, Grayson inhales deeply and changes direction. He shifts to his wolf and darts away. Hunter and I follow suit and take off after him. I can feel the emotions of both of them through the bond. Grayson is confused, and hurt, but also filled with rage. And Hunter is just lost. I feel the darkness as it tries to dig its claws into him.

Don't, Hunter. There is a reason she's gone. I push comfort through the bond at my brother. She wouldn't have left us unless there was a reason.

We'd known there were other shifters checking out the compound. At first, I thought it was a group of rogues passing through, but the same scents were discovered repeatedly. Maybe they could smell an unmated female in a clearly marked wolf territory and were curious. But I should have known after that first day I had found their scents at the fence that the one Lila feared was coming for her.

Lila must have realized what was going on. We knew she was terrified of Alaric coming for her. If she'd thought he was after her, that's the only thing I can think of that would have made her leave.

As we approach the fence, I smell her blood and my hackles rise. Grayson skids to a stop before the hole in the chain link and pushes his nose against the metal. A whine sounds from between his clenched fangs. He pushes against the fence as he tries to fit through the gap, but he's too big.

Find another way, I command.

We split off in separate directions and Hunter's cry soon calls us to where he's found a bigger gap in the metal. We quickly jump through and pick back up on Lila's scent. On this side of the fence, I smell the wolves again and my heart pounds in my chest.

Do they have her?

That thought pushes me on as I hurtle past Hunter and Grayson to take the lead. Stumbling to a stop, Hunter sniffs something on the ground, but I ignore it and carry on.

This is her hoodie. He snarls and quickly catches up with us.

A scream rents the air and I know it's hers. We quicken our pace as another cry echoes around the forest and the scene before us has us all baring our teeth. Lila is lying naked on the floor. Wolves circle around her and a man is poised above her. I don't even think as I aim straight for him and take him to the ground.

My packmates go for the other wolves. We are outnumbered, but nothing is going to stop us from protecting our mate. I look back to Lila and she lies there staring at the sky. The man beneath me shoves me away while I'm distracted and takes a swing at me.

He transforms into his wolf and he's on me. Taking me down to the ground, he sinks his teeth into my flank. A howl escapes my clenched jaws and I swipe out at him with a paw. He backs away a few steps and shakes his head as blood drips down the side of his face.

Teeth rip into my right leg. They crunch down hard enough to break the bone, but he doesn't get the chance. There's another howl as Hunter takes out the wolf attached to my limb. My focus stays on the wolf in front of me, but I hear skin being torn and claws ripping through flesh.

Pain lances down my flank as I grit my fangs together. I struggle to keep my weight on my injured leg. The wolf I found above Lila lowers into a crouch before he launches himself at me again. We trade blows back and forth. I attempt to keep my focus on not only him but also my pack mates. They are both surrounded by wolves on each side.

Lila still hasn't moved from where she is laid on the ground, her body trembling. She doesn't even try to get herself up. Her skin is as white as the surrounding snow and her chest heaves.

I jump onto the rogue's back and my teeth sink into the back of his neck. My claws dig deep and rip into his flesh, rending a howl from his jaws. His body shakes and he tries to dislodge me, but all he does is cause the wounds to deepen. The blood flows down his sides.

Another wolf takes me by surprise, his teeth aiming for my exposed side. I move my hind paws so they are against his chest and push him back away from me before I stumble to my feet.

I feel myself beginning to flag. I need to end this, and I need to end it soon. With one last burst of power, I tackle the wolf that ambushed me to the ground and let my fangs sink into his neck before I rip back, taking his throat with it. His blood drops down my jaws and I spit what meat I have in my mouth into the bloodstained snow.

Whirling on my paws, I'm back on the original wolf once more, and I take him down to the ground. I claw and bite at any part of his flesh I can get at. I want to rip him limb from limb like my packmates have done to the other wolves that attacked us.

"Stop," Lila's voice calls and I turn my gaze on her, my claws still on the throat of the rogue beneath me. She's pulled on a blood-stained jacket, and there's a bloody knife in her hand.

The wolf beneath me is weak now and it wouldn't take much to end him, but her angelic voice stops me in my tracks. All it would take is one little slip of my claws and his lifeblood would spill across the snow.

Lila's hand falls on my shoulder and I stiffen. The wolf under me flinches as my claws nick the skin there. My angel drops to her knees beside me and her hand rests over my paw.

The body under me quivers, the loss of blood forcing his change back to human form. The man under me is a mess, his body covered in claw and bite marks from head to toe. Even his accelerated healing can't close every wound.

"Little bitch." I snarl at his words and let my claws dig deeper, causing the man to grunt. "You wouldn't let the big, bad wolf kill me would you?" He sounds almost sincere. I know now that this must be Alaric, the crazed wolf who planned to force Lila to blood bond with him.

Chapter Thirty Five

Lila

The sound of ripping, growling, and tearing snaps me out of my daze. I'm so cold and my whole body aches. Pushing up from the floor, I lean on my elbows and look around. There are bloody and broken bodies all around me, most back in their human forms.

Three giant wolves, covered in blood and healing wounds, are the only ones left standing. Wolfie—well, Grayson—a sandy color with amethyst eyes—Hunter—and the other is the same russet color as Cayden's hair.

The russet wolf has another beast I'd recognize anywhere beneath his paws. His claws dig into Alaric's neck, blood coating the fur. I rise to my feet and Wolfie—no, Grayson—brushes up against my bare leg. He shifts his head to the dead man only a few feet away. The man's clothes might be bloody, but if I don't put something on soon, I'll freeze to death.

I drop to my knees and wrestle the jacket from him before I sink my arms into the sleeves and pull the material around me. Grayson nudges me with his snout and pushes close to me. I barely feel his warmth through the cold.

When I stagger to my feet, my eyes glimpse the knife sticking up in the frozen ground and I head straight for it. My fingers curl around the handle and I look at the wolf above Alaric.

"Stop." The wolf turns his amber gaze on me as he assesses me. I make my way over to him and lay my hand on his fur, his body stiffening at the touch.

I fall to my knees beside him and reach my hand over until it lays over the top of one of his massive paws poised ready at Alaric's neck. Alaric shivers and I watch the slow transformation back to a man. He's a mess of cuts and bites, all of which are seeping blood.

"Little bitch. You wouldn't let the big, bad wolf kill me would you?" The wolf above Alaric snarls and I tilt my head to the side.

"Of course I wouldn't." A smile pulls up my lips as I reach forward and trail the back of my hand down Alaric's face. He tilts his head into my touch.

The huge wolf beside me whines. I turn to him and nod. He moves his claws away from Alaric's neck and Alaric lets out a sigh.

"I knew you wanted us to be together, really. You loved everything I did to you in the caves, didn't you?" Alaric grins. He believes his own words.

Demi stabbing Rufus over and over as she let out her rage fills my mind. Her screams echo in my ears and I know what I have to do.

When the large wolf moves back far enough, I fling a leg over Alaric's chest. He looks down at my naked pussy against his flesh and smirks. Alaric tries to move a hand toward me, but Grayson pins it down with one of his giant paws. I nod at him and give him my thanks.

My hand moves up Alaric's chest and I lean closer to him. He tries to lift his head, but I push him back down and tilt it to the side. My lips are almost against his ear.

"I'd never let them kill you, Alaric." My other hand moves and I draw the knife against Alaric's neck. "Not when I plan to do it myself."

Without a second thought, I dig the blade deep and slice straight across Alaric's throat. His eyes widen as he stares up at me. Blood pours from his mouth as he chokes on it. If I leave him now, he'll bleed out into the snow, but it's not enough. With the hilt of the knife tightly in my hand, I lean back and thrust it straight into the skin over his blackened heart.

I hit resistance, but push my full weight down onto the knife until the blade completely disappears into Alaric's chest. A cough erupts from his mouth, and his blood splatters over my face as he takes his last breath.

Life drains from his eyes as his body slumps back down to the ground. My fingers slip from the handle of the knife and I lean over Alaric's body.

"You'll never hurt anyone ever again, Alaric. Least of all me." My chest heaves, but I can't take my eyes away from him as I smile. My nightmare is finally over, and I feel a sense of relief.

I just killed a man, not that you could even count him as that anymore. The things he did to other women and me in that cave were beyond horrific. He deserved to die.

A hand rests on my shoulder and I flinch, swiveling my head to look at Grayson. He's naked and covered in blood. That alone should repulse me, but it doesn't. All I feel is numb. The other two wolves transform into Cayden and Hunter; they look as bad as Grayson.

Cayden takes a tentative step towards me, a slight limp on his right leg. I stare at all three of them and back down to Alaric. With my hands on Alaric's still chest, I push myself to my feet, never once taking my eyes from him in case he comes back to life.

"Lila, I'm so sor—" I don't give Hunter a chance to finish his words before I raise my hand to silence him.

"We should have—" My glare cuts Cayden off too.

"I don't want to hear any more of your lies. I saw him shift when he hightailed it out of the cabin." I swivel my gaze to Grayson. "You all betrayed me. I just want to leave."

I step over Alaric's body and start to walk, with no care for the direction I'm going in.

"Lila, wait a second," Hunter calls after me. "At least come back to the cabin and clean up. I'll take you wherever you want to go."

A hand wraps around my wrist and I struggle in Hunter's grasp, but he doesn't let go. My emotions hit me all at once. I want to rage, scream, cry. After everything I've been through, the nightmares that have chased me are finally over.

The adrenaline coursing through my veins dissipates and I sag to the ground. I never hit the snow as arms reach under my back and legs.

"Don't worry. I got you, Lila," Hunter's voice whispers close to my ear.

When I come to, I'm sprawled out on Cayden's bed, wrapped tightly in blankets. I struggle out of the material and draw my hands to my face. Most of the blood is gone, but it's still caked under my nails. The rest of my body has been cleaned and someone has dressed me in sweatpants and a baggy t-shirt.

Alaric is gone. I don't need to fear him anymore. And I was the one who got to end his life. There is a sense of satisfaction in that. Raised voices come from downstairs, and I remember the three men shifting from wolves to men. The lies. The betrayal. They all hit me at once.

I rise to my feet and stomp across the loft, looking out over the living room. Cayden and Grayson are standing in each other's faces throwing accusations, whilst Hunter stands to the side, ready to jump in if needed.

"We should have fucking told her!" Grayson barks.

"Did you really want to risk that after everything she went through?" Cayden growls, his fists clenched at his sides. "She'd have run."

They are too fixated on each other to even notice as I slip down the stairs. The only one who does is Hunter. His amethyst gaze flickers to me and a small smile rises on his lips, but he sees something on my face and it quickly drops.

"Guys." Hunter tries to cut in between Grayson and Cayden, but they both throw glares at him and he backs away.

When I reach the bottom of the stairs, I head straight for the door. I pick a random pair of boots and shove my feet into them. Next, I grab a jacket and throw it on before I grab my backpack, the only thing I still own that is officially mine.

"Lila..." Hunter moves closer to me leaving the other two to argue.

I ignore him as I slam open the door and stomp outside. Slinging the backpack over my shoulder, I take the steps quickly and head into the snow. The storm has calmed, but the snow is still thick.

"Please, Lila. Let me keep my promise and take you back to town." Hunter falls into stride beside me.

"Fine. Just get me the fuck out of here and away from you three." I don't have a plan, but I need to get away from them. I can't trust them.

Hunter gently takes hold of my arm and I shoot a glare at him. "You were going the wrong way," he mumbles.

I let him take the lead and he changes our direction, heading around the back of the cabin and into the trees. We walk a few miles at a steady pace until we reach the fence that surrounds the land they have claimed as theirs.

In the middle of the metal sits an inconspicuous door. Hunter lets go of my arm as he approaches it. He lifts a metal cover and keys in a code; the lock disengages and the door swings open.

Hunter holds it open allowing me to step through it. He makes sure the door locks behind us before he continues walking and I trail behind him. It doesn't feel like we cover much distance before we hit a road and Hunter takes my hand. I stiffen and he quickly withdraws.

We walk down the road and find a truck swerved into the gravel off the tarmac. Hunter leads me around to the other side and helps me inside. I drop my bag onto the bench seat and Hunter gets in beside me. The keys are still dangling from the ignition.

"Not exactly secure," I chastise. "You could have easily had it stolen."

Hunter grips the wheel, his knuckles turn white as he lets out a breath. "We realized you were gone. Cayden was on his way back from the store." He releases the wheel and motions to the snow-covered tarp covering the back of the truck.

My eyes follow his hand, and I remember the fact Cayden had told me what he was doing that morning. This was my fault.

"I'm sorry," I whisper.

"It wasn't your fault, Lila. We should have told you." Hunter rushes out the words. "We should have told you everything. Instead, you had to find out on your own and it made you run."

I'm taken aback by his comment. "I'd still have run, Hunter. But I wouldn't feel so betrayed. After everything, you said you wanted me, but you didn't want me enough to tell me the truth," I rebuke.

Hunter grasps the key and starts the engine. He looks over at me and I settle back into the bench, my hands clasped together in my lap.

"I'm sorry, Lila." Hunter pulls onto the road. "We didn't want to lose you."

"Looks like you did, anyway." I end it there. I want to have the last word, and Hunter doesn't even try to challenge me. He keeps his eyes on the road, and I do the same.

The drive back to town seems to drag on as we sit in silence. Before long, civilization comes into view. It's just a speck in the distance that gets bigger as we get closer. We drive halfway into town before Hunter pulls into the lot of the small motel.

I'm out of the vehicle with my bag before he can say anything. I hear the door of the truck open and close, but I refuse to look back.

"Please don't give up on us, Lila," Hunter implores. He gets the last word after all.

Tears form in the corner of my eyes as I do my best to blink them away. I won't let him see how hurt I am. I push through the door into the lobby. An older woman sits behind the counter, but she perks up when I enter. She drops her glasses from her face and they dangle on a gold chain around her neck.

"Good morning, welcome to Blackwell Motel," she chirps. "How can I help you?"

"I need a room," I announce. "Any room. I don't mind."

"Of course. Can I take your name?" She taps the button on the mouse attached to the computer.

"Lila Moore," I answer. She clicks her tongue and smiles before she busies herself with a small box behind her.

"Ah, Miss Moore. We have a room ready for you already." I'm hit by confusion as she speaks.

"What do you mean?"

"Your room has already been taken care of, Miss Moore. I received a call fifteen minutes ago from a..." The woman looks back at the computer screen. "Cayden. He's paid up till the end of the month." The woman turns back to me. My mouth hangs open as she drops a key onto the counter and I stare at it. "Room seven."

I want to refuse the offer. I want nothing to do with them, but I barely have any cash at all. Begrudgingly, I take the key and thank the woman before I walk out of the lobby.

The truck and Hunter are gone. I hold the key tightly in my hand and move past the rooms that are in numerical order until I hit room seven. It's the closest to the forest and beyond the parking lot is the tree line.

I push the key into the door and shoulder it open. It's a simple room with a queen bed, a microwave, and a small fridge freezer, with a coffee maker sitting on the desk beside them. At the other end of the room is a door that I assume leads to the bathroom.

Nudging the door shut, I engage the deadbolt and perch on the edge of the bed. My bag slips off my shoulder and onto the mattress. I let my body fall back onto the mattress and close my eyes. All I see are the three men that came into my life: their smiles, their laughs, their touches.

You should hate them, Lila. They betrayed you.

But it's harder than I thought it would be to hate them. They saved me from Alaric. They took care of me and made me feel alive and safe again. A knock on the door startles me. I push up from the bed and head to the door. Checking the peephole, the woman from the lobby stands on the other side.

Releasing the deadbolt, I open it slowly and take her in. Her arms are loaded with paper bags and she looks like she's on the verge of dropping them. I step out of the door and take a few of the bags from her.

"These arrived for you," the older woman announces.

"But I didn't order anything," I exclaim.

"Then someone is a lucky girl. Now, let's get this stuff inside and in the fridge before I end up dropping everything." The woman scurries past me and straight to the kitchen area.

As soon as she puts the bags on the floor, she unloads them. There isn't much to go in the small fridge freezer. A few bottles of soda, milk, butter, and an assortment of deli meats. She drops the tiny freezer compartment and adds the small microwave pizzas and tray meals before she closes it back up.

Looking down at the bags in my arms, I find sugar, chips, candy bars, and a box of cereal. There's enough for me to be able to feed myself for a few days, but beyond that, I don't know what I'm going to do. Tears prickle my eyes. Even now the guys are still trying to look after me.

The older woman stands straight and gathers the empty bags. I quickly wipe away the tears that are threatening to spill before she can see me. She takes a step towards me and places a hand on my arm.

"Oh, honey. Please don't be sad. It might seem hard right now, but things will turn out right in the end." With that she turns and leaves, closing the motel room door behind her.

Slumping back on the bed, I have no idea how anything will turn out okay. I don't have enough money to leave, and I've left my heart at the cabin I fled only a short while ago.

Chapter Thirty Six

Lila

The sound of next doors' extracurricular activities drills into my head and I want to slap my hands over my ears so I don't have to hear them anymore. It's been over two weeks since Hunter dropped me off at the motel. I spent a whole week with my emotions ranging from anger to sadness before pulling on my big girl panties.

After speaking to the motel owner, she put me in touch with Burt from the gas station who towed the wreckage of my car into town. There was nothing salvageable. My next stop was the diner on the main high street. They needed a dish cleaner and that's what I've been doing for the last five days. It's enough to distract me from them.

With a shake of my head, I drag myself over to the fridge freezer. My fingers grasp the fridge door firmly. I give it a yank. Dropping open the small freezer compartment, I grab the first box I can get my hands on.

Another day, another microwave meal. Nothing like the food Hunter and Cayden were making in the cabin.

You chose to run; my inner monologue reminds me.

Watching Grayson transform from man to wolf broke something inside me. I thought I'd found my freedom with these three men, but they were the same as all the other wolves I'd met. Liars. I ran from them like I had done the other, but I ran straight into the arms of Alaric.

I'd been so stupid, but Grayson, Cayden, and Hunter had all lied to me. They knew about the caves, and the wolf that had wanted to force me to be his blood mate, yet they still made the decision to leave out one vital piece of information. All three of them were the very thing I was running from.

My heart races as I remember the bays of the wolves as they chased me. I ran straight into Alaric's arms. I bet the hunters they mentioned were really Alaric and his men getting closer, another lie. Another thing they hadn't told me.

Hello, my sweet little bitch. I finally found you. That voice in my head still sends shivers through my entire body.

I had ended my nightmare, though. I'd taken a life. One I don't have regrets over. But Alaric still plagues my dreams at night, when it's quiet and there is nothing left to distract me.

Ripping open the small pizza box, I tear away the rest of the packaging and shove it inside the microwave. The door slams closed in time with another of the motel room's doors being closed. With the push of a few buttons, the timer is set and I hit start. I stare at my hands absentmindedly. I still see the blood dripping from them, Alaric's blood.

Moans drift through the thin walls from the room next door and I fall into the memories of them. The time we spent together, the kisses and the touches. How they made me feel. My heart cracks and I feel it again, the tug in my solar plexus that has been plaguing me since I left them.

The incessant beeps of the microwave pull me out of the memories of traveling along the road to the town. That's why I'm here now, in the only motel in the small town of Blackwell, eating crappy, microwaved food. Hunter had brought me here. I knew he didn't want to leave me alone, but I ran from his truck before he could say anything.

Dolly, the owner, keeps dropping by with bags of food and drinks from the small store down on the main high street. She never asks me for a penny. If I wasn't in such dire straits, I'd refuse her, but I'm desperate.

I open the microwave door, pull out the pathetic-looking pizza and move it to a napkin, taking a bite. The cheese tastes like rubber and the tomato sauce is the least tomato-tasting thing I've ever eaten.

Moving over to the window, I look outside. He's still there. Grayson sits in his wolf form at the edge of the property that borders the tree line. It's where he's been every day and night since Hunter first brought me here.

The loss of the three of them sinks into my very soul, but I'm hurt and confused. The need to continue my journey to the demon sector is minute compared to my need to stay and be with my wolves.

My wolves.

Is that what they have become? Will it truly break me to leave them? Or is it for the best?

I sink my teeth into another bite of pizza and chew it slowly as I turn my back on the window. I can't watch him out there anymore. My resolve crumbles to ash around me. When I left them that day, I didn't have a plan. My only thoughts were leaving.

My job at the diner is the only way for me to get enough money to head to my cousin Addi's place in the demon sector. A one-way ticket out of here. But now I'm not so sure.

Leaving half of my pizza, I throw the remnants and the napkin into the trash and drift toward the bathroom. I turn on the taps and leave the water to warm before I drop the plug in and let the bath fill.

One thing that came in the bags left by the owner was a bottle of jasmine bath salts. I scoop out a handful and drop them into the flow. The water turns a light shade of lilac as the floral scent envelops the room.

Disrobing, I climb over the side of the bath and sink into the steamy, fragrant water. Every muscle welcomes the heat, easing the aches and pains of my tired body. Closing my eyes, I let myself relax and think of my wolves. The way they touched me. The way they smelled. The way they kissed me.

Being surrounded by them felt like home. My face grows damp. At first, I don't even realize I'm crying, but now I let the tears out. They track down my cheeks as I lose all sense of time. I lie in the bath long enough that the water has cooled, leaving my skin pebbled and slightly pruned.

I dunk my head under the water to wet my golden locks and quickly wash my hair and body before I slip back under the water to clear away the suds. My hand reaches for the cloth I left on the side of the bath and I dry my face, then climb out. I lean against the toilet. My whole body feels weak, like all the energy has left me.

The two towels I left on the side are still there. I grab one and wrap it around my body before I wrap the other around my hair. I stagger out of the bathroom, not even bothering to empty the tub. It's a problem for later. I make it to the bed before I collapse onto the hard mattress.

With my eyes already closed, I grope around for the comforter and pull it over my tired body. As darkness claims me, so do dreams of my wolves, my men, as we run through the forest. The leaves of the shrubbery brush past my naked body, leaving my skin tingling. Then they surround me, morphing back to their human skin as they stalk toward me. All three of them descend on me and I welcome them with open arms.

Scratching on wood pulls me out of my dream, and I stumble to my feet. Shoving a long t-shirt that reaches down past my ass, I make my way to the window. I look out beyond the car park to the edge of the tree line but he's not there. My heart and soul shatter in unison. Grayson finally left me. I crumple to the floor, sobbing as I clutch my knees to my chest.

The scratching comes again and I realize it's coming from the door. Without thinking, I push to my feet and fling it open. Grayson, in his wolf form, fills the doorway. His large head is lowered to the floor before he lifts those silver eyes to mine.

Tears prickle my eyes at the sheer relief that he isn't gone, he'd only moved closer. Stepping back from the doorway, I leave him enough room to come inside, hoping he will enter.

"Please," I murmur and he pads inside. He jumps straight onto the rumpled bed and lies down like he used to at the cabin.

I close and lock the door and make my way back over to the bed. Crawling up beside him, his warm body curls up against me and I push my fingers into his fur and breathe in his scent.

My heart flutters in my chest. That feeling of home fills me once more. Grayson's rough tongue licks up the side of my face and it's only then that I realize I'm still crying as he licks my tears away.

"Grayson..." I whisper. "Please, I need you."

Bones crack and fur recedes to leave golden skin behind. Then his hands are on me, pulling me against him. His legs tangle with mine as he holds me close. Burying his nose into my neck, Grayson takes a deep breath.

"Not as much as I need you," he whispers against my ear. Wrapping his arms around me, he holds me close and I mold my body against his, breathing in his scent.

He's home, he's safe.

For the first time since the rogue wolves took me and my torment began, I feel like I can fully relax and my body does exactly that. Letting out a long sigh, I close my eyes. Grayson runs his hands over my skin and I let sleep take me.

The sun filtering through the thin curtains of the motel room pulls me from my dreams. I feel Grayson behind me still. His warm breath fans the back of my neck, sending shivers through my entire body.

Encased in his arms, I shift and turn to face him. He looks so peaceful in his sleep. There are no stress lines marring his features. Then I feel him fully, hot and hard, through the thin material covering my body. I can't stop myself from rubbing against him.

A soft moan slips from Grayson's lips from the movement. His words last night pierced me straight through the chest, and I know I want him more than I've ever wanted anyone before.

Pushing against his shoulder, his body falls back on the bed and I climb on top of him. My hot core brushes against his cock and he twitches below me as I rub myself against his hard length.

Grayson is still half asleep, moans slipping from him as I press against him. His eyes snap open and he lets out a growl before lunging up and pressing his lips against mine.

Then I'm lost as our tongues explore each other's mouths. His hands trail up my bare legs and I rock against his cock, dragging more growls from his mouth. His fingers leave my thighs and trail up my sides and over my arms. He reaches for my hair, his fingers tangling in the strands as he takes control of our kiss.

I'm already wet for him, coating Grayson's cock with my juices as I rub against him. He nips at my lower lip, sucking it into his mouth and biting down on my plump flesh.

A wanton moan rushes out of my mouth before I can stop myself. I rock myself harder against him, his mushroom head pushing through my lips and brushing against my clit, sending electricity through my entire body.

Chapter Thirty Seven

Grayson

From the first moment my wolf realized she was our mate; I've craved her more than the air I breathe. But as a man I was too dangerous to be around her, I wanted nothing more than to drag her to the floor and claim her as my own.

Breaking the kiss and reaching up, I drag her t-shirt over her head and marvel at the sight before me. She's pure perfection and made just for us.

Mate, my wolf whines.

"Mate..." I gasp as her pussy drags along my length. Her eyes sparkle as she looks down at me.

My hands move up her stomach and grasp her breasts, a soft moan rushing from between her lips as I stroke my fingers over her nipples. Taking the hardened peaks between my index fingers and thumbs, I add pressure to them both, squeezing them tight. Lila's hands brace against my shoulders as she continues to rub her wetness up and down me.

"If I'm your mate, then shouldn't you be claiming me?" Lila asks between her moans.

Releasing her breasts, I grab onto her hips, pulling her up and positioning her hot entrance right over my throbbing cock. I stop right there, begging for her permission without words. She doesn't say a thing as she pushes down on me. The head of my cock pushes through her lips and the moan that escapes her mouth leaves my balls tingling.

I want nothing more than to thrust deep inside her. My body trembles as I force myself to let her take the lead. When she was held captive, she was assaulted against her will. I won't force her to do anything she doesn't want to do. Lila takes over, lowering herself further down my length. Her moans fill the room as I sink deeper.

When I'm halfway inside her, she rises until only my mushroomed head remains within her before plunging back down and taking me further. Her walls clamp down hard and I can't stop the strangled moan that bursts from me. My eyes connect with hers and she's smiling as she moves up and down my length.

With each rise and fall, more of my cock sinks inside her welcoming heat until I'm fully seated within her. Her clit sits flush with my pubic bone. Lila's breathing comes out of her in pants, her skin is covered in a fine layer of sweat, and I feel her walls pulse around me. My wolf pushes against my skin, begging me to claim her.

"Please, Gray, fuck me." Her words are whispered, but I hear them over the frantic beating of my heart.

Dragging her against me until I lay her flush with my body, I flip us so she's on her back beneath me. I tower over her, looking into her eyes, but I see no fear, only lust, as the blackness of her pupils overwhelms her irises. Drawing back my hips, I thrust back into her, keeping up a punishing pace as her cries of pleasure fill the room.

Lila's fingers claw at my back, sure to leave red marks before my ability to heal can knit my skin back together. Grabbing onto her left leg, I draw it up, changing the angle of my penetration, which leaves Lila screaming out my name. My grip on her is bruising, but I'm too far gone, swept away by the pleasure of being inside her at last.

Keeping up my pace, I grunt with each thrust. I feel my balls drawing up wanting to release inside her. My teeth ache, begging to lengthen and claim her. To place my mark on her neck for all to see. My mouth opens as my fangs burst through my gums. I hear a whimper from Lila, forcing me to look at her.

That's when I see it. She might say she wants me to claim her, but there is a small amount of fear still tinging her scent. After what she has been through, it's no surprise. Her walls clench around me as she screams out her release, and I'm so close to my own. I feel my knot beginning to swell as I pump inside her delicious body.

Pulling my cock from her, I spray my cum across her belly and sink my teeth deep, not into her neck but into the pillow beside her head. My knot fully swells and I feel it between us, rubbing against her clit and prolonging both our orgasms.

My wolf whines at me again for not claiming his mate, but until we've spoken to her properly, I can't let myself do it. She was tortured and abused and nearly forced into a blood bond. As much as her words tell me this is what she wants, the thought of bonding herself with us still scares her.

"Why didn't you complete the bond?" Lila's whispered words throw me off guard and I push myself back from her. I brace my arms on either side of her as I look down at her.

"I won't force you into something that you aren't entirely sure you want." My voice is gruff and strained.

"But I want it, Gray." Reaching up her hand, she strokes down the side of my face and I nuzzle into her touch.

"You're telling me you do, but I can sense your hesitancy. Your words may say it, but your body is still remembering *him*, fearing *him*." I lean down and kiss her lips far more softly than I ever thought possible. "I don't want our bond to be tarnished by what *he* did."

Pushing back, I roll onto my back beside Lila and sit up. My cum coats her stomach and my cock aches. My knot still has not gone down. Lila pushes up onto her elbows and her eyes fall straight onto my length.

Without a word, her hand reaches forward, her fingers brushing against the knot at the base of my length. I let out a growl and her eyes move to my face.

"If you keep touching me like that, Lila, I'm not sure if I will be able to control myself." Lila quickly pulls her hand away.

"Why did I never feel that with *him*?" Her question is so innocent.

"You were not *his* true mate. It's the same with Hunter and Cayden. Even when we fucked to stave off the curse, our wolves are never fully satisfied. As much as they are my pack, they aren't you."

"I never felt it with Hunter either. Does that mean I'm not his true mate?" I see the tears forming in the corner of her eyes and I quickly brush them away.

"It's nothing like that. Hunter was close every time, but he pulled out before he got too far. He wouldn't have bonded with you, not without your permission," I explain to her.

Her hand reaches for mine and she laces our fingers together. My thumb strokes the back of her hand. "As wolves, our bodies want to procreate with our mates. Our knots swell to keep our seed inside." Lila lets out a gasp. It's another reason I won't bond with her until we've talked.

"I... I didn't know. I've never wanted children, not in this world. I would never want to bring a child into this world, not the way it is." I understand her words. This world is fucked up. I'd never want to drag a child into it.

"I feel the same way. While I would love nothing more than to have a child with you, I wouldn't want to risk them." Lila smiles at my words. "Come on, we better shower. If you agree, I'll take you back to the compound. The others will want to see you." I reach across the bond over the pack link but there is only silence from Cayden while Hunter lets me know he'll be outside.

A subtle nod is all she gives me. I push to my knees, taking Lila in my arms and lifting her from the bed. A squeal escapes her lips as I carry her into the bathroom and straight into the shower.

Turning on the water, I put my back to it as the water flows cold before heating. Once it's warm enough, I lower Lila to her feet and push her under the spray.

The water sluices down her body, soaking her from head to toe. I grab the small bottle of shower gel and squirt some onto my hand before my hands are on her. I wash away any traces of our coupling from Lila's body with reluctance. A part of me wants to at least leave this mark on her body, even if it isn't my bite.

Once I'm done, she returns the favor. Her movements are careful and precise as she cleans every inch of my body. Just the sight of her doing such a simple task has the blood rushing to my cock, but she doesn't comment on my hardening length as she wraps her hand around it. A moan bursts from between my lips when she moves her hand up and down my cock.

When we are both clean, I grab some towels off the rack, ignoring the fact that I want to sink back inside her. I wrap one around my hips, before enveloping Lila in the other and helping her dry. She watches my every movement. My cock twitches from her intense gaze but I do my best to ignore it.

Interlocking our fingers, I pull her from the bathroom and guide her to the bed. Taking a glance around the room, I throw the clothes strewn across the room into a bag while Lila finishes drying off and getting dressed.

She uses the towel to dry as much of her hair off as she can. When she's done lacing up her boots, she looks at me still standing in a towel with her bags in my hand.

"Wait, you've been outside as a wolf. I'm guessing it's a no to clothes." She lets out a giggle and I shrug.

Opening the door, I grab her hand with my free one and walk outside in only a towel. A car door slams and feet approach us.

"Lila..." Hunter calls. Lila grips my hand tightly before ripping it away and taking off toward Hunter.

The next minute she's in his embrace and he's kissing her. His arms come around her and lift her from the ground, spinning them both. Shaking my head, I approach the truck and throw her bags into the bed.

"If you're done, we need to get back," I grunt. Hunter breaks their kiss, letting Lila slide down his body until her feet are back on the floor.

"You're here," Lila squeaks out. I checked in with Hunter a few times and knew he was nearby. He was confident that she would come back to us. More so than Cayden and I were, but he never lost hope.

"Of course. I knew I had to give you time to think. But every time I tried to go back to the compound, my wolf wouldn't let me leave. I've been sleeping in the truck on the other side of the street, waiting and hoping, but trying not to push." He looks over at me. "This big lug, however, was even more determined to stay close. I told him to leave you be, but I guess it's a good thing he completely ignored me."

"I was going to leave. I wanted to leave. I had a plan, but every time I thought about leaving this sector, I just couldn't do it. When I saw Grayson was gone, I panicked. I thought you'd given up on me."

Approaching them both, I box Lila in between mine and Hunter's bodies. My hand rests on her hips and Hunter's arms are still around her shoulders.

"I could never leave you, Lila. If you'd left, I'd have followed you to the ends of the earth. You're mine...ours." I look over her shoulder at Hunter and he grins.

"And I'd have been close on his heels," Hunter exclaims.

"What about Cayden? He's not here." I hear the tremor in her voice and I tighten my grip on her hips.

"He wants you as much as we do, Lila. Never think otherwise." My voice is full of promise. He might not be here. Lila leaving sent Cayden into a spiral. His wolf is mourning her loss as much as the man.

"Okay." Lila's voice still trembles. "Let's go."

Hunter and I both release her before he heads around the other side of the truck, climbing in. Holding the door open for Lila, I help her inside. Leaning behind the bench seat, I grab the spare sweatpants and pull them up my hips. The towel drops to the parking lot floor and I climb in behind Lila, slamming the door behind me.

Once I'm situated beside her, she grabs my hand and laces her fingers through mine. As soon as Hunter has pulled out of the lot, she does the same with his free hand. I look down at our interconnected hands and I feel the calmest I have in a long time. We have our mate, and at some point soon we will claim her. She'll be part of our pack, she'll be ours forever.

Chapter Thirty Eight

Lila

With Hunter and Grayson on either side of me, I'm where I'm meant to be. We fit together like a puzzle. I'm wrapped in their warmth and safety. However, there is still one piece missing and I'm nervous about seeing him. Cayden.

We have never gone beyond kisses; he kept his distance, unlike the other two. They both pushed my boundaries but gave me full control, a thing I will always be grateful for. I glance from Hunter to Grayson and our interlocked fingers.

After we pull out of the motel lot, we pass the gas station. Burt is outside, pumping gas. He raises a hand to us as we pass and Hunter gives him a small nod before moving his eyes back to the road.

It seems so long ago since I took this exact route through the town and beyond. When we reach the thick line of trees at the end of the town, my gaze falls to the side of the road as we pass the tree I crashed into. The space is now void of the car the magic born gave me. I tighten my grip on Hunter and Grayson's hands, and they both squeeze my fingers back.

That one incident set off a chain of events I never saw coming. Who would have ever thought that the very species I was running from would become my saviors? But the three men had shown me that not every shifter was the same.

A few more miles down the road, we drive off the tarmac and through a gap in the trees. We hit a small path that leads through the forest. I came this way before on foot, when Hunter brought me back to the town a few weeks ago. I close my eyes, remembering the feelings that rushed through me as I turned my back on them and left.

A single tear tracks down my cheek and a finger wipes it away. I turn my gaze to Grayson and he leans towards me, kissing where the tear once was.

"Don't even think about it, Lila. You had every right to leave. We didn't tell you what we are. We were too scared after what you told us." Hunter speaks from my other side and I look over to him. "But you came back. That's all that matters."

Grayson pulls his hand from mine and wraps an arm around my shoulder. I lean my head against his chest, breathing in his scent as Hunter continues to drive us to our final destination. It doesn't take long before we make it to the edge of the compound. To the only real entrance. Hunter pulls the truck into a wooden shed hidden among the trees and kills the engine.

Grayson clambers out of the cab and I scoot over to the edge of the bench seat, ready to jump out. His arms embrace me and pull me to his chest. My legs wrap around his waist and he kicks the door shut before he moves around the back of the truck. The other door slams closed, and Hunter appears beside us, my bag firmly in his grip.

"I can walk, you know," I chide, but Grayson ignores me and nuzzles his face against my neck. His breath tickles against my skin.

"Let him have this, Lila," Hunter replies. "His wolf needs to feel you close by."

I give a small nod and settle my head against Grayson's chest as he carries me. My eyes slip closed as my hands link behind his neck. The gentle sway of his walking makes my body relax. I don't even notice the distance we travel until Grayson strides up the steps of the cabin.

Hunter opens the door to allow us entry and follows us inside. My eyes open as Grayson slides me down his body and I feel every dip and bulge. The warmth and smells of the cabin soothe my very soul. But when my feet hit the floor, I glance around the open plan room.

My mouth drops open at the sheer devastation around me. The coffee table is in two pieces and there are deep gouges in the floor. The chairs from the dining table are scattered around in the room; only one remains standing. I continue my perusal; the curtains are torn, and shredded clothes are scattered around the room.

"What the hell happened?" I gasp at the sight before me.

"Cayden," Hunter mutters as he steps beside me. "His wolf wasn't happy that he let you leave. The darkness is riding him hard."

"Darkness?" I question. My eyes flicker up to the loft, hoping that Cayden is there, but there are no other sounds in the cabin apart from us three.

"The curse, as humans call it. Come on, we'll explain." Hunter beckons as he takes my hand and leads me to the couch. Like the floor, there are claw marks running through the fabric, but I take a seat anyway. Hunter takes a seat beside me.

I don't know much about the curse. All we are told is that some sort of curse drives male wolves to find their mates. Since my abduction, I have garnered that without their true mates, it drives the male wolves insane. Alaric and the other wolves that took me are perfect examples of the madness that affects them.

"There's a darkness." Grayson crouches down in front of me. "It begins to dig its hooks into male wolves once we hit maturity. It's like a voice in our heads. Pushing us to kill, even those close to us." His eyes flicker to Hunter and he swallows hard. "Sometimes it demands we take what isn't ours."

"We left our pack without an alpha," Hunter adds. "Cayden attacked Beck, one of his betas. We didn't want to risk the pack's safety. The darkness was already beginning to affect us as well, so we all came here."

"The fence. It's to keep you in?" I think about the fence at the boundary with the top bent inwards.

"Yes." Hunter nods. "To keep the outside world safe as much as we could."

"We agreed," Grayson adds. "We stay together for as long as we can. We love each other. Being together has helped a little. But when the time comes..." His words drift off and I whip my head around to Grayson.

"When the time comes, what?"

"We die." Hunter's answer makes me flinch. "We went to balls for years. We never found our mate. After Cayden's attack, we couldn't stay any longer. The pack thinks we're looking for our mate. But we'd given up. Well, that was until you."

"But you three don't seem affected. How do you know the darkness has you?"

Grayson jumps to his feet and paces across the floor. "It's the voice, it speaks to us all. When I first found you, it wanted me to kill you." My eyes move to him, and I gasp. I see it now, the strain in his features. "It wanted me to fuck you and claim you that morning in the loft. If Hunter hadn't interrupted, I would have. But even then, the darkness still wanted me dead. It demanded I bond with you and then kill you, which would inevitably end me as well."

My mind whirls as it tries to understand what Grayson is saying. I never realized how the curse affected them, or even that these three were afflicted. I thought Grayson was just a moody bastard.

"That's why you saw Wolfie more than Grayson," Hunter adds. "It was the only way he could stop himself from claiming you in the beginning. But being around you curbs the darkness."

That's why Grayson began appearing more in his human form. My very presence helped him.

"But what about Cay? Where is he now?" I beg.

"He's staying in his wolf form. We've hardly seen him since you left." Hunter gestures to the room. "The darkness has been sinking its claws in quicker and faster. He tried to attack us both when we've been with you. It wants us dead."

"You could have bonded with me at any time while I was here, but you all waited." I look between the two men. "You could have saved yourselves."

"No," Hunter interjects. "We wanted to give you time, Lila. You didn't even know what we were. We weren't going to just force the mating bond on you. Alaric already tried that." Hunter drops his gaze to the floor, and Grayson nods in agreement with his friend.

"I need to find Cayden. Please," I beg. "Tell me what I need to do."

"You're our true mate, Lila. You are our savior," Hunter answers. "Once we have all bonded with our true mate, the darkness can't keep its hold anymore." He sounds almost relieved.

The darkness, as they call it, has been clawing at them for as long as I have known them, but not once has any of them fully claimed me. Even in the motel room, Grayson refused until we had a chance to speak first. Well, now we have. I've heard enough and I need to save Cayden.

"I'm going to find him." I rush to my feet, and Hunter quickly stands beside me.

"I'll go with you." Hunter's hand wraps around my arm, pausing my movement as he holds me back.

"No, I don't think so. You just told me his darkness has wanted you both dead. I'm not risking either of you," I shout. My anger rises to the surface; I won't let them get hurt.

"But you'd be risking yourself, Lila." Hunter steps closer and his hand rests against my cheek. "We can't lose you now."

"You won't. He won't hurt me." Or at least I'm hoping Cayden won't hurt me. I pull away from Hunter and look over to Grayson; he nods at my assessment. With that, I grab a thick coat from the hook and rush out of the door.

"At the very least, let us take you to him." Hunter pads down the steps with Grayson as they both strip out of their clothes, leaving the material in a line on the porch.

I give Hunter a nod, rushing down the steps, and run straight into the forest. I have to find Cayden. I need to save him from the darkness. My feet crunch against the snow on the ground as I dash through the tree line. Two shapes fall into step with me on either side.

A howl splits the air. It's full of sadness and I quicken my pace. Hunter and Grayson keep up with me and use their huge bodies to take me on the best path through the tree-laden forest. It's not long before I have to slow down to a walk, but my two wolves continue to guide me. We weave through the trees and bushes until the hard ground beneath us gives way to rocks and I stop suddenly.

A beautiful lake sits in front of me. It's clear enough with the lack of trees for the moon to shine through fully and illuminate the entire area. Then I spot Cayden on the far right. His huge body sprawled out on the rocky ground. Grayson nudges his muzzle against my hand. I run my hand over the top of his head.

"You both need to stay here." Grayson flashes his fangs at me but Hunter nips gently at his neck before he falls back onto his haunches and Grayson follows suit.

I take a tentative step forward and then another. I give the two wolves one last look before I turn back to the lake and focus on Cayden. I move slowly towards him watching as his chest rises and falls quickly. The rocks shift under my feet each time my foot hits the ground.

"Cayden..." My voice is a whisper, but his ears flicker at the noise.

Chapter Thirty Nine

Cayden

The darkness claws at me. I'm losing myself to it. Since Lila left, the voices have been getting stronger. They demand I track her down and claim her. I can't let them take control. I don't want to think what I would do if I went after her.

Take her.

No.

Claim her.

Not without her permission.

Fuck her till she's yours.

I can't.

What are you waiting for?

Her to come back.

She's never coming back unless you force her to.

I howl into the night sky. It's filled with pain and the longing I have for my mate. I'm struggling in both forms. The voices are there no matter what, but if I run as my wolf for long enough, I can collapse from exhaustion and sleep until the process starts all over again once the sun rises.

My paws thunder against the ground as I eat up the distance. The fence comes into view, and I veer alongside it. What I wouldn't give to be on the other side. To run for miles in any direction and not be caught in this cage. But I'm too dangerous to go beyond the man-made structure. It won't be long before I have to beg one of my brothers to put an end to my misery.

Lila left me. She left us.

I shake my massive head, pushing the thought away. We shouldn't have lied to her. We should have told her what we were as soon as she told us her story. Instead, we erred on the side of caution and now she's gone.

The wind brushes against my fur, and the cold seeps into my body. How could things have been different? We could have started by not lying to her. She had every reason to leave. I can't say I blamed her. We lied about what we are; we didn't tell her about the fact we had smelled other shifters on the perimeter and inside it.

Visions of that psycho above her naked body rip through my head. My teeth gnash together as a snarl escapes me. With a shake of my head, I force the image away. It's replaced by her in the snow, twirling in a circle as me and Hunter watch her laugh and smile. The way her cheeks and nose are red from the cold, even as we sat in front of the fire, make her even more beautiful.

Every moment I've spent with Lila pushes its way into my head, like a movie playing from beginning to end on repeat. It's enough to drive anyone crazy. Then I smell her; roses and jasmine. It invades my senses and I stumble. My huge body hits the floor hard and I roll a few times before I come to a stop on my side.

My breaths come out in pants as I lie there and close my eyes. I tilt back my head to discover I'm by the watering hole. The rocks dig into my heaving sides, but I can't bring myself to care. My ears flicker to the sound of rocks shifting underfoot as her scent gets strong.

"Cayden..." It's a whisper in the wind but it's her voice.

My eyes crack open and I lift my head. The madness must have finally taken over. Not only can I smell and hear her, I see her, too. My wolf groans and my head sinks back down to the rocky ground. Steps get closer, the sound so real to my ears. A hand touches my flank and my body flinches. My eyes spring open again and I let them focus on her form.

The moon glows behind Lila, giving her a halo of light around her head. I must have died and she's an angel coming to claim my soul.

"Cayden...please." Lila leans closer, her hands running through my fur.

My ears twitch toward her voice again as I continue to stare at her. When her arms come around my neck and her scent envelops me, then I feel her body against mine and know she's there. My body creaks and groans as the shift takes over, and my arms come around her back. The body against me is real and not a figment of my imagination.

"Lila." My voice is raspy from lack of use.

"I'm here, Cay. I'm so sorry I left." Lila's head falls into the hollow of my neck as we both lie awkwardly on the rocky ground. Her breath is warm against my neck and I shiver each time it hits my skin.

I take in a deep breath, letting the roses and jasmine wash over me. My hands move all over her body that's wrapped in a thick jacket and jeans. Her hands skim over my shoulders and down my arms. Every part of my body feels alive, in some places more than others. As my cock rubs against the rough fabric of her jeans, I groan.

Lila pulls back and her eyes connect with mine. Tears line her lower lashes and it breaks my heart to see them there. Tracing my thumbs under both of her eyes, I wipe the tears away. My fingers brush through her hair and tangle with the strands as I pull her lips to mine and kiss her hard.

Our tongues tangle together and I devour her like a starved man. Her fingers grip my shoulders, her nails digging deep as she clings onto me for dear life. Without another thought, I gather Lila in my arms, rise to my feet, and stride away from the lake.

My brothers' scents hit my nostrils and I know they have been here recently. They must have led Lila to the lake, she wouldn't have found me otherwise. I let the thought slip away. Our lips are connected still but I don't need to be able to see to know where I'm going.

When I stride up the cabin stairs, neither Hunter nor Grayson are close by. They know what I need. Time on my own with Lila. The darkness won't let me share with them right now and until my bond with her has been cemented I won't risk them.

I don't stop as I take the stairs up to my bedroom two at a time. I kneel at the end of the bed and place Lila on the mattress. Her blue eyes peruse my body as I rise back to my feet and stand before her. Her hands move to the zip of her jacket and she lowers it slowly down her body. She slips her arms out of the sleeves one at a time and my cock jerks.

Lila notices and her tongue darts out to wet her lips as she pulls her top over her head. Her breasts are on full display and I can't stop myself reaching out a hand and rolling one of her nipples between my fingers. A tiny gasp comes from her lips as the bud hardens beneath my touch.

"Lie back," I command, and she does without question.

I brace myself over her lithe body, my arms on either side of her. My lips trace down the side of her neck as I nip and bite at her pebbled skin. When I reach her nipple, I take the bud between my teeth and bite down. Her arousal and moans flood the room.

My tongue moves around the peak of her nipple. "That's a good girl," I whisper against her skin.

I lean on one arm and move my other hand down her side to the waistband of her jeans. With a single movement, I pop the button and lower the zipper. Her entire body trembles beneath me, and I know as soon as I touch the apex of her thighs she will be wet for me.

My wolf whines inside my head. Our mate is so close and he wants her but I need to take my time and worship her. I drop to my knees at the end of the bed and latch my thumbs into the top of her jeans and panties. With a yank I pull them down her legs until they snag on her boots.

My fingers fumble with the laces on the front of the boots and I groan in frustration. Lila lets out a small laugh and I look up at her. My claws spring free and I cut straight through the offending laces until I can tug her boots from her feet. Once I have removed them, I yank her jeans and panties the rest of the way down her legs so she's bare before me.

With a hand on either knee, I push her legs apart. She's already so wet, her juices leaking from her hole. I pull her to the edge of the mattress and dive straight in. The first lick of Lila's pussy has me groaning. She tastes amazing and I want to devour her.

I attack her clit like a man starved and push two fingers into her pussy. Her walls quiver around the intrusion. Lila's fingers grip my hair and as she pulls at the strands I groan again. I speed up the thrusts of my fingers. My teeth scrape against her clit and she shatters. Her cries of pleasure are music to my ears.

My tongue licks up every drop. I shove my fingers between my lips and suck her cream from both digits.

"Fuck. You taste so good."

"I need you, Cayden. I want to be your mate."

Any thought of worshiping her flies straight out of the door with her words. I climb to my feet and push her up the bed before I follow her down. Pre-cum drips out of my tip and I smear it around the head before I push my cock against her folds. What's left of her release covers my length.

"Are you sure?" I ask.

"Yes." Her answer is so sure.

Without further words being needed, I push through her folds. Her walls still clench from her orgasm and like a teenage boy, I almost come right there and then. My hands lift her hips and I slip further inside her. My large girth stretches her and her breathing increases as she bites on her lower lip.

Everything about her body calls to me as I thrust in and out of her wet heat. Her fingers grip the comforter as she tries to stifle her moans.

"Just let go. Let it all out," I encourage her and her teeth give up their grip on her lower lip.

Lila's moans and the slapping of our skin fill the entire cabin. With each thrust, I come back to myself. The darkness pushes and pulls against me. It wants me to claim her, but it also doesn't want to lose its tether on me.

Lila bares her neck to me and my fangs push through my gums. Her small nod is all the encouragement I need and I sink my teeth deep into her flesh. Her blood explodes across my tongue and my hips speed up. My cock thrusts deep and her walls tighten. It's a mixture of feeling like she is trying to expel me and pull me deeper all at the same time.

She reaches her peak and screams out my name, her nails digging into my shoulders. My balls tighten and my knot begins to swell. It's like a bolt of lightning has struck me and I pull my teeth from her neck and howl. A lightness fills my body and explodes outwards. The claws that were embedded deep in my soul lose their grip as they are ripped from my body.

My hips continue to flex and I roar as my release hits me. My cum floods her insides and my knot swells further. Lila screams out another orgasm as we are locked together. I can't stop my hips from moving and I sink my teeth into her neck once more. It feels like our souls are connected and I sense every emotion that flows out of my mate.

Her happiness.

Her love.

I lick at Lila's neck and clean the wounds my fangs have caused. My arms wrap around Lila and I roll until she lies on top of me. My cock and knot are still inside her. I pull her mouth to mine and we kiss. Our tongues slide against each other, my hand running through her hair while the other lands on her ass.

My mind feels so clear. The darkness is completely gone, and I feel totally like myself again. All because of Lila. The love coming from her wraps us in a cocoon. I break the kiss. “I love you.” I look her straight in the eyes with my declaration and I see the tears that line them.

“I know. I can feel you.” She rocks her hips. “All of you, everywhere, all at once.”

The bond between a wolf shifter and their mate connects them at the deepest level. I feel what Lila feels and she can feel me too. Like two halves of one soul being stitched back together.

You’re mine forever, I speak inside her mind and for a moment there is a look of pure confusion on Lila’s face.

What the hell? Her internal thoughts hit me loud and clear.

“Being the mate of a wolf shifter has its bonuses,” I say out loud.

You can hear me? I give her a nod in response.

Chapter Forty

Lila

Grayson told me about how wolves knot with their mates, but he forgot to tell me about the fact I'd become part of their pack. Or that I'd be able to hear their thoughts as well as their emotions once bonded.

Hunter and Grayson can't make it work yet, though, I can feel their emotions when they are close, and they can feel mine. I hear Cayden even when he's at the perimeter of the compound. It's weird to hear someone else's voice in your head.

I haven't bonded with Grayson or Hunter yet. They came back to the cabin a few hours after Cayden and I had finished, but he wouldn't let them anywhere near me. The bond was too fresh, too potent. Now, though, not twenty-four hours later, they watch me with heated gazes from the kitchen and I clench my thighs together.

Hunter rounds the counter and stalks toward me. I feel like he's hunting me even though I haven't moved from my place on the couch. When he stops in front of me he drops to his knees before me.

"Lila." His voice breaks as he says my name.

I uncurl my legs and place one on either side of him as I scoot to the edge. His fingers link with mine and he kisses the back of each hand. His lips send tingles through my body. Another figure appears behind me. Grayson climbs onto the couch so he's sitting behind me.

The inside of his thighs presses into mine. His body sculpts against my back. Grayson's hand brushes my hair from my neck and his lips press against my skin. Hunter breaks contact with my hands and runs his fingers from my ankles up the insides of my legs. The cabin is warm enough to wear shorts and right now I appreciate the fire that burns in the stove.

Hunter curls his fingers around the waistband of my shorts and I lift my hips. He slowly lowers the fabric down my legs, leaving me bare.

"No panties?" Hunter smirks.

Grayson breaks his lips away from my neck and looks down the front of my body. A small gasp rushes from his lips. "It's like she's been waiting for us."

Grayson lifts my tank top so that it sits above my breasts and palms my chest. His rough skin sends tingles through my nipples and straight to my core. Hunter sniffs the air and lets out a groan. Gripping under my thighs, he opens my legs and dives straight in. The first lick up my slit leaves my body quivering all over.

Hunter's tongue delves in and out of my pussy with the odd nip at my clit and I moan. I feel Grayson's bulge against my back as he rubs himself against me in time to his stroking of my nipples. My hands lace through Hunter's hair as I grind against him.

"Please..." I whisper. "Don't torment me." My head falls back against Grayson's shoulder as Hunter pushes two fingers into my soaked pussy.

Grayson's mouth moves to my neck and I rock my hips against Hunter. My body feels like it's already on fire. Their lust sparks through the connection I have with Cayden and amps up my own.

"Come for us," Grayson whispers against my ear. I scream their names and my walls clench down when my orgasm hits me hard.

Hunter continues to lap at my pussy as he pulls his fingers from me and offers them to Grayson. He opens his mouth and sucks on Hunter's fingers. I watch as his tongue wraps around the digits and licks away my essence.

With one last lick, Hunter pulls away and reaches over me for Grayson. Their lips press together as they taste each other. My belly flutters at the sight of the two of them together, and I remember that day when Hunter licked me out while Grayson thrust into him.

"I want both of you together." I rush out the words, and they break apart, both staring at me with a look of shock. "Right now."

Hunter grabs onto me and pulls me to his waiting lips, his tongue tangling with mine. He lifts me to my feet and into his chest. His bulge rests against my throbbing clit and I rub my body against him.

"Anything for you." Grayson stands behind me, his bare chest flush with my back. At some point, he took his shirt off.

Grayson yanks me away from Hunter and into his own arms. His mouth presses to mine, his tongue licking at my lips until I allow him access. There's a thunk as something hits the floor. I pull away from Grayson and my eyes track to Hunter, who is yanking off his boots and letting them drop.

I stare as he lifts his shirt straight over his head and throws the top on the floor. Next, his fingers reach for the button on his pants, deftly snapping it open before they move to the zipper. When his jeans are undone, he pushes them to his ankles and kicks them away. His erection bobs as he straightens.

My tongue darts out to dampen my lips as I take him in. The metal in the end of his cock glints in the light. A bead of pre-cum sits over his slit and I want to taste him.

"Take her to the bedroom," Hunter rasps, his eyes completely blown with lust.

Grayson doesn't say a word as he carries me down the hallway and into the first room. Hunter walks in after us and goes straight over to the bed. He lies down on the edge of the mattress, his cock standing stiff and proud in the air with his legs dangling over the side.

"Come here, pretty Lila." Hunter beckons me over and Grayson slides me down his body.

I stalk towards Hunter and climb straight into his lap. His cock nudges against my folds and I rub my wetness up and down his length. I can't wait any longer. I need him inside me. Filling me. Claiming me.

"Make me yours," Hunter whispers as one hand falls on my hip and the other guides his length to my entrance.

The wide head of Hunter's cock pushes through my lips and I let out a sigh as his piercing rubs just inside me causing a delicious friction. As I sink lower, a groan escapes his lips and both his hands move to my hips. Holding me, but not controlling my progression, I slip further down his length.

"What a sight." Grayson's voice rasps behind me and I turn my head to look over my shoulder. He's on his knees between Hunter's open legs, licking his lips as he watches Hunter enter me.

My body lifts slowly before I drop back down on Hunter's length, taking him further inside me. I lean forwards and brace my hands on his chest for balance. Hunter lets out another groan as my body sits flush with his.

As I move up and down Hunter's length, Grayson's hands grab my ass cheeks and squeeze the mounds of flesh. When I raise my body again so only the head of Hunter's cock is inside me, Grayson's tongue hits the outside of my pussy and I groan. My fingers dig into Hunter's chest and his eyes roll back into his head as his teeth dig into his bottom lip.

I plunge myself back down on Hunter's length. Grayson's tongue moves with me licking Hunter's cock as I work myself up and down. Hunter's fingers dig into my hips as I ride him. On my next upward movement, I swirl my hips and as Grayson's tongue pushes in alongside the head of Hunter's cock.

"Gray..." His name whispers across my lips and I freeze as he continues to thrust his tongue inside me. I feel him pushing between my walls and Hunter's cock. I throw back my head in pleasure.

"So beautiful." Hunter gasps between moans. He lifts a hand to my hair and tangles his fingers in the strands, pulling me down over the top of him as his lips connect with mine.

Grayson removes his tongue and lies over the back of my body. I feel his cock as the wet tip pushes between my ass cheeks. I restart my movements up and down Hunter's length as one of Grayson's hands travels down my side. The touch sends tingles through my body.

When he reaches over my ass cheeks, he pushes a finger against my pussy and slips it inside alongside Hunter's cock. The stretch isn't much more, but it's enough to make my toes curl. My pussy is already drenched, and he uses my wetness as a lubricant.

A gasp rushes from my lips as Grayson pushes another finger inside my pussy, curling them until I'm quivering. My body stutters and I can no longer control it. Hunter takes charge and thrusts up into me. The sound of flesh smacking and groans fill the room, and my orgasm hits me out of nowhere.

My walls clench around Hunter's cock and Grayson's fingers, and I slump over Hunter. The intensity of my climax soaks mine and Hunter's thighs. With how Hunter flexes his hips against me and ravages my mouth only serves to turn me on more. Grayson slips his fingers from my pussy. I'm craving so much more from them both I quiver at the loss.

"Taste yourself." Grayson's fingers appear next to me and I break my lips from Hunter's to wrap them around them. I can taste myself all over him and I groan as my tongue licks around his digits.

"Don't think we're done with you yet." Hunter nips at my neck, his tongue licking over the bites, soothing my skin.

Yanking his fingers from my mouth, Grayson twists my head until I'm looking at him. He stares at me for a moment before claiming my mouth as Hunter thrusts back into me, his balls slapping against me. Grayson swallows my moans as Hunter ravishes my pussy with his cock, my walls still clenching from my release.

When Grayson pulls his lips from mine, I feel his cock against my back. He trails his hand back down my spine. His fingers curl around his length as he guides himself to my asshole.

A whimper escapes me. "Please," I beg.

Grayson doesn't enter me there, though. Instead, the broad head of his cock moves down to my pussy and Hunter stops his thrusts. The stretch engulfs me, a mixture of pleasure and pain as Grayson sinks his length inside me alongside Hunter. The burn and stretch barely even registers before they are both thrusting inside me.

My body is beyond overstimulated as they move in and out of me. When one pulls out the other thrusts back inside me, neither of them leaving me empty for even a moment. Grayson holds onto my hips, his fingers now tipped with claws that dig into my skin. Grabbing onto my hair, Hunter pulls my mouth to his.

I shiver and thrash as they ravage my body, lifting me higher than I've ever been. My mind is blank and all I can do is squirm as they touch me and nip at my skin with their teeth. I'm spiraling one more time as the pleasure becomes too much. The friction inside me plunges me head first over the threshold and I scream. My walls clench and they follow me over the edge.

I know exactly what is coming next. They shout my name before their teeth sink into both sides of my neck, puncturing my skin and making me crash further over the cliff as their knots swell inside me. The stretch is unreal and I feel their cum as it floods my pussy, filling me to the brim and spilling over the edges.

Their thoughts hit me all at once. Grayson howls my name inside my head and Hunter says it over and over as his hips continue to thrust as he spills more of his release inside me. Pulling his fangs from my neck, Grayson laps at the blood dripping down my skin. His body covers mine and he plants his hands on either side of me and Hunter.

Hunter takes one drag of my blood before his fangs slip from my skin. Like Grayson, he laps at the blood until he's satisfied.

Ours. Their voices speak in unison in my mind.

Grayson wraps his arms around me and Hunter and rolls us so we are all on our sides, their cocks still in my pussy. Their knots are locking us together and I've never wanted to be anywhere else but where I am right now. Wrapped in their arms, with their cocks deep inside my fluttering walls–heaven.

The voices are gone, Grayson says. His voice sounds a little unsure. Like he's expecting them to return.

You're mine now, Grayson. Always and forever, I say across the bond and Grayson kisses the back of my head.

I love you, Lila. Hunter's voice echoes and I kiss him softly.

We stay there until their knots finally release me but even then, they refuse to pull out. Their cocks are both still hard and they flex their hips as I lay on the bed, putty in their hands. We spend the rest of the day and most of the night in the bedroom.

Every time we join, their knots swell, keeping me locked to them. Something has changed since we have bonded. Something to do with the bond has allowed my mates to knot with each other.

Even as Hunter thrusts inside me and Grayson takes him, Grayson's knot now swells deep inside Hunter's ass.

The howl that fills the air from Hunter has me quivering as his own knot swells inside me.

We lay on the bed, a pile of limbs. My pussy aching and my heart swelling with love for my mates. As my eyes close and I drift off, I feel Cayden's mind brush against mine, sending his love through our connection. Happy and content, I let sleep take me.

Chapter Forty One

Lila

When I wake the next morning, I find myself back in Cayden's bed. My body aches but in the most delicious way. My thighs rub together as I remember bonding with Hunter and Grayson. Their minds both brush against mine and soothe my soul.

I push up on the mattress, still naked from the previous night. I shuffle to the edge of the bed and pull the sheet with me as I stand. Wrapping it around my body, I let it trail slightly on the floor as I creep to the edge of the loft.

When I look over the side, Grayson is sprawled across the couch. A book is grasped in his hands, but I can't see the cover from where I'm standing. I slip down the steps and his eyes look over the back of the couch to me, a smile breaking across his lips.

"Good morning." Grayson's voice is light and cheerful. There is still a gruff edge to it, but he no longer sounds strained. His features are brighter, and the crinkles at the edges of his eyes are relaxed.

Morning. I use the bond to reply to him.

Turning to the kitchen, I spot Hunter and Cayden are preparing breakfast. They laugh and joke as they move around each other. Hunter punches Cayden in the shoulder, but Cayden has other ideas pulling the smaller wolf against him.

When they pull apart, Cayden's eyes slip to me and he grins. "You're going to need more clothes than that unless you want us to fuck you."

A giggle slips from me as I shake my head at him. "I'm a hot mess. I need a shower." I glance at Grayson and then Hunter. "Blame those two. I have cum in places I never thought it could go."

Grayson lets out a snort as he pushes up from the couch and jumps over the back of it, landing gracefully on his feet. He strides over to me and pushes me against the bottom post of the stairs.

"I can find so many more places for my cum to go. All you need to do is ask," he mutters against my lips before he kisses me. My mind begs for his touch and I feel his acknowledgement in my head.

The kiss is short and sweet, and the next minute I'm being lifted from the ground. Grayson throws me over his shoulder, the sheet slipping from my body. My head stares at his back as I pummel at his ass and laugh. He carries me down the hallway, the laughter of the other two following us.

When he gets inside the bathroom, Grayson kicks the door closed and carries me straight into the large shower cubicle. He turns on the taps and waits for the water to warm before he drops me down under the stream. He steps back and slowly strips out of his damp clothes. My eyes fall to his cock as it bounces against his stomach.

With a growl, he prowls towards me, his eyes flashing silver and his tongue darting out to wet his lips. His hands grasp my hips, and he pushes me against the wall. The contrast of the cold tiles and the warm water of the shower shoves a gasp from between my lips.

Without further ado, Grayson lifts me and sinks his cock deep inside my aching pussy. There is a pinch of pain that is soon taken over by pleasure as he fucks me against the tiles. There is no softness from him, only the need to claim me all over again.

The room gradually fills with steam as he takes his fill. Our moans echo around the small room. He ruts me, his balls slapping against my flesh. Claiming my lips, he nips his teeth against my lower lip and I dig my fingers into his shoulders as he takes me.

With a shout, he empties himself inside me. The same knot I felt last night swells and locks us together. The stretch sends me over the edge and my walls squeeze down on him. He locks his lips over my skin in the same place he bit me last night. Grayson sucks hard, sure to leave a bruise on my flesh.

When his knot shrinks and Grayson's cock slips from me, his cum drips down my inner thighs. He lowers me to the floor of the shower and I drop to my knees. His eyes track me as I move to his cock, engulfing his length with my mouth. My tongue swirls around him, lapping up the remains of both of our releases.

"You're a vision on your knees with your mouth around my cock." Grayson brushes his hand through my hair. "How do we taste?"

Delicious. My mouth is too full to respond out loud.

Licking our combined cum from his length, I let his cock slip from my lips with a pop. Grayson drags me to my feet, pushing his tongue inside my mouth, tasting both of us on my tongue.

You're right. Grayson smiles against my lips. "Time to get clean before Cayden storms in here to drag us to breakfast."

Grayson breaks the kiss and grabs the soap from the tray. He foams up his hands and runs them over my body, cleaning every part of me. His fingers dip into my pussy, pushing his cum back inside. He keeps his fingers there as he drops to his knees and cleans my legs with his other hand.

When he's satisfied, he pushes back up to his feet and turns me, his fingers slipping from my pussy. His hands move across my shoulder, down my back, and over my ass. He squeezes hard and I let out a small yelp, followed by a giggle.

It doesn't take him long to clean both of us, shutting off the shower, he wraps towels around our bodies. Grayson guides me out of the shower and helps to towel dry my wet body. His hands rest on my hips and he turns me to face the mirror.

It's the first time I've seen myself since they marked me. Three bites adorn my neck, one from each of my wolves. Two on the left side, one high on my neck and close to my ear, the other sits on the juncture of my neck with the bite on the right-side mirroring it.

My fingers drift over the broken skin and a twinge of pleasure lances through my body instead of pain. Grayson steps up behind me and wraps his arms around my waist. His lips drift over the bite I know is his from the added bruising that is blooming over my skin.

Grayson trails his hand up my body and shifts my hair from my neck. I automatically tilt my head back to give him access. His tongue laves over the puckered flesh and my thighs clench together. His other hand pulls me tight against his body.

"You wear our marks so beautifully." Grayson's lips trail up my neck and he whispers the words into my ear. "Everyone will know you are ours."

"But how will they know you're mine?" They marked me but there is nothing to show they are mine. "I don't think I'll be able to fight off any she-wolves."

Grayson laughs and nibbles at my ears. "Oh, everyone will know we're yours. We're covered in your scent."

If it's the only way others will know I have staked a claim on all three men, it's enough for me. I turn in Grayson's arms and smile up at him. He returns it with a grin of his own as he leans down and kisses my cheek.

"Come on." He laces his fingers with mine, walks us out of the bathroom, and down the hallway to his room. I hear my other two men laughing in the kitchen. I know they heard everything and I can feel their lust through the bond.

When we get inside, he stops at the drawers and opens two of them, selecting boxers and socks from one, and a t-shirt from the other. Grayson passes them to me before he walks to his bed and grabs a pair of gray sweatpants, pulling them up his legs as I drop the towel and pull on his clothing. His scent drifts to my nose and I can't help lifting the neck of the t-shirt to breathe in his scent.

A chuckle sounds and I throw a glare at Grayson before joining his laughter. He takes my hand again and leads me back into the living room. We head straight to the dining table where Cayden and Hunter are already waiting for us with amused expressions on their faces.

"Glad to see you could both finally join us." Hunter snorts as he pushes a plate filled with bacon, eggs and toast and a coffee cup towards me.

Grasping the cup in my hands, I take a swig of the delicious nectar and hum out my pleasure. I dig straight into the food. I'm going to need all the energy I can get with these three.

"Lila..." Cayden utters, grabbing my attention. "There is something we need to talk to you about." I feel a twinge of apprehension through the bond, but they all bombard me with comfort.

"What is it?" My words are mumbled.

"The darkness is gone," Cayden proclaims. "We are safe to return to our pack."

A wave of panic hits me. I never thought beyond saving them from the darkness that was taking them over. Of course, now the curse is gone they can return to their pack and I'd go where? Would I want to go with them and end up surrounded by that many wolf shifters? My heart plummets and the fork in my hand drops to the plate.

Grayson lays his hand on my thigh and squeezes. "We aren't leaving without you, Lila. We love you. We want to know what you want to do."

"We'll follow you wherever you go, even if that means leaving the pack for good," Hunter announces.

"Always and forever, Lila," Cayden adds. I see the truth in his eyes.

What do I want? Do I want to carry on my journey to the demon sector? Can I really take them away from their pack?

"When I left the vampire sector, all I could think about was heading as far East as I could go. And getting away from both the vampire and wolf sectors." I think about my cousin, Addi, and how I was going to New Haven in the demon sector to see if I could stay with her while I got back on my feet. The decision hits me like a ton of bricks. "But I can't take you from your pack, Cayden. You're their Alpha. I go where you go. Your pack needs you."

"Are you sure?" Cayden asks. His eyebrows pinch together as I nod. "We don't have to if it's too much for you."

"I'm sure."

Hunter shoots to his feet and rounds the table. He pulls me straight up from the chair and into his waiting arms. Lifting me from the floor, he twirls me around a few times. My laughter fills the room as he holds me tight.

"You're our home, Lila. Never forget that." Hunter nuzzles into my neck.

When he slowly puts me back on my feet, Grayson and Cayden are both staring at me from where they sit, and I smile.

"Let's finish eating and we can start packing." I drop into my seat, grab a slice of toast, and take a bite.

"Not so fast." Cayden laughs. "We need to head to town and contact Beck. Let him know we're coming back." He quickly adds. "And that our mate is coming with us."

"How far away are your pack exactly?" I ask between bites.

"The town of Blackwell used to be part of pack lands. This was long before wolf shifters made themselves known. My great grandfather was the alpha. More of our males became affected by the curse, so he pulled away from the town," Cayden explains. "He wanted to protect the humans, so they headed North to the other side of the mountains and rebuilt."

"Since the supernaturals made themselves known to humans, it's been better for the males of our pack. With the balls, more of them have found their true mates," Hunter adds.

"And now we have ours." Grayson speaks up.

A grin spreads across my lips. I have a future now. One with these three men and their pack. The thought of being surrounded by that many wolves is daunting, but I won't let them give it up for me. I'll find a way to adjust, of that I have no doubt.

When we finish our food, Hunter takes the plates to the kitchen and Grayson kisses my cheek as he heads for his room. Cayden watches me from across the table and I make my way over to him and sit on his lap, my arms wrapping around his neck.

"Are you positive you're okay with going to our pack?"

"I'll have you three to protect me." Just like they did with Alaric.

"You'll have no problems with our wolves. Like Hunter said, most are mated now. The fact you are ours will make any of the unbonded have second thoughts." His hand brushes through my hair and he curls his finger around a small strand.

"Then I'll be fine." I brush my lips against Cayden's. "Promise." His lips part for mine and I sink into him.

Chapter Forty Two

Hunter

It took us exactly three days to get the cabin packed up, cleaned, and secured, as well as make plans with Beck for our return. The interim alpha had been ecstatic to hear that we had found our true mate. It took a little effort on my part to calm him down with all the plans he had.

"We'll have to update all your houses," Beck exclaimed. "You and Grayson, with your bachelor pads, there's no way you can take your women back there."

"There are no women, Beck." That stopped him in his tracks.

"But you said..." Beck's voice trails off.

"I said we've found our mate, singular. Lila is ours," I announce.

"A shared mate," Beck utters. "You three wouldn't have had it any other way. I should have known. I'll tell the pack. When should we expect you back?"

"Give us a few days." After exchanging a few more pleasantries and finalizing plans, I end the call.

My eyes drift to Lila, she's curled up against me, with Cayden beside her on the bench of the truck. Grayson and our belongings are in the truck bed. It was the only way to do it when there was barely enough room for three people in the cab.

Her eyes are closed and her breathing tells me she's asleep. I'm not surprised in the slightest. She's spent the last few days giving all three of us jobs to do before leaving the cabin. She even pushed a list of the books she wanted from the bookshelves. What I didn't realize until I was putting them in the boxes was that she wanted all of them.

It didn't take much to convince Cayden. Grayson and I came back to the cabin after taking some of the boxes to our truck to find Lila on her knees in front of him. His cock was deep in her throat whilst he moaned and groaned. We watched as he exploded and once she finished swallowing his cum she licked her lips.

"So, I'll get more boxes for the rest of the books." Her eyes had twinkled as she rose back to her feet. Cayden leant breathlessly against the kitchen counter, without a single objection on his lips.

I chuckle at the memory and glance over to Cayden who is shooting me a glare. We've long since left the cabin and the small town of Blackwell behind and we're halfway up the mountain that separates the pack lands from the town.

The journey from the cabin to the beginning of pack lands takes most of the day, but Cayden is taking the treacherous roads through the mountains at a snail's pace. I feel his apprehension of returning to the pack through the bond. The last time most of them saw him had been when he'd attacked Beck.

Cayden might have trusted Beck to take care of the pack in our absence but he still feels guilty for what happened when he attacked him. Things got out of hand, and for the first time ever Beck had reeked of fear.

The car glides over to a lookout point and my eyes flicker over to Cayden. His knuckles are white from clenching the steering wheel so hard. He kills the engine and hops out of the truck. The sound of the door closing makes Lila bolt upright.

"Are we there?" Her words rush out. She brushes loose hair out of her face as she looks at me.

"Not yet, pretty. I think Cayden wanted to stretch his legs." I gesture to Cayden as he leans on the front of the truck.

"You're shifters, you don't need to...oh." Realization crosses her features and her lips draw in a thin line.

Without another word she climbs over my lap, stopping for a moment to brush her lips over mine. Pushing the door open, she hops out and moves around to where Cayden is. He looks at her and offers her a small smile before he takes her hand and they walk to the edge of the lookout point. I look through the back window at Grayson and he shrugs. I climb out too and join Grayson in the bed of the truck.

"He's nervous about going back. When have you ever known Cayden to be nervous?" Grayson moves over to give me room to sit with our backs against the cab, the only space we can fit with the boxes in the bed.

"There was that time he asked Alison to prom," I quip. We'd been seventeen at the time. Still pups.

Grayson laughs. "He definitely wasn't nervous when her dad found them in the barn." My barked laughter follows his.

I remember the night well. Cayden had come banging on my bedroom window and threw himself through it. His suit pants had been half undone and he looked an absolute state with straw sticking out of his hair.

"I may have told him her dad was going to kill him." I laugh and Grayson joins in.

The fear I could smell coming off Cayden, I had been impressed he hadn't pissed his pants. It took me forever to calm him down, and I'm fairly certain that Alison's dad knew exactly what they'd been up to.

"Then you called me and told me everything. We ate so much junk food that night, I was surprised none of us were sick," Grayson reminisces.

"Alison's dad gave Cayden the death stare for months after that, but he never did anything in retaliation. Probably a good thing, or our pack wouldn't have an alpha anymore."

Grayson leans his body against mine and sighs. We can hear Cayden and Lila's quiet voices from where we sit, but we do our best to ignore their conversation. But from what I pick up she's trying to convince Cay that his pack will be happy to have him back. She's not wrong.

The two of us sit there basking in the sun when we hear a faint gravely moan from behind us. Grayson smirks and raises an eyebrow as he looks my way.

"They're having fun without us again," Grayson announces and pushes to his knees.

With his head barely above the top of the cab he looks over to where we last saw Cayden and Lila. I quickly join him when I feel my mate's lust tease the edges of our bond. Spying over the roof, I find Lila with her back to us on her knees, her mouth firmly around Cayden's cock.

Like he knows we're looking, Cayden opens his eyes and stares straight at us. Beckoning us over with his eyes, I jump over the side of the bed and Grayson joins me. We all but run over to the pair. The sight of Lila's red lips locked around Cayden's length has all my blood rushing south.

With a pop, Lila pulls her mouth from Cayden and stares up at me and Grayson. "It's about time you guys joined us. I was just helping Cayden relax a little."

My alpha grunts when Lila wraps her lips back around his length, his eyes rolling back into his head as she kneads his balls between her fingers. Grayson closes the distance and tangles his fingers in Cayden's hair, dragging their lips together.

My cock throbs in my pants as I step closer to the three of them. I palm my length through my pants and lower my zipper, letting myself free. My hand wraps around my length and I pump myself a few times. My eyes are set on Lila's mouth as she moves up and down Cayden's cock.

Lila's eyes lift to mine and I see the wicked look that crosses her face. She pulls her mouth from Cayden and sinks straight down over me. Her tongue laps the metal at the head and my legs nearly give out. With his lips still on Cayden's, Grayson wraps his fist around him and we both moan.

We're all lost in the passion, the mate bond making everything so much more intense. Lila moves her mouth between mine and Cayden's lengths. Her hand never leaves my cock, and Grayson's never leaves Cayden's. Moving his lips from Cayden's to mine, Grayson's tongue thrusts into my mouth with little warning.

Ripping his lips from mine as Lila moves back to my cock, Grayson drops to his knees in the dirt in front of Cayden and takes his length into his mouth. My fingers tangle in Lila's hair holding her against me as her tongue swirls around my length.

Cayden grunts as Grayson takes him all the way to his base and Lila does the same to me. Heat rushes down my spine and my balls tingle and then tighten. Lila's throat squeezes around my length as she moans. The sensation sends me over the edge and I pull back slightly so my knot doesn't swell in Lila's mouth.

With a groan, my cum spurts down her throat and Lila swallows every drop. Cayden soon follows me as he thrusts in and out of Grayson's open mouth. With one last groan he shoves his length to the point just before his knot down Grayson's throat. The beta grips onto Cayden's hips as he swallows our alpha's release.

We're all left panting. Lila licks her lips as she releases my length and grins up at me and Cayden. Grayson grabs Lila and pulls her mouth to his and kisses her. They both moan and my eyes widen. Without a single word, Grayson wraps his arms around Lila and lifts her into his arms, never once breaking the kiss.

Grayson rushes back to the truck and Cayden and I glance at each other. Our eyebrows raise as we tuck ourselves back into our pants. With a quick kiss we saunter after the other two. When we make it back to the truck, Grayson has Lila spread out in the back.

Grayson pulls her to the edge, his claws extend, and he makes quick work of her sweatpants. Lila's body trembles with anticipation. Grayson pushes his jeans down his thighs and thrusts straight into Lila's waiting pussy. Her moans turn to groans as he pumps in and out of her.

Cayden and I watch the two as they join together. He climbs up into the trunk, his hands moving up her t-shirt and gripping her breasts as his lips press to hers. I sit on the edge of the bed, my hand working its way down her side to her clit.

The first brush of my finger-tip over her swollen bud has Lila's hips rising into my touch as Grayson pounds into her. She's so wet already and my fingers move over either side of Grayson's cock and her lips. I keep my thumb on her clit and push down.

Lila's whole body is shaking and I feel her pleasure soaking through the bond, turning me on again. My cock is hard already, but it's not about me anymore. Grayson's thrusts push and pull at Lila's body as she claws at his chest, her legs wrapped tight around his hips.

I pinch Lila's clit and her scream is muffled by Cayden's lips. I feel her wetness increase as she finds her release. Grayson roars as he plants himself deep within her pussy, finding his own release within her tight walls.

When we part, Lila is a sweaty mess. Her lips swollen are from Cayden's kisses and her skin is flushed a rosy red. Grayson is locked deep inside her, his knot keeping them together. Her breathing slowly returns to normal and she chuckles.

"Well, this is going to make traveling difficult." Lila hums as she looks to where she and Grayson are joined and we follow her laughter.

"I got this." Grayson smirks as he gathers Lila into her arms.

A moan rushes from her lips at the change of position. Grayson carries her around the side of the truck, holding her up with one hand as he opens the door with the other. He steps into the truck and shuffles onto the bench.

When he's settled, Lila is in his lap, her legs on either side of his thighs, his cock still inside her. I grab a blanket from the truck and throw it at Grayson. He wraps it around Lila's waist and lets the fabric drape over her to cover any of her exposed flesh.

Cayden and I shake our heads at each other and climb into the truck alongside Gray and Lila. When Cayden starts the truck, Lila lets out another moan and I stare at her. She gives me a small shrug and curls up against Grayson as we pull away from the lookout and back onto the main road. Every bump leaves Lila gasping as she waits for Grayson's knot to return to normal.

I no longer feel Cayden's nervousness over the bond. Instead, he is sated and happy. Whatever Lila said to him has calmed him, the blow job was an added bonus.

Chapter Forty Three

Lila

With the amount of stops the guys make along the way, the journey over the mountains takes twice as long as it should. After our impromptu break at the viewpoint, I end up needing to pee, which then becomes Hunter fucking me against the sink in the small bathroom at the rest stop.

After that we get on our way again, but twenty minutes later, Cayden wants to pull over so we can have lunch. What he didn't tell me was that they all planned on making me dessert. One more stop and I put my foot down and tell them no more. Hunter pouts, Grayson groans, and Cayden admits defeat.

They want me all to themselves, but heading back to the pack means them all having to take up their previous roles within it. Cayden as the alpha, Grayson as their enforcer, and Hunter as their accountant. They're worried that restarting those will give them less time with me.

"Please say we're almost there?" I whine from my spot on Grayson's lap. Hunter chuckles from the driver's seat. "I don't know what you're laughing at. You're not the one with cum stuck in their ass crack."

Grayson pulls me closer to him. "Don't worry, we're almost there. You can grab a shower as soon as we get to the house."

I let out a sigh and sink down on Grayson's lap. The last place they stopped wasn't exactly sanitary and there's only so much a wet wipe can do. A shower sounds amazing right now. Then again, so does a bed, or even a couch to have sex on. Sex outdoors is definitely not my favorite thing.

I focus on the road; the trees are thicker here. Even more so than near the town of Blackwell. There's hardly any light cutting through the dense overhang of branches and leaves. The road in front of me distorts slightly and I blink my eyes a couple of times to clear it, but it doesn't go away.

As the shimmer envelops the truck, I feel it. Multiple connections explode from the bond and what feels like a hundred muffled voices are in my head all at once.

"What in the world?" I gasp, my hand clutching my chest.

Cayden takes my hand. "It's the pack. We just crossed the boundary. This is my fault, I didn't even think about the fact you'd be able to hear the pack as soon as we crossed." There are voices overlapping, my ears are ringing. "Take a deep breath. It's pretty overwhelming at first. Push them away, let them know you don't want to hear them anymore."

I follow Cayden's instructions, taking several breaths in and out. I push against the voices in my head and they fade, becoming a barely audible whisper.

"It'll take some time, but we'll help you learn to build a wall against them," Hunter offers and I smile over at him.

Now I'm looking back at the road, the trees are thinning out and I see the brightness of the sun a little further ahead. The truck breaks out of the forest and the road turns from tarmac to gravel. The wheels bounce as they run over some of the larger stones.

We pass a few smaller cabins on either side of the road with people gathered outside them. A few raise their hands as we pass and the guys wave back in greeting. I sink back against Grayson and he wraps his arms tight around my waist.

"You'll be okay, Lila. We won't leave your side." I look up at him and smile at his words, but it doesn't stop my nerves entirely.

As we crawl past more cabins, more people emerge. When we reach the end there is a huge log cabin, not that I'd call it a cabin given its size.

On the porch is a tall man with short brown hair and tanned skin. There's a woman next to him who's a few inches shorter and her black hair is pulled back in a tight bun at the nape of her neck. There's a swath of blankets clenched in her arms.

"Welcome to the Blackwell Alpha house," Cayden announces.

As we pull to a stop, the man jumps down the steps and slowly approaches the truck. Hunter kills the engine, leaps down from his seat, and bounds straight over to him. They wrap their arms around each other and hug.

"That's Beck," Grayson whispers and I give him a small nod. "He's the interim alpha and has been looking after the pack while we were gone. The woman on the porch is his true mate, Sophia. I'm guessing that's their baby. Sophia was pregnant when we left."

Grayson opens the door and shuffles us to the edge of the bench. He slides me down his body but keeps me close. Cayden follows us out. Striding around the truck, he heads over to the one Grayson called Beck.

Hunter steps back and Cayden clasps his hand around Beck's forearm; the man reciprocates. My focus ends up on Sophia who is still standing on the porch. Now we are outside the truck, I hear the soft wails of the baby in her arms.

Sophia's eyes fall onto me, and she smiles before she pulls the baby up and rests it against her chest. She pats the baby's back and hums to it as she slowly moves down the steps.

"Hi, I'm Sophia." She stops humming for a moment so she can introduce herself.

"Lila." I keep my voice low, unsure of the woman in front of me.

"I'm so happy you're here, I think everyone else is, too." She looks over my shoulder and I turn to see the growing crowd.

I'm taken aback by the semi-circle of people gathering around the truck. I can't stop the involuntary step back I take. I slam into something hard and turn to realize how close Grayson is standing to me.

"Sorry," I quickly apologize.

"It's okay. They're just curious." Grayson looks at the crowd as an older woman splits away and approaches us. A huge smile beams across her face. Grayson steps around me and the woman throws her arms around him.

"Grayson, you're home," she exclaims. "And you brought your mate." She holds his cheeks between her hands and looks up at him, before her eyes move to me.

"Hi, Mom." As soon as the words slip from Grayson's lips, I see it.

While the woman's hair is mostly gray, she has subtle streaks of black throughout—the opposite of Grayson's. Her eyes are more of a gunmetal instead of the liquid mercury of her son's, but there's no denying the familial similarities between the two.

"Mom, this is Lila." The words are barely out of Grayson's mouth before the woman flings herself at me. Her arms come around my shoulders as she pulls me into a tight hug, making me flinch.

"Grayson, she's beautiful. You must tell me everything." Grayson's mom stares at me as she speaks.

"You know Lila can hear you, right?" Grayson lets out a chuckle and his mom releases her death grip on me.

"Of course. That was rude of me." His mom still doesn't release me entirely. "I'm Nora. It's such a pleasure to meet you, Lila. You'll have to come for breakfast tomorrow. I can make your favorites, Gray."

Nora continues to natter but I miss most of what she says. Instead my focus has shifted to the crowd as they get closer. Some move over to where Cayden, Hunter, and Beck are still talking, but I notice a few of the women being drawn to where Grayson, Nora, and I stand.

"I can't believe Cayden is finally mated," a voice behind me says.

"I told you they would be successful finding their mates...well, mate." Another voice says; this time to my left.

The pack doesn't know that Cayden, Grayson, and Hunter went to die, and I won't be the one to tell them, it's not my place. Everyone sounds so happy but a small part inside me wants to run away. I know that a lot of those present are wolf shifters and while they seem nice, I don't know them. They still set my nerves on edge.

An arm wraps around my shoulders, pulling me away from Nora. The scent of old books and coffee tells me it's Hunter. The voices still chatter away as he steers me towards the house. Sophia comes up on my other side as they both lead me up onto the porch.

"Is it too much?" Hunter asks.

"Yes." The word slips out of my mouth and Hunter pulls me closer.

"Come inside." Sophia heads for the door. Holding the baby with one hand, she opens the door with the other and waits for Hunter to guide me inside before she lets it close behind us.

Hunter leads me to a sectional couch to the right of the door and sits me down. The voices are back in my head. Whatever I did to quieten them down stops working and they are now overwhelming me once more. There are too many voices for me to pick out any singular one and my head hurts.

Sophia sits beside me with the now sleeping baby and lays her hand on my arm. I flinch at the sudden touch.

"Lila, I need you to breathe for me okay. I know what it's like." Her voice is soft and soothing. "I'm human, the same as you. When I first bonded with Beck, I almost passed out because of the pack's voices suddenly invading my mind."

"What did you do to make it stop?" I grit out between clenched teeth.

"Beck and I had to move a little further away from the pack for a while," Sophia explains. "Still within pack lands, but far enough away that the voices quietened. It was easier after that, but you need to build a wall around your mind. One to keep the voices out."

I take a few steady breaths, but I can't seem to get away from the voices in my brain. My hands grip either side of my head. The headache is getting worse. The couch shifts beside me and Sophia stands. I hear her whispered voice but I can't make it out over the chaos in my head.

I keep pushing at the voices and they quieten down, but only a fraction. When Sophia returns, she's holding a steaming mug. She sits down next to me and holds the mug out towards me.

"What's this?" I take the mug from her and inhale. It seems like herbs, with a hint of nuttiness.

"It's something I've been working on. The pack has found a lot of human mates, each one having different levels of struggles with closing off the pack link." Sophia folds her hands over her lap. "Wolf shifters have had these voices in their heads their entire lives, they've had time to build their connection with the link and learn to close it off. It doesn't taste the best at first, but it helps."

I don't need much more explanation; I only need the voices to stop. I take a tentative sip; it's bitter at first but then a sweetness takes over. I keep drinking until the mug is empty.

One by one the voices melt away and my body finally relaxes. My shoulders slump and Sophia quickly takes the mug from me.

"It's going to make you sleepy at first, but the more it builds up, the less it should affect you. I'm going to get you some supplies of the tea to take with you. Hunter, you better sort moving to mine and Beck's old cabin near the hot springs. Go take care of your mate."

Sophia rises from the couch again and moves away. I yawn and my eyes drift closed. The tea is working quickly and the voices are nearly all gone now. The couch presses down on my other side and arms wrap around me, pulling me into their body.

"I got you, Lila," Hunter whispers. "Welcome home."

I feel my body being lifted and I snuggle deep into Hunter's embrace. My head lies on his chest and I can hear his heartbeat against my ear. The soothing sound is enough to send me over the edge into sleep.

Chapter Forty Four

Lila

The tea that Sophia gave me has been a lifesaver this last week. Cayden moved us to the same cabin that Sophia had used when she first arrived with Beck. It's a good distance from the main pack cabins, but still close enough that the guys can get back and forth when needed.

Sitting on the bench seat outside, I sip on a mug of herbal tea and look out over the forest. From here I can hear the waterfall that's close to the back of the cabin. The birds are tweeting and the leaves rustle in the breeze.

It's still cold, but the air is refreshing. I relax back on the bench. The voices are quiet now. Between the tea, Sophia, and the guys, I've been learning to block them out. I can finally function without the constant noise in my head.

Cayden and Grayson left at first light, heading back to the alpha house to deal with some of their duties, but Hunter is inside the cabin with his laptop. He's been there all morning sorting out the pack's accounts.

Rising from the bench, I head inside, leaving my mug on the coffee table. I head towards the small room at the back of the cabin that Hunter has turned into his office. The door is slightly ajar, and I peer inside. Hunter hunches over the desk sifting through paperwork before going back to his laptop.

I watch him work as I rest against the door frame. Hunter's t-shirt stretches around his chest as he switches back and forth between the laptop and sheets of paper. With a pen gripped firmly between his teeth, he only removes it to add notes to the sheets of paper in front of him.

"Are you going to stand out there all morning?" Hunter quips, keeping his eyes on his screen.

I push through the door and pad over to him. Leaning over the back of the chair, I wrap my arms around his neck and kiss his cheek. "I didn't want to distract you."

"Too late." Hunter swings me around the chair and straight into his lap. I squeal. His amethyst eyes rove over my face and I feel my skin heating under his intense gaze. "Hey."

"Hi." My arms curl around Hunter's neck and he leans in for a kiss.

Hunter's lips are soft against mine as he runs his fingers through my hair. I shift slightly on the chair, trying to get myself comfortable but sprawled across his lap on the wooden chair isn't the best.

Hunter's tongue traces across my lips and I open for him. He delves inside my mouth and tastes me. A small moan slips from my lips, the sound muffled by Hunter's lips on mine. When he breaks the kiss, I'm panting slightly.

"You are definitely a distraction, pretty Lila." My body trembles at his words and I let out a sigh.

"I can go if you like?" I go to move but Hunter keeps his arms locked firmly around me.

"Not a chance, I need a break anyway. I was thinking we could go to the hot springs." My eyes light up at Hunter's suggestion. "I'll take that as a yes."

I nod enthusiastically and finally Hunter lets go of me as I jump to my feet, rushing out of the office and into the bedroom. Cayden took me there the morning after we first arrived. The voices were still in my head though muted with the help of the tea, but it didn't stop me from pacing up and down the living room.

The guys had made sure the cabin was fully stocked, including some clothes in my size. Cayden had told me to go find something suitable for swimming in and after questioning the fact he wanted me to wear so little even with the cold temperatures outside, I shrugged and went to get changed.

We left the cabin and Cayden guided me through the trees. As we walked, the sound of a waterfall got louder and when the trees opened up there was a steaming body of water in front of me. A waterfall on one side cascaded down into the water below.

Even with snow dusting the ground everywhere else the small patch of ground around the hot springs is untouched. The heat from the water is enough to thaw the snow for a few feet around the edges.

I smile at the memory as I strip off my clothes. I let them fall to the floor and grab the small shorts and tank top I've been using already to swim in. I don't know what it is about the water in the hot spring, but I feel relaxed when I'm there. The voices in my head melt away, along with the cold.

We've definitely gotten up to more than just swimming there. The guys really do know the best way to make me relax and this is it. I'm not going to deny the offer to go to one of my favorite places in the pack lands.

When I'm ready, I pull on sweatpants and a thick hoodie. Pushing my feet into my boots before retrieving a towel from the en-suite bathroom, I head into the lounge. Hunter is already waiting for me, his body on display apart from the swim trunks he's wearing. The advantages of him being a wolf include that he doesn't need the extra clothes to walk to the hot springs.

"Ready?" Hunter questions.

"Yep." I dash past him and out the front door and down the steps.

Hunter bounds up behind me and links his hand with mine as we join the path that takes us to the hot springs. I can't wait to sink below the warm waters. As soon as we emerge from the trees, I throw the towel at Hunter and he laughs as I quickly strip my clothes off, leaving them in a pile by the edge of the pool.

I'm in the water before Hunter has even made it to the edge. As the warm liquid envelops my body, I let out a sigh. My entire body relaxes as I lie back in the water, floating just on the top. The steam cocoons me in a layer of warmth. A splash lets me know that Hunter has jumped in too.

Hands wind around my waist and tug me into Hunter's hard body. My legs encase his hips and my arms go around his neck as he holds me up in the water.

"This is perfect." I let out another sigh.

"I know what would make it more perfect," Hunter purrs against my ear.

One of his hands trails between us. Dipping beneath the waistband of my shorts, his fingers skim over my clit and a moan rushes past my lips. His fingers delve deep as he slips one finger inside me.

Hunter doesn't stop his movements as he thrusts the digit in and out of me, adding more until he has three fingers inside me. My hips move in time with his thrusts, trying to take him deeper.

My head falls back, but Hunter keeps one hand around my back. I've been horny all morning and it doesn't take me long before my walls tighten around him and I cry out my release. When he pulls his fingers from me, I whimper at the emptiness but he soon replaces them with his cock.

The metal at the tip brushes against my sensitive clit, before he pushes through my folds and seats himself deep inside me. I let out a rush of air and pull myself back up so my chest leans against Hunter's.

My lips brush against Hunter's as he opens them for me. My tongue thrusts in time with the rise and fall of my hips. His arms lock around me as he lets me take the lead.

We collide, our bodies rubbing together as we take our pleasure from each other.

Moans slip from my mouth as Hunter nips down the side of my neck, taking over the thrusts as my body turns lax. More hands trail up my legs and my head tilts back to see Grayson behind me. I don't know when he appeared, but I'm too overcome with lust to even care.

Fingers trace between my ass cheeks and between my legs. Two slip inside me alongside Hunter's cock and my heart thrashes against my chest, trying to break free. They move in time, pushing me closer to the edge. When I'm about to fall over the precipice they both stop and I whimper in frustration.

Hunter holds me close, not moving a single muscle and Grayson's fingers slip from my pussy and move back to my asshole. One pushes against the tight ring of muscle before pushing inside, my teeth dig into my lip to restrain the sound that wants to break from my lips.

After a few thrusts, Grayson slips another finger inside me and the walls of my pussy quiver. Hunter moans and his hips jerk involuntarily, sending shocks through my entire system. I try to move, but Hunter holds me still as Grayson fucks my ass with his fingers, scissoring them to stretch me wider.

Another finger pushes inside and I can't stop the scream that has been building up inside.

"Fuck, Grayson, I can't take much more. She's squeezing my dick like a vice." Hunter's voice is husky and breathless.

A whimper is dragged from my lips as Grayson pulls his fingers out of me, it turns into a moan as he notches the head of his cock with my asshole. As he pushes against me, his lips trace up the side of my neck.

"Relax for me." Grayson's tongue licks the shell of my ear and I do as he asks.

The mushroomed head of Grayson's cock slips past the tight muscle and my fingers grip Hunter's shoulder tight enough for my nails to leave marks on his skin. Grayson inches inside my ass. The stretch of both their cocks makes me cry out with every shallow thrust Grayson does.

When Grayson's pubic bone brushes against my ass cheeks I let out a loud sigh and my body slumps against Hunter's chest.

"Are you ready, pretty Lila?" Hunter's fingers curl under my chin and lift my head so I'm looking at him. I give a small nod.

Grayson thrusts first, then Hunter. They take it in turns until they hit the perfect rhythm. One drives inside me as the other withdraws. I'm soon a mess in their arms as my orgasm builds again and I writhe between the two of them; I'm so full.

There is the edge of pain along with the pleasure. Their fingers dig into my flesh, sure to leave their marks all over my skin. They build me higher, until there is nowhere else for me to go other than over the edge.

My walls clench around them as I fall over the precipice. My orgasm detonates through me and they both strike, their fangs piercing the flesh on either side of my neck. I scream as the rush of pain pushes me further into my orgasm.

My vision blurs as their knots swell inside me and it feels like I lose consciousness for a moment. Their hips continue to move with small thrusts as ropes of their cum coat my insides and fill me to the brim.

I slowly come back to reality with two of my wolves wrapped around me. Their tongues lick over the fang marks they have left on my neck and they both groan against my skin.

Hunter pulls away from my neck. My blood stains his lips and he licks up every drop before he kisses me. The kiss is savage as he claims my lips just like he claimed my body. Grayson's fingers grip the back of my neck and he pulls my lips from Hunter's, tilting my head to face him.

Grayson attacks my lips with the same savageness as Hunter and he nips at them with his sharpened teeth. It's a ferocity I have come to accept from my men. They are fiercely protective of me, and while sex with them might push some of my boundaries, they would never hurt me on purpose.

Grayson pulls his lips away from mine, his silver eyes black with unbridled lust. He tilts his hips, and my body quivers as his knot moves inside me.

"Well, this is awkward," Hunter jokes and I smile at his ridiculousness. "We probably should have taken this to the grass bank."

"You've never complained before," Grayson grunts as his hands trail up and down my arms.

"Usually not in the water, when there are two of us." Hunter barks out a laugh and I listen as the two argue jokingly with each other.

My body is too relaxed to care as I lean against Hunter. Their knots are locked inside me and there is no way any of us are going to be able to move for a while. The heat of the water seeps into my muscles even now, helping to soothe them before any soreness can sink in.

Exhaustion overtakes me and I curl myself against Hunter's chest with my legs still wrapped around his waist as my two men talk. The sound of the waterfall crashing down into the hot springs sends me into oblivion.

Epilogue

Lila

Sitting on the couch with the phone pressed to my ear, I listen to my cousin ranting down the phone. She was surprised to hear from me at first, shocked when I explained everything. Addison even offered to buy me a plane ticket to get me out of the wolf sector.

I hadn't even called her before I began my journey to the demon sector, but now I had told her what had happened, she was more than happy to let me stay with her. Then I told her about Cayden, Hunter, and Grayson.

"You're mated to how many wolves?" Addison's voice hits high as she finishes her sentence.

"Three," I mutter.

"Holy crap, Lila. That's a lot of dick." Addison chuckles and I shake my head at her comment. "For someone who wanted to get out of the wolf sector, it sounds like you've changed your mind?"

"I have. I'm staying. I never thought I'd end up back here, with the balls, Mom and Dad dying. I thought I needed a fresh start. It didn't exactly go to plan." She knows everything about Alaric, the caves, and then him following me. "But I'm happy, Addi."

"As long as you're sure," Addison implores. "You better tell those mates of yours if they ever hurt you, I'll be out there like a shot with my shotgun."

"You don't even own a shotgun." I exclaim, laughing at her ridiculousness.

"I'm pretty sure between here and there I can get one." The laugh that follows tells me she isn't entirely serious. But I don't doubt that when Addison puts her mind to something, she will make it happen.

"Anyway, that's enough about me. How's Jamie?"

"Asleep, he had a rough night. He keeps being sick and his temperature is a little on the high side. I'm hoping it's something he's picked up at school." Addison sighs. "We have a doctor's appointment in a few days."

"Oh, Addi. I'm so sorry. Give him all the hugs and kisses from his Auntie Lila. And call me if you need me. You have my number now." Hunter had decided I needed my own phone.

I hadn't had one since I'd been kidnapped, but that changed as soon as the guys realized.

"I will. Anyway, I gotta go. It's nearly lunchtime and I want to try and see if I can get Jamie to eat something."

"Love you, Addi."

"Love you too, cous." Addison hangs up and I drop the phone into my lap.

The door creaks and I look over as Grayson walks inside, he's been back at the packhouse all morning. Jumping from the couch, I run over and wrap my arms around his neck.

His lips instantly fall on mine. Every kiss with these men is like kissing them for the first time. I probe at his mind, but his wall is firmly in place just like my own now is. Sophia has spent a few hours here every day since we moved into the cabin near the hot springs, teaching me how to block out the voices.

I've been improving every day, and the voices are barely even audible anymore.

Grayson breaks the kiss. "We have a surprise for you."

“Is that so?” I smile up at him, and I see the sparkle in his eyes. “Well, you’d better show me what it is.”

I pull away from Grayson and he laces his fingers through mine. With a small tug, he leads me to the door and straight outside into the trees. We walk in silence and I let him take me wherever he wants to go.

We walk for about twenty minutes before Grayson stops and I stand beside him. “You need to close your eyes.”

My eyes slip closed and Grayson moves behind me, resting his hands on my hips. He continues to guide me forwards and I feel the sun heating my face, the light getting brighter behind my closed lids.

“Okay, you can open them now,” Grayson whispers against my ear.

My eyes snap open and I gasp. In front of me is a larger replica of the cabin back at the compound. There’s even a fire pit about fifteen yards in front of the porch, only this time it’s lined with stones and there are log benches in a semi-circle around it.

“This is...” My voice trails off.

“Amazing? Wonderful?” Grayson asks. “You love it? You hate it? Come on, Lila, you’re going to have to give me something,” he teases.

“I can’t believe it. When did this happen?” I move away from Grayson and head closer to the cabin. I take the steps slowly up to the porch.

“Cayden had already laid the foundations before we had to leave.” Grayson follows me. “With the entire pack helping, we managed to get most of it finished. There are still a few things we need, but we couldn’t wait to show you.”

A porch swing hangs from the roof on one side and there are four rocking chairs on the other side of the raised area. I push through the door and my mouth drops open. The setup inside is almost the same as the other cabin. There are even steps leading up to a loft only this time the loft takes up the entire width of the cabin.

"Cayden made sure there is a bathroom in the loft this time. There's a bed big enough for all of us." Grayson stands behind me and wraps his arms around my waist. "There are still separate rooms on this level in case any of us need space."

"It's perfect." I smile. "It's home."

"You're our home, Lila. Never forget that." Another voice cuts in as Cayden strides into the cabin. Hunter follows close behind him.

My lips curve up again as I pull away and smile at all three of my men. They are my home now. I've been wolf kissed, after all, but my true mates found me and saved me from a fate worse than death.

"Now, what was that about a bed big enough for all of us?" Hunter chuckles at my comment and rushes towards me.

Arms slip around me and lift me clean off the floor. I let out a giggle as Hunter runs for the stairs leading up to the loft.

"I say we need to make sure." Hunter laughs and the others join in his laughter as he takes two steps at a time.

We reach the top and I barely have time to take in the whole room before Hunter throws me down on the bed. Then all three of my men are on me and I welcome them with open arms.

Acknowledgements

It took me a little longer than I wanted it to, to get to the end of this book. At this point, it's been a longtime coming for those readers who wanted the second book after Vampire Kissed, but we got there in the end. Things happening in my real life meant that I had to take a step away for a little while, they are still ongoing, but it's getting better every day.

This book honestly wouldn't have happened without the amazing team I have standing behind me.

My amazing cover designer, Hajer, from Blue Crescent Covers. She's been amazing throughout and even when I didn't contact her for a little while, she was there ready and waiting to get the wrap cover sorted on a cover we designed what feels like forever ago.

My alphas, Hayley and Amanda who are more than happy to point out where I messed up, which can be a lot at times. I absolutely adore them both and swear my stories wouldn't be what they are without them.

Tori, my editor who made sure I didn't have any fragmented or run-on sentences as well as possibly questioned my sanity at points. I think we only broke this document twice.

Mich, my proofreader. The one and only! I'm sure she's just happy I got through a story without adding the words channel or rosebud.

And lastly, to you, my amazing readers who have stuck by me even through my long absence and still wanted to read my words. If you are a new reader to me, welcome.

I hope I didn't traumatise any of you too much and you'll stick around. More books will be coming and I can't wait for you to meet the characters within.

About the author

Powered by tea and sarcasm.

S Lucas is a self-published indie author, who lives in the UK with their significant other. When they are not writing they can be found either reading, blogging, or sitting behind a sewing machine making costumes for various events around the country.

After completing NaNoWriMo for the first time in 2020 with the finished story of Against the Odds, they were set on the track to publishing their very first book.

You can find S Lucas at:

Facebook Page – https://www.facebook.com/authorslucas
Facebook Readers Group – https://bit.ly/2VucxSE
Amazon – https://amzn.to/3wuOEbJ
Bookbub – https://www.bookbub.com/profile/s-lucas
Goodreads – https://bit.ly/2VnBoHT
Instagram – https://www.instagram.com/slucasauthor/
TikTok – https://www.tiktok.com/@slucasauthor
Website – https://slucasauthor.wixsite.com/home

If you want to find out more about me, my books and my characters then please join my Ream – https://reamstories.com/slucasauthor/public

You can also join my newsletter if you want to hear the inner ramblings of my mind: http://eepurl.com/hqyy8P

Also by

Odds and Expectations

Against the Odds
Defying the Odds

Supernaturally Yours

Vampire Kissed

Shared Worlds

Taming Wrath – Sons of Satan
Leo Blessed – Dawn of the Zodiacs

Printed in Poland
by Amazon Fulfillment
Poland Sp. z o.o., Wrocław